Lucy Roth is the pseudonym for author Lucy Nichol – a writer with a love of flawed characters and tales from the darker side of life. Her debut thriller was *When Sally Killed Harry* ('witty and dark' *The New York Observer*). Under Lucy Nichol, she has written *Girls to the Front, No Worries if Not!*, *Parklife* and *The Twenty Seven Club*.

Praise for *The Party to End All Parties*

'This book has got everything! Juicy, glamorous and you will find yourself really, really rooting for . . . a goat'
Caroline Corcoran, author of *Tiny Daggers*

'With an opulent backdrop to rival Saltburn, and despicable characters you'll love to hate, this book delivers fun of the darkest and most delicious kind. Roth proves herself to be a talented and twisted author to watch'
Lisa Timoney, author of *The Lies Our Children Tell*

'Packed full of delicious family drama and sordid secrets, *The Party to End All Parties* is a wild ride from start to finish!'
Tess James-Mackey, author of *The Perfect Wedding*

'Decadence, scandal, murder, and an adorable goat: what's not to love?!'
Naomi Kelsey, author of *The Burnings*

Praise for Lucy Roth

'Incredibly pacy, funny, oh-so-dark, devious and dare I say, relatable . . . I loved everything about it!'
Noelle Holton, author of *His Truth Her Truth*

'I couldn't put it down (I barely slept!). Lucy Roth is officially brilliant and I am obsessed'
Lucy Vine, author of *What Fresh Hell*

'Wow! I loved it. Devoured it in two days. It was dark, delicious and deadly' Louise Swanson, author of *End of Story*

'Delightful malice and menace'
Robin Ince, author of *I'm a Joke and So Are You*

'Dark and funny' Jackie Kabler, author of *The Murder List*

'I couldn't put it down' L.M. Chilton, author of *Don't Swipe Right*

THE PARTY TO END ALL PARTIES

LUCY ROTH

avon.

Published by AVON
A division of HarperCollins*Publishers* Ltd
1 London Bridge Street
London SE1 9GF

www.harpercollins.co.uk

HarperCollins*Publishers*
Macken House, 39/40 Mayor Street Upper
Dublin 1, D01 C9W8, Ireland

A Paperback Original 2026
1

First published in Great Britain by HarperCollins*Publishers* 2026

Copyright © Lucy Nichol 2026

Lucy Nichol asserts the moral right to be identified as the author of this work.

A catalogue copy of this book is available from the British Library.

ISBN: 9780008803971

This novel is entirely a work of fiction. The names, characters and incidents portrayed in it are the work of the author's imagination. Any resemblance to actual persons, living or dead, events or localities is entirely coincidental.

Set in Sabon LT Std by HarperCollins*Publishers* India

Printed and bound in the UK using 100%
Renewable Electricity at CPI Group (UK) Ltd

All rights reserved. No part of this publication may be reproduced, stored in a retrieval system, or transmitted, in any form or by any means, electronic, mechanical, photocopying, recording or otherwise, without the prior written permission of the publishers.

Without limiting the exclusive rights of any author, contributor or the publisher of this publication, any unauthorised use of this publication to train generative artificial intelligence (AI) technologies is expressly prohibited. HarperCollins also exercise their rights under Article 4(3) of the Digital Single Market Directive 2019/790 and expressly reserve this publication from the text and data mining exception.

*For my beautiful friend Kassie,
and in memory of Iggy the cheeky goat*

Prologue

Sunday 24th August

06.17

Angel wings lie spreadeagled on the grass, punctured by scorch marks and ash. Tab ends and a burnt-out roach decorate the netting like trashy beading. The camera points upwards to a sky streaked with soft ribbons of lilac, pink and pale orange, treetops moving gently beneath. A tuft of white hairs occasionally obscures the lens. Quick, short sniffing sounds overwhelm the audio before a magpie revs up its angry chatter in the distance. The camera points downwards towards the grass and a grating sound can be heard, like a train on the tracks. The grating stops and the camera pans around to where a fountain stands in the distance, shaped like petals atop a smooth stone column. Water trickles down gracefully like liquid silk. Neat gravel paths and well-kept lawns frame the fountain – the intense green interrupted by wine bottles, sunglasses and small pieces of discarded food. A twisted wooden dome with a covered entrance and latticed sides stands tall to the left, while to the right is a vacant stage with speakers either side of a table.

The lens stops and shakes. Violently. A fast, scratching sound.

A grand house is almost fully in view now, large and imposing. It is bordered by low-level structural hedging and stone-covered walkways. The camera moves towards the house, its brickwork bold and solid. A grey-white statue to the right reveals an amalgamation of stony human forms, a bare bottom beaming proudly into view.

The camera manoeuvres to the left of the house, heading up a small slope at speed – trip, trap, trip, trap – and then it turns to the right and enters the building. A raw stone floor is decorated haphazardly with patterned cushions and people. Endless human bodies drape across each other like layers of fleshy rock. A half-empty bottle of something cradled in broken glass, its dark blue label only partly visible, exposing fragments of gold script. Bare feet hug bare feet. Someone is snoring . . .

A human face comes into view, its pointed nose twitching and its top lip shiny with sweat. Its owner lets out a low guttural groan and the camera backs away. The view moves towards spiral steps, swerving to avoid a doll hanging from the wall – its eyes staring. The camera heads down the steps and stops. A pink mass fills the screen. The camera jolts in and out, a white furry chin prodding at the soft texture. The focus moves, and wiry black hair fills one half of the view, some kind of fleshy mound, flopping among the hair, completes the other half of the picture. The view moves again, scaling a limb, before panning out to reveal a hand, its fingers forming an impossible, backwards, mangled V shape.

The camera reverses once more. A tongue sticks out and licks the ground, lapping something. Whiskers and white fur appear in the top of the screen, globules of a bright red substance lodged within them. Thick red liquid spatters the lens.

Chapter 1

Kassie

Friday

I grab my Dr Martens from beneath the cherrywood bureau and collapse onto the rug as I slip them onto my feet. I jump back up, wafting out the hem of my dress, and pluck the wicker basket from the hook where it hangs among a pile of coats.

I open the front door to my cottage and step onto the path outside, the morning sun immediately warming my pale skin. I turn to close the door and catch the scent of the jasmine climber next to me. I take a deep and satisfying breath.

Mmmmm . . .

I adore the dark cottage-core thing I've got going on and I'll play up to it as much as I damn well want, *Steven*, I think, remembering my brother's pointless taunts. I squint and smile at the same time, looking towards the blood orange star in the sky. God – I love days like this. And then I remember . . .

This weekend we'll be over-run with rich drunken arseholes. Costumed-up, coked-up, boozed-up arseholes. Great.

Stay in the moment, Kassie . . .

I glance between my quaint cottage and our gigantic family house looming in the distance. The main hall sits face-on, while cloisters jut forward on either side, their hollow archways like missing teeth in a gaping jaw.

It's obscene, really, that all this belongs to us.

But my cottage, while not of a good enough size or standard for any of my siblings, apparently, was perfect for me. Sure it was a little rough around the edges, but I've made it pretty as a picture, with jasmine, ivy and clematis growing up it, a solid wooden front door that I painted violet and adorned with a heavy iron knocker in the shape of a hare's head, and front and back gardens well off the beaten path. Even when the grounds are open to the public I rarely feel like there's any intrusion on this part of the estate.

Not like in the main house.

Being holed up in the west wing as members of the public wander around the rest of the building always feels a little intrusive. We're like ghosts in our own home. But we need the income to contribute towards the upkeep of the place, and we're not exactly doing the best job of it since Dad got ill and, rather infuriatingly, stopped living.

Steven, as the eldest and our self-appointed leader, did manage to get me a lump sum from Granny to make the cottage 'fit for purpose' as he described it. I was shocked by his help, which made me highly suspicious given how much of a curmudgeonly bully he usually is. Regardless, I took the money, and I gave the place a makeover.

I glance up towards the sunshine, forcing a smile as

I wander down the little stone path and turn right into the rundown cottage next door to check on Iggy. It was a condition of me moving in here almost a year ago now – Steven was to allow me to keep my little goat Iggy next door, and I'd stay out of Steven's way by holing up in the cottage.

To be fair, I'd have moved here in a heartbeat. It's so much nicer having my own space. Bar the occasional family meeting and the expectation that we all dine together when Caitlin or Granny visit, I'm pretty much left in peace.

I walk towards Iggy's quarters and can hear her scuffling around behind the crude replacement door with its cute little 'Iggy's Place' sign attached to it.

Before moving her in I completely gutted the adjoining cottage, which had been in a state of dilapidation for years since the fire. It all happened before I was born – jackdaws nesting in the chimney or something. Dad was always planning to get it renovated, to turn it into a visitor café and let the cottage that I'm now in as a holiday home. But Steven seemed hellbent on defying his ghost. Which I guess worked out OK for me in the end.

I push the door open and, as soon as she sees me, her little tail starts wagging and she skips towards me across the hay-scattered stone floor. Her small black and white body lurches at me, giving me a wiry-haired cuddle that almost knocks me backwards and makes me drop my basket to the floor. Laughing, I regain my balance and hug her back tightly.

My baby girl.

She's the closest any of us have got to having a child since none of us have ever shown any interest in having actual human babies. Morland spawn would be pretty horrific. There's enough shit happening in the world.

I look around the space, checking she still has enough bedding in the far corner and making a note to muck the place out before dinner later on. I moved Iggy here from out of the ramshackle goat pen she used to live in since she was a teeny baby Bagot goat. It's all on one floor, thanks to the stairs collapsing and being taken out, and it has enough air circulating due to the windows not being in a fit state. But, while that might seem like slumming it for us, it's perfect for Iggy. I cleared out the debris – burnt furniture and the like – and I got a structural engineer in to check that it was stable enough to keep her safe, warm and dry. And so here she is.

I continue to hold Iggy for a moment longer before straightening back up and batting away the hay that's now clinging to my dress. She follows me close at heel as I stock up her hay feeder, check on her water and unlock the Iggy-sized cat flap I had installed so she can come and go to graze on the lawn and scamp around as she pleases during the day.

'Come on then, baby girl,' I say, picking my basket back up as we wander towards the herb garden and past the greenhouse.

Our greenhouse, well, *my* greenhouse seeing as I'm the only one who really uses it, is a long narrow room built out of an old brick structure with a slanted glass roof that meets the ground to form the side of the building. I keep the most gorgeous flowers on show in there. The exotic primeras, with their pink spiky flowers sitting among dappled green leaves shaped like long wilting tongues. The flame lilies are also absolutely stunning – despite reminding me of arthritic fingers all coiled up like something on a villain from *Doctor Who*. But I kind of like the strangeness. There's the cantaloupe melons I currently have resting in hessian hammocks like babies in slings, and the cyclamen with their twisted stems reminiscent of musical notes. And then I have my special project – my chacruna plants with their deep red berries and the soul vine, which generally needs a lot of pruning before it takes over.

I walk along the path by the side of the greenhouse, looking in through the window at the mushroom tent, which is set back behind the big, showy plants. Mushrooms thrive in the dark – which is a good job seeing as we're not supposed to grow this particular kind of fungi. Peering in you wouldn't have a clue what's cultivating beneath the dark grey fabric of my little grow tent.

I spend a lot of time in the greenhouse and I just knew I had to keep it to myself when I did it up. And that was even before I became a purveyor of hallucinogenics. It's the solitude and the cultivation for me – consumption of the finished product I can take or leave to be honest.

We've actually kept the greenhouse private since 2016 when it needed a refurb. It was deemed unsafe after the cottage fire spread to the roof, and then, when we finally got the work done, I said I'd take on the tending of it if I could keep it as a passion project – and keep the public out of the area.

Shame us Morlands don't stay out of view – everything we do seems to play out in public.

I walk past the greenhouse and towards the herb garden. As much as I love Iggy, I have to draw the line at access to my herbs. I've cordoned that off, too, and she's happy enough trotting about in the small paddock next to it while I gather the herbs I need for tomorrow's party cocktails. I keep my greenhouse goat-free as well. To be honest, I try to keep it family-free, too.

I take the scissors from my basket and kneel beside the mint plants, snipping at the stems in sharp, clean cuts before placing the harvest in one area of the basket. Then I scooch around past the lavender, where bees are out early buzzing around the small flowers that always remind me of tiny purple pineapples. I've had enough lavender cuttings drying out by the kitchen for a few weeks now, so I don't need to get any more of that – it's just the coriander I need. Paul loves a spicy marg and the coriander sets it off perfectly.

After gathering everything I need, I leave the herb patch and open the little gate to the paddock, whistling for Iggy to follow me towards the house.

As you face Morland Hall there are steps leading up to the main doors – the grand entrance – but our family doesn't use those. The building consists of the main hall ahead, and two wings on either side reaching out towards the sprawling lawns that meet the estate's roadside entrance. I enter the west wing by the unassuming door that opens directly into our main living space and close it behind me once Iggy's safely inside. Then I turn left and head towards the kitchen with Iggy in tow. As I approach, I can smell freshly baked bread and can hear our housekeeper, Mrs Davies, closing cupboard doors and chatting to our chef, Brian.

'Yes, to the left of the entrance. They'll probably need help with the glasses, too, so if we can both be on hand for that mid-morning . . . oh, hello, Kassie my love.'

'Morning,' I chirp. Brian gives me a silent half-smile that barely creeps out from under his huge gingery beard, then he quickly glances away again, needlessly rearranging the condiments with his big bear-sized back to us. Mrs Davies' eyes glance up to the ceiling and she shakes her head with a knowing smile on her face, her cropped salt and pepper hair unmoving. There's a reason she's always on catering team liaison duty while Brian is hidden away in the kitchen. He's a great cook; social skills leave a lot to be desired. Paul once joked that he could stand in for Father Christmas during our festive events programme, but, as Mrs Davies pointed out, his demeanour might add a sinister edge. I couldn't see him ho-ho-ho-ing in any case.

I smile back at Mrs Davies, who moves towards the island top with purpose, gathering papers that she scoops up and holds in front of her crisp white T-shirt and navy tailored trousers.

'Are they the cocktail menus I put together?' I ask.

'Yes. You made quite the impression there, you know. The mixologist said he's tempted to add your version of the spicy marg to his own menu.'

'It's all in the herbs,' I say, tapping my nose and placing my basket on the side. Mrs Davies positions her nostrils in the air above the basket before taking a couple of short, sharp sniffs and wafting her hand beneath her nose in a precise manner.

'That mint is delicious,' she says, gently squeezing my arm. 'Brian, love, would you mind finding a container for Kassie's herbs and keeping them fresh for tomorrow?'

Brian nods, another half-smile threatening to escape but not quite making it out alive.

Mrs Davies manages the running of the house and kitchen, and Brian reports to her – albeit with creative culinary autonomy – most of the time. Mrs Davies also serves our food and drink daily, whips out the Dyson after a party and cooks up a home-made lasagne when one of us is feeling down. She's a real gem.

As Brian takes my basket to one side, Mrs Davies puts

her arm around me and holds me close. 'Your mother would be so proud of you, growing those herbs. You're a natural,' she says, holding on to me. I might be almost thirty but Mrs Davies' hugs have been a staple since I was a kid. She's my comfort blanket.

'Oh what a beautiful morning, oh what a beautiful day, I'm gonna get fucking arseholed, everything's going my way . . .' My middle brother, Paul, dances into the kitchen wearing only lounge shorts and singing at the top of his voice in an accent even more affected than his natural one.

'Hey, how come I never get a hug?' he says, running up to Mrs Davies, forcing her to release her grip of me and scooping her awkwardly up off the floor. She grimaces and I giggle as he places her carefully back down on the tiled floor, realising he's overstepped. As always.

'Morning, sis.' He turns his attention to me and kisses my head. 'And good morning to you, little Iggy Piggy Pop!' he says, his tone reminiscent of a hyperactive kids' TV presenter as he grabs Iggy's face and gives it a wiggle. She waggles her little tail in appreciation and he purses his lips towards her, his freckled nose wrinkling as he shakes his head.

'The mixologist is apparently impressed with my take on the spicy marg,' I say to Paul.

'Not surprised,' he says, ripping a corner of bread from the fresh loaf on the side. Brian looks like he could explode; his veins are popping in his neck, making his tattooed angel's wings flutter. Mrs Davies clocks his discomfort, walks by and slaps Paul's hand. 'Nobody's too posh to cut their own bread,' she says, pointing to the knife.

'I know,' he says. 'But I'm eating with my hands. Like a natural-born savage.' He makes a strange animal noise in Iggy's direction and she skips around in delight.

'Did you get that DJ sorted in the end?' I ask.

'Hm?' Paul says, still chewing on the bread and pulling daft faces at Iggy.

'The DJ? From that place in town?'

'Don't even go there,' he says, straightening up and lifting his hands in front of him.

'Why? What's up?' I ask, noticing Mrs Davies leaving the kitchen through the back door. Paul's boundless energy can be too much first thing in the morning.

'You've not looked at the family WhatsApp yet then?'

I pull a face and take my iPhone from my dress pocket, lighting the screen up with my thumb. I swipe left to locate the little green app and open up the family group chat – entitled 'Morland Twats' – only to find an angry exchange between Paul and my sister, Caitlin. I scroll through the messages while Paul watches me expectantly, still chewing frantically on bread.

> Caitlin: Got us a superb DJ.
> Paul: FFS! Seriously?!
> Caitlin: You might sound more grateful.
> Paul: Control freak.
> Paul: You'll have to cancel cause I've already booked someone.
> Caitlin: Don't worry – I cancelled yours this morning. All sorted. Xx

'Eh? Why has she cancelled your DJ?' I ask.

'Because it's what she does,' he says, letting out a deep sigh.

Paul was supposed to be our one-man entertainment committee for our party tomorrow. Caitlin's supposed to be in charge of the costume and décor. Me the cocktails and natural party treats. And Steven, as ever, took the monopoly over the guest list. He'll not be best pleased when Paul and Caitlin's lot turn up when the sun goes down, as they inevitably will.

'When's she getting here anyway?' I ask, dread rising in me at the very thought.

'Sometime this afternoon. Granny and Caitlin in one day. Deep fucking joy.' He grabs more bread from the fresh loaf and sneaks out of the kitchen before Brian can chastise him with a terrifying look.

'Just going to grab some of that lavender,' I say to Brian, not really expecting an acknowledgement. I wander out through the kitchen and towards the utility room at the back. The lavender's hanging over a high line that's stretched between the walls, just as you might hang weed.

Lavender has a truly calming smell, and I love how it can create the prettiest cocktails. A nice, refreshing lavender lemonade cocktail.

I place my basket on the wooden sideboard and step onto the little wooden footstool to reach the hanging flowers. I'm just gathering the dried-out stems when I hear hushed urgent voices outside beyond the half-open door. I place the lavender I've just plucked into my basket and listen intently.

'You know why you can't.' It's Mrs Davies. She sounds angry. And not just a bit grumpy either, but genuinely angry. It's a tone I rarely hear from her.

I stop what I'm doing and concentrate. The only other sound is Iggy sniffing around between the stone tiles of the floor and the bottom of the tall cupboard door. I strain to hear as Steven's impersonal, formal voice hisses in response.

'If you had your way . . .'

'You've had your way all your life. But when it comes to this . . .'

'You'd do anything, wouldn't you?' he jumps in, interrupting her.

'Yes,' she snaps, her voice rising. 'So you know that it will never be yours.'

I bite my lip in concentration. What the hell are they arguing about? What will never be his? The estate? Granny's coming to speak to us about our inheritance later on – could it be to do with that? But why wouldn't it be Steven's? As the eldest, he's the natural first choice. Unfortunately.

And I've no idea why Steven is letting Mrs Davies speak to him like that. I mean, not that she shouldn't – he's a right twat at the best of times. But he's usually such an authoritative, totalitarian bully. Although, saying that, she probably had to wipe his arse when he was a kid so maybe, when push comes to shove, she really can hold her own with him. I've just never heard her speak so . . . aggressively towards him before.

He comes back at her, but his voice has lost its usual confidence.

'It's rightfully mine.'

'No,' she says. 'You should be locked up for what you did. Pure evil.'

What on earth are they talking about? Pure evil? Curiosity sets my brain whirring at a thousand miles per hour but just then, there's a huge clatter. I turn and can see Iggy has managed to force open the cupboard door with her nose, an ironing board falling out and making a racket against the stone tiles and everything else that was propped up with it. Iggy runs at full pelt out of the door.

'Who's that?' Steven yells.

'It's just Iggy,' I call through. Then I go towards the door and poke my head out, pretending I haven't heard anything. 'Oh, morning, Steven,' I say. 'Just been sorting the cocktail herbs.'

Quite distinct from Paul's casual vibes, Steven's morning attire consists of a preppy white polo shirt with smart jeans and tan shoes. Paul once ironed creases down the middle of all Steven's jeans to prank him and, honestly, while he openly reprimanded Paul, I think he was secretly pleased.

Steven chooses not to comment on my herbs and instead silently drops his cigarette onto the path and puts it out quickly with his foot. He stares at me for a moment, his brown eyes appearing almost black and his brow pinched. He says nothing, then storms off to the left.

'Right, I better make sure Caitlin's room's ready,' Mrs Davies says, then she walks off quickly too and I stand there, completely bemused.

What exactly has my big brother done?

Chapter 2

Paul

Friday

I can feel Caitlin's upcoming presence like acid reflux. I try to distract myself by pointing the remote control at the widescreen TV that sits on top of our heavy antique drinks cabinet. I flick through the channels aimlessly, then stop at *Homes Under the Hammer* – an intriguing show. Steven appears in the corner of the room. I've never known anybody look stiffer than a porn star and as nonchalant as a lemming on a cliff edge simultaneously, but Steven pulls it off well. Perhaps that's the problem – maybe he needs to pull it off more frequently.

He looks at me, says nothing and heads to the bureau by the door.

I fix my gaze back on the TV. 'Smoking in the house again, Steven?' I say, imitating the old woman and keen to irritate the shit out of him. He says nothing but I can hear the spark of his lighter and soon the smell of burning tobacco floats over to me. I remain fixed on the TV, intrigued as to why the presenter, who looks like a car salesman, suggests the sorry-looking terraced house he's standing in front of is a bargain. I chuckle, then – feeling irritated by Steven's silence – I turn to look at him.

'You know what she's gone and done?' I say forcefully.

Steven just looks at me and takes a long drag of his cigarette.

'You know we're not meant to be smoking in the house,' I say, circling my pointed finger in the air. 'Insurance or whatever.'

'We have farmyard animals running around the kitchen and you're worried about a cigarette. Besides, it wasn't a cigarette that caused it.'

I raise my eyebrows. 'Whatever,' I say, exhaling noisily and turning back to the TV. The presenter is now standing in the middle of a kitchen surrounded by cheap melamine units. 'Crikey,' I say. 'How *do* the other half live?'

'So what's she gone and done then?' Steven says, tapping his ash in the ceramic key tray on top of the bureau. Mrs Davies'll give him grief about that later, I'm sure.

'What's who gone and done?'

'You tell me – it was your pointless story,' Steven says dismissively. And then I remember what I was so angry about before losing myself in *Homes Under the Hammer*.

'Caitlin,' I say, sitting back up and knowing full well Steven won't have seen the WhatsApp message. He has us on mute. He uses that group chat to summon us, but other than that, he pretends it doesn't exist.

'You're bickering again I take it? She's not even here yet.'

'She cancelled my DJ. Booked her own.'

'That's it? Jesus, Paul, in the grander scheme of things . . .'

'Fine. I'll uninvite some of your guests.'

'Not exactly the same though is it,' he says, his patronising tone making me sneer. 'DJs, or potential investors. I wonder who we need the most.'

'Your investors won't be happy if the party's purely wank,' I say, staring back at the terraced house on the TV and putting my feet up on the Italian marble coffee table in front of me. I study its intricate giltwood edges, then look back at the TV screen. That coffee table cost more than the bargain house on TV. I remove my feet and put them up on the sofa instead.

I wonder, would it be better living somewhere like that terraced house on TV alone than living in this huge fuck-off house with Northumberland's very own Caligula breathing down my neck?

'When's she due anyway?' Steven asks.

'Why does everyone think I've got access to Caitlin's diary?'

'Because you probably have.'

'Mid-afternoon or something,' I say, even though I know she's expected between three and three thirty.

'Well, what can I say? Take it up with Caitlin.' He extinguishes his cigarette. I could do with one myself to be honest.

If I argue my case, I know he won't help and he won't bite. So there's no benefit and no entertainment. I change tack.

'Got your pitch for Granny ready?' I ask.

'Hm?'

'I bet it's on PowerPoint. You using a pointer? Or a laser? Or are you just going to use your pencil dick, seeing as it won't be able to contain itself at the prospect of financial gain.'

'Look, Paul,' he says, exhaling a plume of smoke as he speaks. 'Given I'm already running the estate single-handedly, there's not really a need for me to peacock around the old woman, is there.'

'There'd be no need for anyone to peacock around her if we all stuck together,' I say.

'But where's the fun in that? Besides, it's a test. You know what she's like. If we all stick together she'll suggest we haven't got the balls and give it to a dog's charity or something.'

I refuse to laugh at that because he does have a point. Granny loves baiting us, divide and conquer and all that. It's her sport. And that's exactly what she's doing with the estate.

Tuesday marks five years since the death of our father – and so this month is Granny's deadline to hand the estate over to one – or all of us. The rules are simple. If we all agree to run it together, she'll hand over an equal share to each of us. If just one of us refuses, we all have to make a play. Separately.

And of course, Steven – being the arrogant sociopath that he is – refused to join ranks. He's created a bear pit. I just don't think he realises quite how much competition he's got.

Chapter 3

Kassie

Friday

My peaceful reading session hidden away in my late father's study is interrupted by the start of a new story. A horror, no doubt. The beginning of which opens with the crunch of stones under the wheels of a Bentley Continental GT.

Leaving the Romanovs' final days behind in the pages of my book and re-entering my own reality is a daunting prospect. A prospect that, should Anastasia Romanov have endured it in those final days, would no doubt have helped her come to terms with her impending death.

And the death of all her family.

I close my book, place it on the arm of the chair and take a deep breath as I watch my sister Caitlin and her husband, James, park their car, the sun glaring blindingly from their windscreen.

They walk towards the steps of Morland Hall, Caitlin in

glamorous oversized sunglasses, and, unlike the rest of us, they go to enter through the main doors as though they're royalty. Iggy, lying on the rug, lifts her head curiously.

They don't know I'm watching them as Caitlin leads the way empty-handed and lips pursed, maxi dress flowing behind her – along with James who is overloaded with bags. Mrs Davies comes out to greet them and Caitlin waves towards their car. There's clearly more to be carried into the house.

As much as Caitlin's presence irks me, she alone is not the full horror story. She's simply a puzzle piece of our horror story. Once we are all back in the grounds, rubbing up against each other, a chemical reaction occurs. A really shit one.

It was when I was in school with the other kids that I realised my life wasn't exactly typical. And I don't just mean the huge amount of money we have. I mean the huge amounts of narcissism and psychopathy that seem to co-exist in this household like jam and cream on scones. And just like jam and cream, it's hard to work out which comes first – the narcissism or the psychopathy. They definitely complement each other, though. They definitely work together. And no, I'm not claiming to be an armchair psychologist. You don't need to be in this case. Their traits are bright and extreme and impossible to miss.

I look up at the huge, framed paintings hanging on the walls in the study flanked by elaborate gold frames. The first is a portrait of our parents, my mother sitting on a dark green armchair, her wavy hair tied up neatly in a style that, according to Cailtin, she never really liked. My father is posed behind her, pinstripe suit and tie, nothing out of place. My mother's eyes appear empty and I wonder if that's really what the artist saw that day? I never did have the chance to look into them myself.

The other frames capture a generation at a time, starting with Granny and our late Grandpa (who Paul's convinced was murdered by Granny – his sudden death aged forty-seven always did seem suspicious), and then the rest of our ancestors all standing tall with round, porcelain faces, ruddy cheeks and gentle eyes. The portraits make my ancestors look dreamy and soft in nature – which is far from Morland reality. Our temperament goes way back. It didn't start with Granny, but it might end with us. There are no baby Morlands to keep the sociopathic nature of who we really are going strong.

But they could never fully hide the truth. If you look closely at the portrait of my great-great-grandmother Anna, you can see a mark that covers a hole in the canvas. Rumour has it, it was created by a champagne cork flying out there at warp speed. We weren't the first to party hard in this place – but perhaps it's time we were the last.

I leave the peaceful confines of the study and walk down the stairs towards the main hall. I can hear them all before I see them.

'Sweetheart. *So* lovely to see you.' Caitlin's voice is thick with artificial sweetener as she draws out her syrupy words.

'We've missed you, Linny,' Paul says to Caitlin, kissing both her cheeks. Caitlin always balks if we shorten her name to Cait, so, a few years ago, Paul decided to go one further, miss out 'Cait' entirely and extend the final part of her name. Caitlin doesn't react. She knows it's better not to indulge him.

I wave over to Caitlin and smile but keep my distance for now. James, however, approaches and kisses both my cheeks and, from the smell on his breath and the greying of his lips, I can tell he's already been at the Merlot. 'For his nerves'.

Iggy head-butts James' thigh enthusiastically and his face suddenly looks as grey as his lips. James is terrified of Iggy, which is why her instinct propels her towards him first. Goats love a bit of mischief.

I follow them through to our wing where they gather in the living room, Iggy trotting ahead of me. When we get in there, I feel instantly amused to find James backing away from Iggy, pressing himself against the bookcase while she wags her tail at warp speed. She would move away if I call out to her. I don't.

'Look at you, Kassie.' Caitlin faux squeals, holding out her arms, her beautifully layered dress flowing out beside her as if it has a life of its own. Her body language, however, is in stark contrast to her tone, and she air-kisses me with precision.

Caitlin squeezes my shoulders theatrically, pulls back and holds my arms out. 'Kassie. What *are* you wearing? You look . . .'

'Delightful.' It's the authoritative voice of Mrs Davies that instantly puts me at ease. She walks in with a tray of drinks. Steven, following close behind, a scowl on his face, heads straight towards the bureau and picks out his cigar case. He lights one up and offers his open case to James, who accepts.

As Mrs Davies continues to walk through the room, tray in hand, she winks at me. We both know she's saved me from another of Caitlin's abrasive remarks. Mrs Davies places the drinks tray on the table and everyone, bar me, grabs a gin and tonic. I choose not to partake. I need my wits about me among this lot.

Caitlin looks me up and down, an expression of bemusement on her face as she takes in my almost black, long 'shullet' haircut, dark green smock dress and Dr Martens. 'I'm so excited to show you your costume, Kassie,' she says. I catch Mrs Davies rolling her eyes and I smile inwardly. 'You're going to look divine.' Caitlin beams.

The party, which will take place tomorrow night, has been in the planning for months. It's kind of a D-day blowout. Our last weekend before we find out who's going to be handed the responsibility of running the estate – and deciding everyone else's fate.

We're also hosting Granny overnight tonight. She announced she was coming only the day before yesterday, so we've been feeling on edge ever since. Someone must have tipped her off about the party. And while Granny knows her DNA hasn't exactly spawned strait-laced grandchildren, she doesn't know quite how debauched things can get at Morland Hall when Paul and Caitlin are let loose.

We always theme our parties and go to town on the costume and decor. The first big bash we threw after Dad died was inspired by *Alice in Wonderland* – an obvious choice. They gradually got stranger and more obscure as time went on, with Steampunk and messed-up mythical creatures until eventually we came to this year's theme . . .

The party tomorrow is to be a heaven and hell themed costume party inspired by the famous Hieronymus Bosch painting – *The Garden of Earthly Delights*. So we're not just talking angels and devils – we're talking naked people emerging from broken eggs with their legs spreadeagled; birds sitting on top of thrones devouring other human figures like a snake might; and a pig wearing a nun's veil while trying to get off with some poor fella.

Perfectly normal stuff.

Caitlin and James visited the gallery where it hangs in Madrid last summer and she's been obsessed with it ever since. She's even gone as far as to invest in 'companion pieces' from Christie's. She spent over a hundred thousand on *The Harrowing of Hell* and I swear James is as scared of that as he is of Iggy.

'I've carved some pumpkins,' I say proudly. 'In homage to Bosch.' I was inspired by a focal point in the painting that's like a face, but with arms and legs, and its hands are pulling its huge mouth wide open, revealing a black abyss. It looks like the rest of the painting is being puked up out of it. So I created some pumpkins with strange little limbs that look as though they are puking their insides out – seeds and gunk everywhere.

'Pumpkins?' Caitlin says, releasing a deprecating laugh. 'I'm not sure that *pumpkins* are really an homage to Bosch, darling.'

'Oh I don't know,' James says kindly. 'I'm sure they—'

'I'm sure they'll be great for the kids,' Caitlin says, interrupting him and throwing a death stare. Her sweet voice cracks into something more naturally sinister when she's caught off guard. 'Will they last until October, though, Kassie?'

Paul downs his G&T, places it back on the tray and picks up the one that was meant for me. He moves towards Caitlin and I. 'But, Caitlin, I thought our party roles were fluid.'

'Fluid? That word coming from you makes me want to gag...'

'And thinking about your pulsating throat makes me...'

'Give it a rest,' Steven says. 'It's boring and we've only been in the same room five minutes.'

Caitlin always talks to Paul like dirt. And Paul always gets thrown and struggles to come up with something intelligent when Caitlin's on his case. Don't know why – he's king of the riposte usually.

Paul persists, ignoring Steven who is standing to his left now, continuing to puff away on his gross cigar. 'Seeing as how you decided to make a move on entertainment, I'm sure Kassie can have at least *some* say in décor.' Paul looks at me now and I wonder whether being drawn into their bickering can ever be a good thing.

Regardless, Caitlin's glare transforms into a smile. Not that you could tell she's happy by looking into her eyes. 'Of course. Of course,' she says animatedly, her hands clasping in faux delight. 'Why not place them outside of your cottage, hm, Kassie? That'll do nicely. There. Sorted. Can we move it along now please?'

The fact I'm almost thirty seems to have bypassed Caitlin. And the rest of them for that matter. Being the youngest has always been a drag in this house. When did décor have to become so stiff? Surely using natural resources is better than spending a fortune on whatever Caitlin's got planned?

'So what's the plan for the décor?' I ask her. 'It better be sustainable.'

'I have the most wonderful designer working on it,' Caitlin says. 'She's drawn up some fabulous plans, created some amazing structures and she's arriving with it all for the big installation tomorrow morning.'

'But is it—'

'Yes, yes, yes,' Caitlin replies, waving her hand in my face while looking away. 'It's guaranteed to be . . . show-stopping.'

Paul makes a noise as if he's clearing phlegm from his throat. Caitlin narrows her eyes before looking back at me and moving her arm slowly through the air like a ballerina might. 'Birth. Death. And everything in between,' she says, as if she's got those three things dancing delicately on her fingers as she speaks the words. This outward delicacy isn't born of sensitivity; it's born of control. I swear, if you found an opening in the back of an old wardrobe, you'd find Caitlin poised in a diamond-studded sleigh slaughtering woodland animals, a deluge of blood trailing in the snow behind her.

'James,' Steven says formally, clearly keen to change the subject. 'Did that property come through?'

'Yes. It's currently in for planning. Keeping everything crossed,' James says, wandering over to Steven, both still *avec* cigar. The smell makes me want to gag. Of course, James doesn't need to keep anything crossed. He has the financial power to sway council decision-making.

They're about the same age, James and Steven. Steven's forty-three and I think James is maybe a year or two older at most. Given the proximity in age and wealth, there's a definite competitiveness between the two. I mean, there's a competitiveness between all my siblings, but it's different between Steven and James. There's a mutual respect as well, but it's always dampened by a need to outdo one another. And now, with James being Caitlin's not-so-secret weapon in inheritance-gate (Granny simply adores the link to James' much wealthier family) Steven will be keeping his cards close to his chest. So, they will inevitably spend this evening playing snooker and boasting about their latest cars. Steven's just bought the new Aston Martin Coupe. James has his Bentley. They'll be out there later on, each with a glass and a cigar in hand, lifting up the bonnets of their respective vehicles as if they've any clue whatsoever as to what lies beneath them.

Of course, they don't actually *like* each other.

'I take it you're going to manage your intake tomorrow?' Caitlin says to Paul, sipping her gin and tonic slowly. Meanwhile Paul's already finished his second.

'It's a party,' Paul says. 'You might be in charge of costume but you're not in charge of consumption. Besides, there's only room for one killjoy at a party.' He glances in Steven's direction and Caitlin's eyes follow.

'Fair point,' she says. 'Just, go easy on the psychedelics. We don't need to be scooping you out of the fountain and mopping up your inappropriate behaviour again.'

'It was *paradoxical undressing*,' Paul says, exhausted by yet another reference to that night. 'Besides,' he adds, 'it's the middle of summer. There's no harm in a bit of skinny-dipping.' I cringe at the memory. Paul's usually the last one standing – booze, coke, whatever, he can handle it. But when he throws more unpredictable substances into the mix, as he's planning to tomorrow, it can go one of two ways. Heaven – or hell. Quite apt really. I've never understood why he insists on taking the risk. But he does love a bit of roulette. And it is our final blow-out, so . . .

'Count me out,' I say, keen not to get drawn into any weird shit that goes on tomorrow night. I might enable said weird shit with my plants and herbal brews, but I don't want a front-row seat to watch it.

'It's OK, Kassie. We know you'll be away for your 9 p.m. curfew.'

'Piss off, Caitlin,' I snap.

Caitlin emits a satisfied smile, and Paul squeezes my arm in solidarity. It's cute that he always has my back, but it feels like a reminder of the eight-year age gap between us. I'll still be considered the baby when we're all geriatric. Which reminds me . . .

'Isn't Granny meant to be here by now?' I ask.

'Dennis has gone to get her,' Paul says of our business manager. I say 'our' business manager, but Granny appointed him. And she's always got his ear. 'She's staying with the Taylor-Bankses again tomorrow night.'

'Why is she staying there?' I ask. 'Isn't it the opposite direction?'

'One of the grandsons is part of the Trust inspection team,' Steven explains, re-entering the conversation. 'So I can't quite decide whether she'll be buttering them up or asking them to catch us out.'

'How so?' Caitlin asks.

'If we don't pass, it gives her reason to play puppet master for longer.'

Caitlin sighs. 'Granny *will* be gone in time, won't she?' she says, placing her now empty glass back on the tray. 'For the party, I mean.'

'I believe she's heading to the TBs early morning,' Paul says. 'I made a point of saying we needed Dennis and the car back early doors to schmooze business contacts.'

'Yes, and you can let Dennis and I lead in that department,' Steven says flatly.

'What department?'

'Business. You'll be even more inept than usual by

sundown.' Steven takes another pompous drag on his cigar, all the while eyeing Paul, who delivers a hard stare back before muttering something barely audible under his breath.

There's a moment's silence, which James fills by cosying back up to Caitlin on the sofa. Meanwhile, Steven calls my name abruptly.

'Kassie. Kass! Would you mind . . .' He's holding out his empty glass. He knows it's the biggest slight he can dish out. I ignore him.

'I'll do that, Mr Morland,' says Mrs Davies. 'It's what you pay me for, after all.' He looks affronted but says nothing as Mrs Davies marches out of the living room and towards the kitchen.

I slump down onto the sofa next to James, squashing him between me and Caitlin. 'Ooh, a Morland-women sandwich. Every man's dream,' he jokes awkwardly and highly inappropriately, trying to right his position while Caitlin rolls her eyes at me in sympathy and then turns to my brother.

'Steven. What's going on with the wallpaper?' She waggles her fingers abruptly in front of her face.

Steven takes the glass of whisky brought to him by Mrs Davies, who then walks back out of the room. Steven sips the rusty-looking liquid slowly, leaving Caitlin waiting. She doesn't take her eyes off him the whole time. 'How do you mean?' he says eventually.

'The new wallpaper design. It's not up.'

Steven glances at the custard-yellow walls. 'Apparently not.'

'And why not?'

'Because it's vile, Cait.'

Caitlin narrows her eyes at his shortening of her name. 'I'll arrange for someone to fit it after the party.'

He doesn't reply, confident that he won't let it happen. Caitlin is equally confident that it will. It's a reflection of their firm belief that Granny will put one of them in charge of the estate. And they'd both bet a million to one on themselves.

Caitlin might no longer live here, having chosen London over Northumberland, but at the end of the day, until Granny makes her decision, we are equally charged with looking after it.

'So tell us who you've bumped my DJ for then?' Paul says to Caitlin. 'Some wanky player from London I'm guessing?'

'Ah yes. He's quite the catch,' Caitlin says smiling. James, meanwhile, looks down at his shoes and juts out his lower jaw. 'He's called Ollie,' Caitlin adds beaming, 'and he's a resident at that place in King's Cross.'

Steven sighs sarcastically. 'Deep joy.'

'Deep *house*, actually,' Caitlin says, while Paul mutters under his breath: 'Fucking dinosaur.' Caitlin and I snigger.

Steven ignores the jibe and looks over to James. 'Snooker?' James nods and stands up from the sofa, placing his hands on mine and Caitlin's knees to lever himself up. I look at Caitlin who gives me a *'what can you do?'* kind of look. Then she beckons and whispers something to James who nods before following Steven out of the room.

Paul waves in my direction to catch my attention. 'Kassie, you sorted the supplies then?'

'I'm not using the strong stuff,' I say firmly. 'I'm not convinced it's ready.'

'But I've been promising people an *experience*,' Paul whines.

'*Shrooms* give you an experience,' I say. 'Can't we just do that?'

'But they're so, I don't know, passé,' Paul says, wafting his hand in front of his face as if the common mushroom is indeed performing a disappointing dance in front of him as we speak. 'It'll do nothing for our reputation if we're offering below-par psychedelics. And the ayahuasca is *so* much more . . .'

'I'm sure the Amazonian people will really empathise with you, Paul,' Caitlin says, rolling her eyes. 'What's wrong with a bit of coke anyway?'

I let the irony of Caitlin's moral stance hang in the air. I'm not sure either of them really cares about the ethical implications of their favourite party substances, to be honest.

'Look, the end result's gonna be the same,' I say, trying my best to deter the undeterrable. 'Except with less vomit.' I sigh. 'Well, hopefully with less vomit. We've got a plan for that. Anyway, just . . . let me cultivate the mushrooms. They've been doing well in the tent this year. And Brian's gonna craft them into something ultra sophisticated for you.'

It feels like a good compromise. Brian is a dab hand with our secret catering requests. You can trust a man who doesn't communicate to anybody to keep your secrets.

'Fine,' Paul says. 'I reckon we could zhuzh things up anyway.' He glances over to where Steven was standing moments earlier. 'Don't you think he'd benefit from loosening up with a mushroom-infused canapé?'

'Yeah, good luck with that.' I scoff. 'He won't touch them with a bargepole. Besides, all the more for you.'

Paul smiles like the Cheshire cat and Caitlin exhales wearily. 'I'm not sorting your mess out again, Paul,' she says, standing and leaving me alone on the sofa.

Paul then stands and follows her. And I have to wonder if his loyalty really does lie with me – or whether Caitlin still has him wrapped around her finger.

Chapter 4

Paul

Friday

She's sitting by the fountain like a queen, refusing to thaw even under this sun. Her tanned legs are stretched in front of her and her stupidly perfect feet dangle in the water. Thank God fuck-face has managed to tear himself away from her for two minutes. He's no doubt brown-nosing Steven over snooker, or Steven's brown-nosing him. They've created their own human fucking centipede, those two.

Caitlin lowers her lit cigarette, clicking her nails with the same hand while staring ahead. I can't hear it for the fountain, but I know she's doing it. She's always done it. Gets right on my nips.

She hears me approach as I cross the gravel in my loose jeans and sliders, snifter in hand. She doesn't bother turning her head to look at me before she speaks, instead lowering her oversized sunglasses to get a better view ahead of her. 'What do you think to the new topiary, hm? I'm not sure . . .'

I glance towards the unimaginatively shaven hedge in front of us. It's kind of a nondescript oblong. It'll be one of the gardening apprentices Kassie suggested our full-time gardener take on. Good for the local community, she said. Clearly not so good for our garden. And given she's obsessed with our natural exterior I'm surprised she's not up in arms over the clear decline in artistic sculpting.

'Insignificant,' I say. 'It's hardly the hallmark of Scissorhands.'

'*Precisely*,' she says. 'Don't we want the public to be wowed?' She says the word 'public' as though she has a bad taste in her mouth. 'I mean, we need reason for them to keep coming back. To keep spending their state benefits at Morland Hall. Tea, scones, ice creams. It should feel novel. Aspirational.'

I nearly spit my whisky out. 'I hardly think they'll be spending their benefits on a trip round our gardens. More likely cigarettes and alcohol. Just like us.' I glance at my whisky and Caitlin's cigarette and shrug off my internal voice. Nobody needs an inner fucking angel if they want to succeed in life. Besides, we've earned our money. It's our rightful inheritance. And if we want to spend it on cigarettes and alcohol then that's absolutely grand.

I shake my head in an attempt to dispel the encroaching arse of my unwanted angel, peddling shame like a bastard.

'Think Granny's come to a decision?' I ask.

'Who knows? Dangling our inheritance in front of us is her only sport these days.'

'We should have got to Dad before she did.'

Caitlin exhales a waft of cigarette smoke straight into my face. 'Excuse me, what? If I recall correctly, you all called me a greedy bitch when I mentioned power of attorney.'

'Well, we could all see you had designs on the estate.'

'Yes. As do we all. But wasting time picking a fight with me instead of responding quickly to the situation is what's put us in this monstrous position.'

I hate to admit it, but she does have a point. If we had acted sooner when Dad's mind was deteriorating, we could have power of attorney right now. We could have complete control of the estate. But instead, Granny swooped in. And now, it's all at her discretion. Playing us off against each other. She's a sick old bitch.

I look ahead towards the gates that are now slowly opening.

'She's here,' I say wearily.

We both look towards the car pulling into the estate. I can feel the cloud of dread washing over both of us. Caitlin clears her throat.

'You know, Steven is just so . . . sour. No, dour. He's dour. He's really fucking dour,' Caitlin says, looking at me now, sunglasses perched on the end of her nose, cigarette still burning between manicured fingers.

'Reminds me of someone close to you . . .' I say, kicking off my sliders and sitting on the lawn, denim pooling out around my legs.

'Fuck you.' She looks away again.

'The only justification I can come up with for you marrying Winnet of Winnet Hall is the hall. Oh hang on,' I say clicking my fingers and squinting at the sun. 'There's also the small matter of that joint Coutts bank account.'

'Oh don't be ridiculous. I have my own . . .'

'But there's always *more*.'

'More' has always been her dopamine. And I know how much Granny loves Caitlin's marital position so it's a plus in that respect as well. James' family have long been admired. For their wealth rather than their personalities, I must say. Granny was so delighted when they announced their impending nuptials that she invited them both to stay with her for a week at her immaculately soulless place on the Scottish border. I don't think the rest of us have ever stayed in that house overnight. Of course, Caitlin didn't want to spend a week under the watchful eye of our vicious grandmother, but you've got to play the game, haven't you. And Caitlin certainly knows how to do that. James is of benefit to her. Shame he doesn't tick all her boxes. Or should I say, tickle her box. Not that Caitlin lets the little matter of marriage vows stop her from getting it elsewhere.

I've heard it first hand, through the walls. My sister wailing like a blissed-up banshee when Steven's golfing pals christened the Morland driving range. Never heard her wail like that when James is in there with her.

Caitlin throws her cigarette on the ground. Defiance has always been part of her MO, too. 'Anyway,' she says. 'He needs to step up.' I give her a look of confusion.

'Steven!' she snaps. 'He needs to look outside of his stunted imagination.' She stands up, sighs, and collects the empty glass from her side. 'If he wants to play little Lord fuck-le-fuck he needs to roll his sleeves up.' She looks up towards the sky and takes a deep breath before changing her demeanour like a demon has just left her body. 'Like us!' she says, a lightness to her voice now. She approaches me with an unnerving smile and bends down towards me. 'What would I do without you, Pauly?' she says, squeezing my chin between her thumb and finger. Contrasting notes of tobacco and expensive perfume engulf me.

All my life Caitlin has swung violently between mothering me and kicking me in the balls. There's only just over a year between us but she's always acted as if the divide were as wide as a decade.

'Don't you think Steven has a point, though? You don't even live here anymore,' I say, letting my too-white feet flop outwards under the baking heat. The sun's scalding. I waggle my toes wondering if the UV rays are strong enough to singe the downy hairs that sprout randomly from the tops of my digits.

'You know as well as I do that until Granny names one of us as inheritor, we all have an equal say,' Caitlin says authoritatively. 'Even Kassie, regardless of Steven's incessant baiting.'

We both watch silently as Dennis drives Granny past us and parks up by the main entrance. There's a collective sigh and then I start picking at blades of grass and throwing them back down. 'What hideous costume have you got for me anyway?' I ask.

'Hideous? You could never look hideous, sweetie.'

I feel my cheeks flush and step up the angry costume chat to disguise it. 'Are you going to tell me or what? I can't believe we let you talk us into this.'

'Into what?'

'You. Being in charge of costume.'

'But I'm the one with the most style. Couldn't have you turning up in some hideous tat from Shein.'

'Oh, come on. And why does Steven get off scot-free?' I say, standing up. We both need to be present and correct for Granny. 'Costume-wise, I mean.'

'He looks hideous in his natural state. It's hardly getting off scot-free. He's got to live with that pointy, angry, ratty little face for the rest of his life. You've just got to get through this party. Besides . . .' She claws at my abs, making me flinch nervously. 'It's the perfect excuse to show off your six-pack, brother.'

She waltzes off ahead of me and I gulp down the remaining drops of my bitter drink, my face burning.

Chapter 5

Kassie

Friday

We all stand in the living room fidgeting as Granny appears to inspect every inch of the place, running her fingertips across the top of the fireplace and pulling a face at the new TV. Even Steven seems on edge, given how he's hovering around the bureau where his cigars are kept but doesn't get one out.

'Your focal point is quite the eyesore,' she says, turning her nose up at the big screen, before facing us. We say nothing but I let out a half-smile because I don't know what else to do. Finally, Granny sits on the sofa, crossing her legs in front of her.

I genuinely have no idea what made Granny so hostile and bitter. It's not as though she ever went without. But she's never been a loving grandmother. I never even knew there was such a thing to be honest. Not until I started school and the other children talked about their families. They would draw smiley, happy faces on stick-people family members with sausage-shaped hair and triangle skirts and make them hold flower-shaped hands. The scene would usually have the sun shining, blue skies and green trees.

My drawings, however, were quite the contrast. I remember being asked once why I was still drawing Halloween pictures in the summer. I said it wasn't a Halloween picture, it was Granny. I kept that drawing. I believe I've even shown it to my secret therapist. The one I used to go to when they all thought I was away to some poxy yoga class. In it, Granny has her hands held above her head, her fingers spread like fat grey, jagged petals and her mouth wide and gaping as she screamed blue murder at us. There was no sunshine. And there were no trees. Just browns, greys, dark blues and black. Similar thing happened one Monday morning in school when I drew Caitlin holding a knife with blood on it. I had to argue that my drawing was valid – this was indeed something I'd seen over the weekend.

'So, how have you been, Granny?' Steven says, attempting to conjure something vaguely sweet, but it just comes off as sickly.

'Where are your brother and sister?' she says, ignoring his pleasantries.

Just then the door opens and Caitlin walks in, leaving the door ajar for Paul, who's a few seconds behind her.

'Still smoking then?' Granny says, sniffing the air theatrically as Caitlin walks past her. Caitlin lets out a small laugh. None of us know how best to react to our grandmother. Paul sits in the leather chair and Caitlin perches on the arm. Steven and I are still hovering. All eyes are on Granny.

'Good Lord. Could you all relax? You're making me feel bilious,' she says. I plonk myself down on the rug cross-legged and let Steven perch next to Granny on the sofa.

Mrs Davies walks in with tea and biscuits and places them on the coffee table. She pours Granny's tea, adds a dash of milk and hands it to her, along with the plate of biscuits. Granny leans forward slowly, her movement as stiff as her dogtooth suit jacket. It takes an age for her to select a biscuit but she eventually goes for the shortcake.

We are all waiting with bated breath but she says nothing as she sips on her tea, swallows, then nods her approval to Mrs Davies, who leaves the room again.

'So how are you, Granny? Are you enjoying your time with the Taylor-Bankses?' Caitlin asks, moving forward assertively to pour herself a cup of tea.

'Hm? Yes, yes. Yes all fine,' she says hurriedly, keen to move the conversation along. 'But I'm not here for small talk. We need to discuss the conditions surrounding your inheritance.'

The room is silent for a moment, then Steve and Caitlin both blurt something out simultaneously.

'I'm so pleased we're close to a resolution,' Caitlin says beaming, over Steven whose approach is a more business-like: 'How would you like to take this forward?'

'One at a time,' Granny snaps.

I see Steven raise his eyebrows in Caitlin's direction and she nods, letting him go first. Meanwhile I look across to Paul who's still sitting next to Caitlin.

'Want a cup of tea?' I whisper. He shakes his head, but I make myself one, using the ridiculous china cups and saucers that only come out when Granny's here.

'So how would you like to take the conversation

forward?' Steven asks again. 'Do you need us all together in the room?'

I can hear Paul sigh, and I don't blame him. Steven's trying to muscle me and Paul out of the equation as per. But Granny's response doesn't please Steven. 'Well of course. You're all Morlands, aren't you? And given how close we are now to decision day, we might as well all hear each other's proposals.'

I gulp. After Steven refused to enable the joint inheritance, which could only be taken forward if we all unanimously agreed, we'd all been invited to speak separately with Granny about our vision and plans for the place should we be named as the main inheritor. Of course, Paul and I already agreed that we intend to share if one of us wins the top prize. Although we have kept that bit of information a tightly guarded secret.

'Want me to get James?' Caitlin says. 'He's just on a Zoom meeting upstairs.'

'Oh no, please don't bother him. He's such a busy man,' Granny says, smiling. 'Besides, I've already spoken to him and I'm satisfied of his commitment.'

Paul kicks his feet against the chair and I know he's still livid about the prospect of James' involvement in the future of this place. I've never known him to loathe another person so much – not even Steven.

Just as Steven looks like he's about to speak, Dennis walks in, his neatly cut beard as tailored as his shirt and trousers. I can't imagine wanting to wear business attire in this heat.

Dennis hands Granny a file and whispers something in her ear. She nods in response. We all remain silent as she slowly places the file on her knee, opens her handbag, takes out her reading glasses and places them on her face in a considered and precise manner. I can practically see Steven's butterflies escape from his gut and flutter madly around the room, a swarm of impatience and angst. He knows that he's taken a huge gamble. He knows he's plunged us all into this unholy situation.

Granny eventually opens the folder and shifts a few pieces of paper around. 'So. Can we confirm that we are going ahead with the sole inheritor model? There is no unanimous agreement to share?'

We all shake our heads silently.

'So in terms of your plans, the headlines are as follows.' We all sit stock-still and I'm sure I can hear my heart pounding.

'Steven,' Granny says, holding her glasses down momentarily as she looks to her side and checks that she has his full attention. 'You plan on uplifting Morland Hall's catering and leisure offer, with a new bistro and golf course.'

Steven nods. 'That's right, I do feel . . .'

Granny holds her hand up to stop him. 'And you plan to turn the cottages into luxury holiday lets.'

My heart plummets. The one thing I can't bear to lose is the cottage. I don't care if I never set foot inside the main house again, but I simply can't lose my home. My real home. That's *such* a classic Steven move. I didn't expect any less, but hearing it read out so factually and formally makes me pale. I look over at him but can see no evidence of compassion or remorse in his face.

'And Caitlin,' Granny says, turning her attention to my sister who shifts forward in her seat. 'You plan to invest heavily into the refurbishment of the Hall and open a five-star hotel and spa.'

We all look to Caitlin who sits there beaming. We've never been able to fully refurbish the Hall. We've never had the funds. Caitlin, however, has James. And James' family have more funds than us and the Taylor-Bankses put together.

'That's right,' Caitlin says. 'Restore the place to its former glory and invite the movers and shakers to experience it. I know a wonderful PR who can really raise the game for us.'

Granny's lips barely move, but there is a slight sparkle in her eye when Caitlin talks. She's always been favourite. I have to wonder if Caitlin's planning on doing me out of a home too.

'And Paul,' Granny says, moving her eyes from Caitlin and up to Paul who crosses his arms protectively in front of him. 'You're looking at developing cultural and entertainment activities on site, with a focus on the Christmas period to boost income, while keeping costs down throughout the rest of the year?'

Paul nods. He knows that Granny's always been unsure of his business savvy, so he adds: 'Yes, I've profiled the budget to fit the seasonal shift. My accountant's looked over it. It definitely works.'

'No need to try to prove yourself. I carry out my own checks and balances,' she says, looking back down to the papers and shifting them around. 'And finally. Kassie. You'd like to work with the National Trust to co-manage the estate, and make our family heritage accessible to the public through educational activities.'

I nod nervously, and I can feel Steven's eyes boring into me from across the room. He loathes the idea of accessibility and he simply can't keep his mouth shut. 'But,

Kassie,' he says. 'Is this simply a ruse because you have no experience in managing the operations yourself? Because if it is . . .'

'Enough,' Granny snaps. And I struggle to hold my smirk in.

Of all the headlines we've just heard, I only had advance sight of Paul's plans. We'd shared them with each other, making sure that they were distinct enough and yet able to complement one another if, indeed, we did go into this together. As the youngest two members of the family, however, we both know it's a long shot.

'I will be reviewing everyone's business proposals forensically over the weekend. And to be clear, in this instance, where the estate must go to one sibling, it is in their gift to allocate suitable accommodation, here or elsewhere, for the remaining three. And that is non-negotiable. Nobody will be left living like a pauper and a minimum stipend will be agreed.'

I have to wonder what 'suitable' means. On the one hand, it would be far too embarrassing to have any of us Morlands living in some rundown property nearby, but on the other, I can see Steven relishing in the power of holding the purse strings – and the decision-making – relating to the rest of our lives. Of course, if Caitlin loses out, she doesn't really lose anything – she married into enough money to keep her happy for the rest of her life. Providing she stays married, that is. *That* will be a challenge for her.

'We also need to ensure the upcoming inspection goes to plan.' Granny sifts through more papers. 'We had a few issues with disability access last time.' She looks up now, lowering her glasses to the tip of her nose again.

Steven clears his throat and I can see that his nervous

energy is still in full flow. 'Yes. We've replaced the ramp on the right-hand side of the Hall.'

'Good,' Granny says. 'And the greenhouse remains out of bounds to the public?'

Steven nods. 'Yes. Kassie is continuing to look after it, and it is now more clearly marked as inaccessible to the public – although they can catch a glimpse of the flowers from the walkway.'

'Good. And leaseholders? All up to date? And the café? Did you involve Brian in selecting the new suppliers and catering team leader?'

Steven nods. 'Yes to both. The café team has introduced a new menu. It's a Northumberland summertime theme. All local ingredients and suppliers. It's all going, well, rather swimmingly, actually.'

'Don't be so naive,' she snaps taking her time to choose another biscuit from the tray that Mrs Davies brought in earlier. I watch as she carefully selects one. 'When the public are involved, nothing goes swimmingly.' She finally picks a chocolate shortcake and puts it in her mouth. It doesn't stop her speaking. 'So I trust everything in this report has been remedied,' she says, tapping the papers in front of her with the backs of her fingertips. 'Meaning that the upcoming inspection to check on progress will result in a swift and positive outcome?' I notice a few crumbs being catapulted from her mouth into the air like dust in front of a sunny window.

'Yes,' Steven says proudly. 'All snags nicely ironed out.'

'Snags, indeed.' She pushes the rest of the shortcake into her mouth. 'Honestly, Steven,' she says through quick bites. 'You were this close to losing your health and safety certificate less than twelve months ago. If you can't open to the public, you can't maintain your income. End of.'

'Oh he's totally on it,' Caitlin says sitting up to attention now. 'Even managed to confirm planning permission to extend the driving range.'

Granny nearly chokes on what's left of her biscuit. 'Excuse me?' She eyes Steven, while Caitlin collapses back in her seat, pleased with herself. She mouths the word 'sorry' at Steven but we all know it wasn't a slip-up. Steven is clearly confused as to how Caitlin got hold of this information.

'I was just future-proofing my proposal,' Steven says defensively. 'It wasn't an expectation of my position . . . more, just, ensuring that my proposals could go ahead swiftly should you wish to award me the estate.'

'And yet, if the estate management goes to one of your siblings, you'll have wasted the council's time and potentially created problems for the actual successor's own plans.'

Steven is furious with our sister whom he side-eyes, a sneer creeping out from his lips. The atmosphere in the room is even more palpably icy now.

There's nothing but negativity when it comes to any discussion about us taking on the ownership of the estate. Dangling it in front of our noses by having it in trust is just the tonic for Granny's increasing boredom. I honestly think, if she had her way, she'd keep the estate herself – until she's ready to leave this mortal coil in peace, at least. She's desperate to be the full-time matriarch again. But that's not the deal. Not unless she can find a loophole – such as us not passing the inspection.

Steven goes on to outline all that *he* has done for the estate so far, positioning himself favourably. There's no 'we' when he talks. It's clearly a ruse to get Granny to see that he is, indeed, the rightful successor. However, while

Granny does have her faults, she has always been a bit of a feminist – in the old-school, not-so-intersectional kind of way. She'll advocate for women *like her*. And, as we all know, she sees Caitlin as the vessel in which to pour her evil spirit after her body has given up the terrifying ghost. I can see Caitlin turning into Granny one day. She's had good training.

But Paul and I have to hang on to some hope. We've made a pact. We're in this together. And our plans are pretty robust and ambitious – and there are many benefits to working with the National Trust and enjoying the promotion and prestige it brings with it. Granny might not be overly excited about the accessibility and educational aspects of my proposal, but the National Trust is a pretty impressive carrot. And I think, given her proximity to her deathbed, she'll enjoy the idea of me creating a strong legacy for our family heritage. Being talked about by the National Trust will feel like a life extension for her. Although, one thing I didn't put in the proposal was my plan to release our family history, warts and all . . .

'OK,' Granny says finally. 'We'll have the final inspection carried next week, with a view to me making my announcement soon afterwards. Providing all is in order, of course.'

'So,' Steven asks. 'When exactly is the inspection taking place again?' He says this as if she's already told us. But of course, Granny hasn't already told us. She enjoys springing these things on us.

'First thing Monday morning. And you can soft-launch by opening back up to the public later that afternoon.'

I feel as though we have all collectively puked our insides into the air. We had no plans to open to the public on

Monday and certainly no plans to host an inspection team so soon after the party. Granny knows we're having the party on Saturday night. She's obviously done it on purpose. Because by Monday, given our regular guests' track records, we'll no doubt still be clearing out the stragglers.

By Monday, we're fucked.

Chapter 6

Paul

Friday

James is buttering his bread like a pig would. Everything about that big stupid shit-cunt makes me want to hurl. I watch as he slathers about an inch of pure fat on his roll, biting into it like . . . a pig. A wild boar. He's a prime candidate for gout – all ruddy-cheeked and moobs.

This man went to the most prestigious school in England. What a waste of his parents' money. Or maybe he just thinks he's better than everyone else so he can eat like a swamp demon pig if he so pleases.

I continue to watch him in disgust and neck another glass of wine. His breathing is heavy and laboured as he snuffles the bread, crumbs dropping on his plate in front of him. I watch Caitlin as she ignores him completely, engaging Granny in conversation. She must have him tuned out of her sound and sight lines. Years of essential practice, I guess.

'So, Granny,' I say, desperate to remove myself from my morbid fascination of James' snuffling, sniffling display of grotesque dining. 'I hear you're leaving us early tomorrow. It's such a shame we don't get to see you more.'

Granny's holding her soup spoon close to her mouth. She pauses just inches from it and looks over to me. 'Paul, darling. We all know why I'm leaving early tomorrow. I'd thank you not to insult my intelligence.'

I let out a small laugh. Caitlin smirks at me, obviously aware of my nervousness.

Granny carefully sips her soup from her spoon, chews on the lumpy liquid as if she has no teeth, then swallows. 'I do know what you have planned,' she says, before taking another spoonful.

The table is silent. Not even the slightest scrape of cutlery on china. I laugh again, a little more nervously this time, thinking on my feet. Is it best to own up? Is it best to make out that it's no big deal?

'Our little party?' I say. 'You're very welcome . . .'

Steven drops his spoon and it clatters onto the tiled floor. Mrs Davies swoops over to pick it back up.

'We both know, Paul, that I don't want to be here for your awful party. There's nothing to worry about there. However, you will do right to remember that there is an inspection and a public opening first thing on Monday.'

Granny, having finished her soup, pushes her chair backwards and excuses herself. 'I'll see you all at breakfast,' she says.

'Aren't you staying for the bourguignonne?' Steven asks.

'No, dear,' Granny says, making no excuse for refusing to eat her main meal. She simply removes herself from the dining table and, eventually, the room. She seems to eat less and less as she ages.

The sound of silver on china starts slowly back up again.

'So, how did the estate discussion go?' James asks.

'As if you don't know,' Steven says, their previous hints of camaraderie having faded dramatically since Steven discovered James' clear and powerful role in Caitlin's plans. The Hall refurb is a major plus for Caitlin.

James shrugs. 'Just trying to make conversation.'

'I think it went rather swimmingly,' Caitlin says beaming. I hate her confidence. But we all know that her financial ties to James are, in reality, just as excruciating for her.

'Well,' I say. 'We'll just have to see. After all, Granny does love springing surprises.'

'I can't believe she's booked that inspection Monday morning,' Kassie says. Although I know deep down that Kassie isn't as concerned as the rest of us. It's always been clear to everyone that she can take or leave our parties. Including Granny. I can't see Kassie getting the blame for any of what goes on here tomorrow.

'It's just a check of the outstanding issues,' Steven says, pushing his empty bowl away from him and picking up his wine glass. 'If we can get Dennis to accompany the inspector, direct him to the specific matters in hand, it should all be over pretty quickly.'

'We'll need to keep an eye on wandering guests,' I say. 'Kassie, you might use your charm on Mrs Davies and ask her to help with that?'

'Sure,' she says. 'Caitlin, you mentioned a costume for me? For tomorrow?' Kassie is clearly keen to change the subject. She's keeping her cards close to her chest. 'Please tell me it's not something you'd wear.'

'No, darling,' Caitlin says, not at all insulted because we know she'd never wear anything Kassie wears, either. 'It's an absolutely angelic costume.'

'Ironic,' Steven says under his breath, but we all hear it.

He's such an incessant bully. I'm not sure there's anything living beneath his skin and muscle besides bone and dust. There's a little superficial charm, sure, but he saves that for the outsiders.

Caitlin turns to Kassie who seems to have batted off Steven's latest insult. Like she's not the most angelic of all of us anyway! 'You're going to look delightful, darling,' Caitlin says. 'I saw it when I went to pick my costume up and I just knew you had to have it.'

'So what are *you* wearing?' I ask her.

'Well, it's in homage to the hell part of the triptych,' Caitlin explains. 'It's a play on Eve, but with a rotten apple, a black thigh-split dress and a sinful glint in my eye.' Caitlin winks at me and I shudder.

'Sinful and impure? *You* surely don't need a costume for that?' Steven says.

'Come on, Steven. It's a big night,' I say. 'Caitlin needs to shine. After all, isn't her ex coming, you know . . . Jack?'

Caitlin slams her spoon into her bowl, letting soup inadvertently splatter onto James. He picks up his napkin and dabs the liquid from his cheek silently.

'Paul, behave,' Kassie says, a half-smile on her face. She doesn't like confrontation. But I also know she doesn't like James. And we both need that marital rift in order to stop Caitlin getting her claws into our rightful inheritance.

Caitlin stands. 'Mrs Davies,' she hollers. Mrs Davies

re-enters the room, an enquiring look on her face. 'I'll take the rest of dinner in my room, please,' Caitlin says, standing and leaving the table.

I look at James and can see the cogs whirring since I dropped Jack's name into conversation. How much more can one man take? I guess we'll find out at the party.

Chapter 7

Saturday 23rd August

10.15

The sound of a car engine gets closer and wheels can be heard crunching on gravel. The camera is shaky and gets faster and faster, the stones coming in and out of view, before it stops, suddenly, and follows the movement of a silver car making its way slowly towards the house. A black Nissan X-Trail with a 2019 number plate. It parks between the Bentley and the Aston Martin.

In the corner of the frame, the car door opens and a pair of brown Birkenstocks plant themselves onto the gravel. The camera stops and focuses on the feet, then moves upwards over the rest of the body, scanning tanned hairy legs, beige combat shorts and a baggy bright white T-shirt with Japanese writing and a small fish motif. The figure turns around and leans on the car, and the camera pans upwards, revealing the back of a man's head, short, wavy hair and phone in hand. He calls a number and, as the camera pans back down, he is kicking at the gravel with his open-toed shoes.

The man speaks. 'Yeah, I'm here. Just outside.' The camera remains on his feet. He kicks the gravel even faster. There's a pause before: 'It's in the back of the car. Could do with a hand . . . OK thanks. Yeah. Yeah.' Another pause. 'You sure this is a good idea? Well, he'll recognise me from . . . Right. No, no, of course, I'm grateful for the . . . Yes, I know, it's just . . . OK, sure. What does he look like? The dude who's coming . . . OK, I'll keep an eye. Sure, yep, see you in a . . . OK, bye. Bye.'

The man leans sideways to place his phone back in his cargo pocket and sighs. 'Fuck's sake.' He opens up the boot of the car. Then he turns and focuses straight ahead, stopping still in his tracks. His eyes widen and he flinches slightly, before stamping one of his feet forward.

'Weird fucking family,' the man mutters.

The camera turns and follows the gravel out towards the grass and the cottages in the distance.

Chapter 8

Kassie

Saturday

We wait awkwardly on the front steps for Granny to appear and say her goodbyes. There's an element of showing up for her, and one of making quite sure that she's left the estate before we crack on with the party preparations.

Caitlin and Steven are both pacing the driveway in the near distance taking private calls, and I sit on the stone steps with Paul. It's still early and the steps are already burning my bare skin. I reposition my skirt to protect myself from the heat and sigh.

'*Of course* she's late,' Paul says, albeit quietly in case Granny suddenly appears from nowhere – as is often the case.

She was supposed to leave at 09.30 and we've now been gathered here, what, almost twenty minutes waiting for her.

Eventually we hear the door behind us and both turn to see Granny, Dennis and James emerging. Paul and I exchange glances.

'We came to wish you a safe journey, Granny,' Caitlin says, her phone call suddenly dropped as she now walks towards the old woman, her hands outstretched. Granny stops short and air-kisses her.

'I've just been having a chat with your delightful husband, dear,' Granny says, her face erupting in pleasure as she turns to James.

'James, darling,' she says, fawning over him. 'Tell me you'll keep an eye on the children tonight.' She takes both his hands in hers and gives them a gentle squeeze. James is literally a few months older than Steven. But his family heritage matters more than anything else. I spy Steven walking across now, a look of pinched concern on his face.

'Granny, seriously,' Caitlin says, her voice faux authoritative and utterly saccharine. 'We know what we're doing.'

'I'd say that's debatable, wouldn't you?' Granny huffs, eyeing Paul to remind him of his previous misdemeanours. 'Anyway, all that matters to me is that this place is in one piece – and you are too.'

'Didn't realise you cared,' Paul says, letting his sarcasm slip out by accident.

'I don't, darling,' Granny says. 'I just don't want any more bad PR.'

'Right,' Steven says, clearing his throat. 'So, you're back at the Taylor-Bankses then?'

She nods. 'Yes. George is on the panel so I'm hoping he'll be able to influence the inspection officer. I'll be having a word with him this evening.'

None of us know if we can really trust her on this. It's not really in her best interest for us to pass straight away, but we know better than to confront her on it.

'We'll see you to the car,' Steven says.

'Fine. I know when I'm not wanted.'

'No, I didn't mean . . .' Steven protests but Granny holds her hand up in front of him.

We all follow her to the car, Caitlin grabbing James' hand in a rare display of affection and catching up with Granny.

'I think Caitlin might have it in the bag, you know,' I whisper to Paul as we lag behind the others. 'James walking out with Granny and Dennis – they must have been talking.'

'It's OK,' Paul whispers back. 'I've got Jack coming tonight. I wouldn't be surprised if that DJ she's booked had already been inside her knickers, too. Won't take much to chuck a massive grenade into the centre of that farce of a marriage.'

I smile back at him. I could feel bad, but I don't. Caitlin and Steven will be playing dirty. A little bit of meddling to simply out the truth of Caitlin's extramarital affairs is nothing in comparison to what they'll be up to. And that takes at least one main contender out of the equation.

'But how are we going to do it?' I ask. 'Get proof to James, I mean.'

'I'm working on it,' Paul whispers, as we both stop in our tracks to see Steven hugging Granny, a pained expression on his face. While Caitlin is all glee and laughter.

'I genuinely don't know what will be worse,' Kassie says. 'Steven playing Lord of the Manor or him moving in.' I point discreetly in James' direction as he hovers between Caitlin and Granny.

'They won't though,' Paul says. 'They'll stay in London. Probably visit occasionally. I reckon they'll just turf us all out and get some hot-shot manager in to do the hard work.'

I feel sick at the thought of my cottage being taken away. And then it suddenly hits me. If we are told to leave, what will happen to Iggy? I know we'll have a new place paid for, but there aren't many going round here complete with goat housing and paddock. My heart breaks at the thought of being separated from her. I have to make absolutely sure that can't happen. I have to make sure either me or Paul are in prime position. But how? Sure we can out Caitlin's affairs – potentially – but what about Steven?

Then I think to the argument between Steven and Mrs Davies that I overheard and make a mental note to interrogate her on it. We need ammunition and we need it fast.

Granny is eventually in the car, Dennis closing the door for her. We all stand, waving over to her, even though we know she won't wave back.

Dennis climbs into the front seat and the car starts moving down the driveway towards the gates. Steven lights a cigarette and walks away, his head down.

I watch as the gates close behind Granny's car, the sun shining off the rear window, and it turns left, disappearing out of sight.

Caitlin snatches her hand away from James and walks towards the house, her face solemn.

'At least we know if Caitlin wins the prize, she'll never be happy,' I say.

'Purgatory with James,' Paul says laughing as Caitlin storms past us, face like thunder.

'Well, this party's gonna get seriously messy,' I say. 'You ready for fireworks?'

'Sure am!' Paul says.

We both walk into the house and I search for Caitlin so I can get my dreaded costume sorted. James is sitting on the sofa in the living room, so I head up to Caitlin's room. I knock on her door, wondering what I'm going to be met with. I haven't properly spoken to her since she stropped off from the dinner table last night following Paul's drunken baiting.

The prospect of wearing Caitlin's outfit is daunting. As much as I think Caitlin's got style, I'm nothing like her. I'd rather blend away into the edges of the party like a dark smudge of ash. Caitlin, though, she'd be happiest if you stuck her on the top of a gigantic twelve-tier cake in the middle of a party and, as long as all eyes were on her and she had a steady supply of fizz, coke and Davidoff cigarettes, she'd happily remain there.

'Enter!' Caitlin twists around from her dressing table stool as I push the door open. 'Oh, Kassie. It's you. I thought you were staff.' She taps the bed, indicating for me to perch, and swivels back round to face her reflection in the dressing table mirror. Her satisfied expression tells me she likes what she sees. 'We've sent what's-his-face out to help with the DJ decks.' She picks up her eyelash curlers and sets about perfecting her look.

By what's-his-face she surely means Brian, who has worked here for years.

Caitlin's room, which has been untouched by anyone since she left (other than weekly cleans to manage any accumulating dust) still has the vile Bird's custard yellow walls that much of our wing does, but she's toned it down with a bespoke Japanese-style mural behind the bed, giving her a focal point and some gentle respite from the overpowering hue.

I'm so pleased the cottage was a blank canvas when I moved in. Walls that needed skimming. Carpets that needed ripping up. The colour scheme was entirely mine for the taking. And I made a point of banning the colour yellow.

I jump backwards to sit onto the bed and put my bare feet up in front of me, dangling them just over the edge so I don't mess up her beautiful white sheets with pale green edging. I watch her as she is now skilfully layering her mascara over her lashes. She's the only woman I know who doesn't automatically gawp her mouth open as she lengthens her lashes.

'Honestly, Kassie. Who does he think he is?'

'Who?'

'Our brother.'

'Oh.'

'Just because he can't keep his own relationships intact doesn't mean he should try to destroy everyone else's.'

'I think he was drinking a lot last night, that's all,' I say. 'Besides, you're as bad as each other.'

'Kassie, babes, much as I hate to admit it, my little brother can handle his drink almost as well as I can. He's just out for trouble.' She stops what she's doing, her hand in mid-air holding the mascara wand nice and steady. 'Seriously, if James was any kind of man, he'd have knocked Paul into oblivion by now.'

I note her disdain for her husband is growing stronger and more toxic as the years go by. On every visit there's a little more distance between them. And when I say years, I'm not talking decades. I'm talking about a handful. It's four, maybe five years that they've been married. Doesn't really bode well but I imagine his bank balance will keep that ring on her finger for a good while. And I can't see Granny handing the estate over to Caitlin unless she's still legally bound to James.

'He does a pretty good job of that himself,' I say.

'Hm? What?' Caitlin says, glancing at me through the reflection in the mirror.

'Knocking himself into oblivion.'

Caitlin laughs. 'Never been so good on the old psychedelics has he? Never knows when to stop. And honestly, one whiff of a party and the powder's making its way up his nose like a rat up a drainpipe.'

'Bus-stop-gate never did calm him down, did it?' I say, referring to the time Mrs Davies found Paul standing at the bus stop one Monday morning stark-bollock naked, scratching at his skin until it bled.

'Considering how much it set us back paying off every local with a bloody camera phone . . .' Caitlin sighs, shakes her head as if to scrub the memory and returns to lash layering. 'There's no wonder we can't get a decent PR agency for love nor money.'

It was two winters ago. Paul threw one of his 'low-key' parties at the house for his uni mates. A reunion or something. And of course, they chose Morland Hall for the venue because, well, it's renowned for it. If walls could talk ours'd be speaking nonsense at a thousand miles an hour and gurning. Anyway, Paul got so wasted on booze, benzos and MDMA that he fell into the fountain fully clothed, passed out on the edge of the water and woke up with some kind of hypothermic phenomenon going on. Paradoxical undressing they called it. Oh, and a decorative map of angry ant bites all over him. Not that the villagers with photographic evidence of a rich boy offering a full frontal to the village during the school run much cared about the medical reasons behind it. It was, after all, a result of him simply partying too hard with no care as to the consequences. And it wasn't the first time the village had to contend with the dregs of a Morland party. But give him twenty-four hours and a hair of the dog and he's usually over it, no matter how shameful. I have to say I admire him for that.

I look around the room at the various dry cleaners' bags hanging around the place. Caitlin's always somehow engineered our wardrobe for big events and parties. It's never been a formal thing – up until now. The assigning of party prep roles in a more formal capacity only came up because Paul was sick of Caitlin taking control of everything when she doesn't even live here. So she divided up the tasks – but it's all just tokenistic. She's already sacked Paul's DJ and I imagine that half the guests who turn up won't have been on Steven's list.

'So, where's my outfit then?' I ask.

'Oh, just you wait, Kass,' Caitlin says, before standing up slowly and steadily placing her dressing table chair back into its position. She walks along the rows of outfits hanging neatly inside sheeny fabric and carefully traces her finger over the bags until she comes to a black one. 'Aha! This is you,' she says, unzipping it and pulling the material away from the costume to reveal what's inside.

I almost inhale my own saliva. 'Sorry, Caitlin, but what is *that* supposed to be exactly?'

'You might sound more grateful. It's Mugler.' Caitlin caresses the layers of the dress. If that's what you can call it.

'Caitlin, I'll look more naked wearing that than I will wearing my full birthday suit.'

'But, darling, I had to wrangle this from the talons of that singer, from that band, you know . . .'

I shrug my shoulders.

'You know, Kassie. The one that's doing so well on TikTok. Anyway, she wanted it for some awards ceremony. But I said we just *had* to have it. It's so on-brand for the theme, don't you think?'

She's holding it now in front of her admiringly, before turning to dangle it in front of me, pulling her head back and squinting to try to imagine me wearing it. What there is of it, anyway. She sighs. 'I mean, if she wants to turn our hospitality down for some crappy awards do . . .'

'Caitlin,' I say moving closer to her and touching the fabric. 'It's basically a pair of sheer tights. Stretched into a dress. With a few sparkles on it. And you know how I feel about sequins.'

'But, sweetheart, these aren't throw-away sequins. They're glass beads. Totally eco-friendly. Besides, we need to match. Well, I mean, contrast. But as a contrasting pair. You know, yin and yang.' She hangs the naked dress back up and unzips the bag next to it to reveal a tiny black shimmery thing with sheer layers and areas that look like they've been slashed open. 'See, you're heavenly, and I'm purely hellish.' She laughs. 'Delightful, am I right?'

'Yeah, well, Steven made it clear last night that I shouldn't be allowed past the pearly gates.'

'Oh, just ignore him,' Caitlin says, like I'm complaining about nothing. 'He's worse than usual at the minute because he's panicking about the estate. Thinks he's made the wrong decision but he can't exactly go back on it now, can he? Granny would think him indecisive. Which is bad for business.'

'But I'm sick of him always having it in for me. I don't even live in the house anymore and he still hasn't let up.' I feel my heart speed up at the injustice of it all.

'Well, you know why. As the eldest, I think it hit him the hardest.' She looks at me now, her eyebrows raised and her head tilted to one side.

'It hit us all,' I argue, my voice instantly louder but threatening to break.

Caitlin just watches me as tears well up in my eyes, a serene smile on her face. She's leaving me hanging, waiting for me to say something. I feel a tear spill onto my cheek and inhale sharply.

'He just needs someone to blame,' Caitlin says.

'But why blame me?'

'Well, I guess, Kassie, because, literally, you did kill her, didn't you?'

Chapter 9

Paul

Saturday

Kassie charges past me, her face screwed up and red. She's heading from the direction of Caitlin's room. Figures. The bitch-queen's clearly been practising her personal brand of compassion again.

'Kass!' I shout after her, but she just ignores me and continues on.

I walk towards the hall, where the interloping DJ is setting up. I'm still furious – even more so since I reached out to my original booking, offered to pay him compensation and was told my sister had already taken care of it. Made me feel like a right mug.

This new one better be up to it.

Aesthetically, at least, I can see why Caitlin chose him. He's maybe late twenties, early thirties at a push. Hair's a bit wild on top, light brown and wavy. Short and neat at the back. He's tanned, with white teeth that stand out but look like he was born with them rather than getting them fixed on a dental package holiday. Stylish – though he'd have to be – unless she's dressed him herself. She's got form. She's dressed all of us tonight and it's not the first time. I swear this place is just one gigantic doll's house as far as Caitlin's concerned.

Oh hello. Who's this?

Mrs Davies is chatting to somebody with the sexiest of auras – and that's not just to do with the striking colour of her hair. She has a clipboard in hand, and Mrs Davies is pointing upwards as they both look towards the ceiling in the far corner of the room. It must be the interior designer Caitlin mentioned last night. To be fair, she wasn't a bad call at all, either. She makes the place look good just being in it. I walk over to them.

'Hi, I'm Paul.' I hold out my hand. The designer shakes it and looks me directly in the eye, holding the look for a few seconds longer than needed. Bingo.

'Naomi,' she says, finally retreating her smooth hand. Her nails are perfectly painted and match her flame-red hair. She smells bloody lovely too. Something kind of citrusy and musky fighting for attention. She's definitely got mine. Mrs Davies grunts and wanders off to the other side of the hall. She never misses a cue; I'll give her that. I let out a chuckle.

'So, you've been tasked with enchanting us,' I say, raising my eyebrows. She smiles and I move a little closer.

'Not that this place needs much – it's simply magical in its raw state,' she says, looking around her appreciatively at the exposed stone walls and pillars that surround us in our main hall. Her voice echoes and it feels like it's going through me.

I try to imagine Naomi in her raw state and feel suddenly excited. I think she notices. She smirks at me and I chuckle, knowingly, looking to the floor and back again, playing the coy game.

Yeah, this is *definitely* on.

'Why don't you talk me through it,' I say, nodding towards the displays already in place. Naomi's smile broadens out at the prospect of discussing her designs.

'So this, inside the hall, this is our hellscape,' she says. I look around me at the twisted wooden structures, decorative ladders propped up against the walls, which I already know Dennis will have a fit about – health and safety and all that. There's a gnarly, fairy-tale type chair, old-fashioned wooden instruments dangling from above and there are birds. Lots of odd-looking birds with too-long legs. And gangly-legged frogs, too. And evil-looking naked dolls sitting on golden thrones or dangling through hoops or suspended from walls.

'You've certainly conjured my idea of hell,' I say, pushing on her arm playfully. 'Well done.'

'Yeah, it's not been my usual booking.' She laughs. 'And it's not *exactly* in keeping with the imagery of the painting, but I think it's certainly hellish enough.' She leans in sideways to me and whispers, 'Those dolls' eyes seem to follow you, don't they?'

I look towards the doll that's attached to the wall next to us with a spear of some kind through its middle. 'Jesus.' I shudder. 'You're right. Honestly though, you should see some of the items in our collection. There's an old puppet that I'm convinced is haunted.'

Naomi laughs. I look around again. The vibe's certainly not average; I'll give Caitlin that. It's kind of odd even by her warped standards. But this is a pretty good blank canvas to work with – our main hall doesn't have much in it. It needed a lot of foundational work doing when things started to crumble. Scaffolding was holding parts of it in place for a few years. Dad had never paid to get it done before he died so we had a lot to do to stop the very fabric of the house disintegrating. Anything on top of that was just too costly, so it's quite the shell, now. Hence Caitlin's renovation proposal appearing so attractive to Granny.

Anyway, that was when Dennis appeared. After Dad died. A right kick in the balls for Steven. I wasn't as bothered – nice to have someone else pick up the boring bureaucratic shite. But even though on paper Dennis works for us, in reality, we know that's not the case. He works for *Granny*. And that can cause us a right ball-ache.

Seriously hope he keeps his trap shut after tonight. He's only in his forties; if he thinks he needs to go running to Granny about a few party drugs then I don't envy his vanilla life.

I look around me at the hall and inhale a deep breath of excited air, imagining the place jumping later on, then glance a sneaky look at Naomi as she continues checking the paper on her clipboard, mapping out which installations or fairy lights go where.

We always have some sort of party décor installed in the public areas, but Caitlin's going to town this time. We never, *never* invite the public into our wing though; that's strictly forbidden. Close friends and family only. A few heavy doors and locks and a bit of genius way-finding signage so visitors don't even acknowledge that there's a lived-in, self-contained apartment in the building.

Even before *our* parties we've always had events here. All those awful medieval banquets I remember as a kid that Dad used to plan in as regular income streams. Those terrible pictures that made their way into the local papers of people grinning ear to ear while some poor pig's head sat directly in front of them as a table decoration, an apple in its gaping mouth and bunches of grapes decorating the silver platter it sat on. But it gave us the gumption to make our own parties pretty spectacular too. So we always decorate the place if we're inviting people over. And I think Mrs Davies prefers that the parties take place in here rather than in our residential wing as there's less to damage. It's pretty much all stone – bar the black and white tiled flooring. But that's tough, too. It's just an empty space, really. A grand empty space, sure. Even the lighting has to be brought in temporarily, and I can see some sitting within the stone fireplace now, flanked by the two ugly statues with missing arms. Not sure why we want to draw attention to those, but they are pretty hellish, so . . .

Naomi points me towards the entrance. 'So this spiral balloon entrance has been designed to conjure imagery of eggs and naked people intertwined as you walk beyond it and into the heavenly garden.'

'I see,' I say, even though I don't. Not really. To be fair, I haven't looked at this painting that Caitlin keeps banging on about. It looks more like a composition of smooth ball sacks to me, but, whatever.

'It has a kind of . . . reproductive vibe,' I say, immediately regretting the cringey word and wishing I'd just been upfront and said 'sexy'.

Naomi clears her throat. 'So, like in the painting that, your wife? Sister? showed me . . .'

'Good Lord, my *sister*,' I say, pulling a face. 'Ugh, the very thought.' My insides contort. 'To be clear, I don't have a wife. Not yet at least.'

Naomi smiles even more broadly. Excellent response. 'Shall I show you what we've done out . . .'

'Naomi. Good. You're here.' Caitlin's bossy tones announce her presence. She strides over, interrupting us, James by her side like the lap pig he is. Caitlin's already done her hair and make-up and she looks good, I've got to say. But she's not in costume yet, just floating around in yoga pants and an off-the-shoulder top. She doesn't practise yoga. At least, not authentically. 'You've got some crap stuck in your hair, Caitlin,' I say, reaching out for the thin and fragile pieces of twisted hazel sticking out of the huge pile of strawberry blonde hair she's got tied up high on her head.

She says nothing, just bats my hand away as if it's a fly, and carries on talking to Naomi. 'This is all looking fabulous, darling.' She kisses both her cheeks and I have to wonder if she's lingered a little too long . . .

When it comes to Caitlin, we all know she's never been one to toe the monogamy line. James, on the other hand, well, I mean, who'd have him? He's not naturally unattractive, not cosmetically, anyway. But he's just so *boring*. And that leaks out into his taste in fashion, and books, and in his dull-as-fuck conversation. Even now he's hovering around next to my glamorous sister in a blue and white striped shirt and chinos. Chinos! She better be dressing him up tonight or he's gonna stick out like a spent beige cock amongst the horny-as-fuck hellscape.

Caitlin goes to walk Naomi outside. 'Hang on, sis!' I say, standing in her way. 'We weren't finished talking.'

'Hurry up then. Naomi and I have much more important things to discuss than whatever your cock's telling you to say.' She turns to Naomi and pats her arm. '*Sorry*, Naomi. But he's like an overexcitable puppy dog, this one. And you're *exactly* his type.'

Naomi looks over at me again, a huge red-stained smile spreading across her face. 'That's OK,' she says, winking discreetly at me as she stands to the side of Caitlin.

'I take it Caitlin's added you to the guest list for tonight?' I ask, knowing full well Caitlin won't have. But Caitlin doesn't even flush. Not in the slightest.

Naomi, however, reddens slightly. 'I . . .'

'Don't worry,' I say. 'Caitlin's never been very organised.' I hand Naomi my card, which she eagerly takes, flashing delicate inner-arm ink and light freckles. 'You're on the VIP guest list for this evening. Bring a couple of friends, if you like. Call me when you arrive so I can make sure you get in OK.' Naomi smiles in return.

'Paul. Shoo! Now!' Caitlin snaps and I laugh and shake my head while she puts her arm around Naomi and directs her towards the 'heavenly' garden. I watch them walk out, Caitlin gushing about her designs. Naomi's pale shoulder revealed by a T-shirt that she's apparently cut the neck out of, and Caitlin, with her hair tied up, revealing her bare neck and its shaded outline of a tattoo running down her spine.

I glance towards the other side of the hall and notice James chatting with Caitlin's hot DJ, their faces to the wall. If he's putting in requests I'll kill him. That prick's got James Blunt and Lewis Capaldi written all over him. I creep up behind them, ready to interrupt whatever it is he believes he needs to discuss with one of London's up-and-coming deep house DJs. But then I notice something . . . James slipping the DJ a big fat roll of notes.

That's not just a DJ-fee-sized roll. That's one hefty payment.

'Now now, gents,' I say. 'What's going on here then?'

James judders violently as if I just jolted him with a cattle prod, meanwhile the DJ tries to casually slip the notes into his pocket, but he struggles to fit it in and turns back to his equipment, roll still in hand, picks up a speaker and lugs it outside.

'Well?' I say to James. 'Stocking up on the party supplies are we?' I eye the DJ as he stops still for a moment on the lawn, places the speaker on the ground and tries with two hands now to conceal the money in his pocket.

'I, ha, no, I . . .' James is stuttering now. The man is a juddery, stuttery mess. Good job he was born into money; he hasn't the nerve to make it.

I tap his arm twice and chuckle to myself but suspicion whirs in my gut. I know full well James won't be investing in drugs. He doesn't partake and would no doubt refuse to have anything to do with supply and distribution. Besides, we've got Dylan coming to take care of that.

But there must have been thousands in that roll. I'm going to have to do some digging there. You never know, I might just find some ammunition.

I watch the DJ saunter back into the hall casually, and hold out my hand to him.

'Paul,' I say.

'Ollie,' he says. It's a firm enough shake.

'I hear we've bagged London's hottest house DJ?'

Ollie smiles. 'Ah. Caitlin does a good sell.'

'Doesn't she just,' I say, looking at James who is still fidgeting on the spot.

Ollie smiles, picks up another speaker, and walks back outside to continue setting up.

'So why's this one off the books?' I say to James.

'What do you mean?'

'The cash. Dennis usually sorts the invoices.'

'Oh, um. Not sure. Caitlin just said, so I . . . speaking of which . . . Better find that wife of mine.'

I cock my head slightly to the side. 'Sure,' I say. James fidgets slightly then turns and heads out of the door in search of Caitlin. Or in search of being in a place where he's not being questioned about why we're paying the DJ a huge amount of cash in hand. There's something not quite right there. I'll get it out of Caitlin though.

And if I don't, if she doesn't know herself . . . Well, that'll ruffle her usually exquisite feathers.

Chapter 10

Kassie

Saturday

There's a knock on the cottage door and Iggy jumps onto her feet. She is standing on the rug, her tail wagging, while I contemplate whether or not to answer. I know who it will be. And I'm not sure she deserves forgiveness.

She knocks again. Eventually, I place my mug of herbal tea on the coffee table, let out a long sigh in Iggy's direction, and move reluctantly towards the door.

As I peer out of the window I can see Caitlin standing there, dress bag in one hand, bottle of wine in the other, lips taut. She is studying the jasmine to the left of her. Not even star jasmine's intoxicating scent can infuse my sister.

I open the door and stand silently. She snaps her head around and looks forward at me, her fine lips breaking into a beaming smile. 'Kassie, darling. Listen, I'm sorry if I upset you. Can I?' she says, moving to come in and gesturing with the costume bag.

I say nothing, but stand aside and let her in. I can see

her appraising the space as she enters. 'You've got this place looking nice,' she says, and I realise at that moment she probably hasn't stepped inside for months.

'Thanks,' I say.

'Listen, I thought, why not have half an hour of sisterly time before the masses arrive, hm? Glass of wine? I can do your hair. Like the old days.'

I nod. 'Sure,' I say flatly. I'm not sure what her memories of the old times entail, but they're certainly not something I want to recall. Your big sister was supposed to look out for you, not catapult you directly into harm's way.

She hands me the chilled bottle, which will no doubt have come straight from our wine cellar rather than her personal supply, and I go to the kitchen to pour us both a glass. 'Are you ready for your transformation?' she says, beaming proudly when I return to the front room. I shudder a little, as I recall her using that word to describe me losing my virginity aged fourteen. She probably recalls using it then too.

I shrug petulantly. I can get away with it right now. She knows just how badly in the wrong she was earlier. Blaming me like that. How could she?

Caitlin stands uncomfortably close to me, glass in hand, and runs her other through my long dark hair. 'Let's see what we can do with this, shall we?' she says, as if my hair is a problem to be solved.

Once she's finished studying my hair, I take Iggy out into the paddock and let her roam around, chewing on hay and jumping on top of her wooden platform. Then I go back inside and prepare to spend half an hour in close proximity to Cruella.

After curling my hair and placing it into a loose up-do, Caitlin attaches the delicate twisted hazel and dusky pink floral headdress and stands back admiring her work. 'Beautiful,' she says. She helps me into my sheer costume and, as I'm pulling on my Dr Martens (which I told her were non-negotiable before she had chance to complain) I hear Caitlin's mobile phone vibrate and catch mine simultaneously lighting up, a tick-tock notification sound in minor notes that always makes me sigh. Because I know who that notification signals.

It's the Morland Twats WhatsApp group.

We both grab our phones. It's Steven.

Steven: All needed at the house
Steven: Pre-party briefing
Steven: Now

'Prick,' Caitlin says sighing.

'I guess we need to plan ahead though, what with the inspection,' I say, hating myself a little for defending Steven's rudeness.

As we walk slowly over the grounds, careful not to trip over the flowing material of my barely there costume, my boots thudding over the grass, I do wonder how Granny's stay with the Taylor-Bankses will influence what happens over the coming days.

'How on earth are we going to get the place cleared in time?' I say, thinking about the aftermath of our parties.

'I know,' Caitlin says, sighing again. 'Mrs Davies has said she's hired some extra cleaning staff. But it's going to be tight. I'd have more hope for Glasto being turned around in time.'

I laugh. I do sometimes forget myself in her company. You have to, I guess. Self-preservation and all that.

We reach the edge of the lawn and head into our wing through the side door. Paul, Steven and James are already gathered.

'Right,' Steven says. 'I just want to run through the guest list with you all.'

'Oh, about that,' Paul says casually. 'I invited a few more last-minute guests. You know, given that our pre-agreed roles don't really count for anything.'

'You mean Jack's coming?' Steven says, unimpressed. 'Already accounted for. I'll have Dennis keep an eye on him.'

To be fair, we all know that Jack can be even more of a ticking time bomb than Paul when he gets the right cocktail of booze and substances down him. But tonight, he's our secret weapon. It won't take much to talk Jack into trying it on with Caitlin. For old times' sake. James shifts uncomfortably at the mention of Jack's name but Caitlin doesn't seem to acknowledge it.

'So, the ones to watch are the Taylor-Banks lad, Will, and his cousin Pete. We need them onside, clearly. We've got Tanya Carroll coming . . .'

'Sorry, what?' Caitlin says. 'You invited a TV journalist? Are you insane?'

'She knows to keep quiet. We pay her well enough.'

Caitlin shrugs a shoulder. 'Fair dos.'

Steven continues, looking down his list. 'There's the usual suspects. Jake and Rhian, Christina, Ed, Suzanne, et cetera, et cetera . . . oh for fuck's sake. Who added Dylan to the list?'

Paul sniggers. 'Just because you don't partake, you can't expect your guests to go without.'

'He's a pretentious dick. It's not the supply that bothers me, it's the bragging about it.'

Paul just laughs. 'He'll be grand. He's never outed us before.'

'No. But he almost outed Jack that time on social media, didn't he.'

'*Almost* being the operative word.'

Steven shakes his head and looks back down at his list. 'Oh, and that TV chef, Miles Thomson. James – I think you were going to introduce me to him?'

James nods.

'What for?' I ask.

'He's keen to open a bistro in the North,' James says.

His use of the word 'bistro' takes me back to Granny's 'headlines' the other day. Bistro was part of Steven's plans. He's literally recruiting his team as we speak. Does he know something we don't? Or is his arrogance just beyond the pale?

Chapter 11

Paul

Saturday

The DJ, Ollie, looks shifty as he walks away from and then back towards his set up on the steps. Shifty or awkward – I'm not entirely sure. I walk over to him, keen to know why James handed so much dosh over to him.

'How's it going?'

'Yeah. Almost there,' he says. 'Just, um, you couldn't show me where the guest room is? I need to get a change of clothes.'

'Of course,' I say. 'I'll walk you over. Did Caitlin not show you? My sister can be so rude sometimes.'

'Yes, she did,' he says, quick to defend her. Just how well does he know her? 'It's just . . . this place is so big.' He looks all around him and takes in our family estate.

'Yeah, and a bit of a rabbit warren too.' I hold out my arm and we begin walking diagonally across the grass and towards our discreet family entrance. 'We've purposely made our apartment difficult to find from the public areas. We didn't want to signpost people to it.'

Ollie nods. 'Course.'

'So,' I say. 'How do you know Caitlin and James?'

'Oh. So, they've hired me before. For their events.'

'Really? For their place in London?'

'Yeah. Some party. A few weeks back.'

'OK,' I say, raising my eyebrows and pausing at the door. 'They didn't think to invite family then.'

'I'm not sure . . . might have been a business thing. In fact, yeah, I think it was.'

I know that this can't be the truth, because I know it's a house rule – James refuses to have business associates in their personal space.

'I take it they pay you well?' I say. Ollie looks puzzled, so I add, 'It was a mighty wad of cash James handed you.'

'Oh, right, yeah so it was to pay for both gigs. This one, and the one before.'

'You must be a shit-hot DJ, that's all I'm saying.'

He shrugs, and I can't tell if it's out of arrogance or awkwardness. He's actually pretty hard to read.

I open the door and hold out my arm again, gesturing for Ollie to enter. I close the door behind me and we take a left, noticing the empty living space. Everyone else must already be buzzing around the steady stream of arriving guests. 'I thought Caitlin might be here actually,' I say. 'But never mind. I'll show you to the room. Just remember, when you come through the green door, you turn left, left again and it's the third door on your right.'

We pause at the door to the guest room. 'I can use this as my signpost,' Ollie says, looking up to the huge framed painting of Granny on the wall.

'Not my favourite,' I say. 'It's our grandmother. And our nemesis.' We both stand silently looking at the old witch who is, as in life, looking down on us with a scowl. 'Anyway,' I say. 'I'll leave you to it.'

He opens the door, and I turn to walk back through our wing and towards the public areas in the direction of the main hall. I figure I better walk out through the grand entrance seeing as how we have guests starting to trickle in.

Even with the sun shining in from outside, there's a cold darkness to the hall, and all those freaky speared dolls and strange creatures top it off nicely. Naomi really has made this place hellish. Which reminds me . . .

I check my phone and can see a text from her from about twenty minutes ago – saying she'll be arriving in approximately twenty minutes. I decide to make my way to the gates where people are being checked in, and so I walk along the side of the hall, turning a corner when I bump into something.

'What the fuck.' I almost jump out of my skin. I stand and find myself face to face with a horse. At least, a horse's head. A white horse's head with a white mane, sad dark eyes and nostrils that my eyes line up with. I am staring deep into the black void of them, feeling as though I have truly been transported into the realms of hell when the nostrils shoot upwards to reveal Kassie.

I place my hand on my chest, trying to steady myself. 'Jesus Kassie,' I say as she perches the mask up on top of her head. She has Iggy by her side. As ever.

'You like it?' she asks.

'Not sure like's the right word but, yeah, it's a pretty effective costume. I thought Caitlin was dressing you though?'

'She has.' Kassie gestures to her sheer dress. She looks great, but it's so not her thing. I can imagine just how uncomfortable she feels.

'So the horse's head is for . . .'

'To take the attention away from the fact that I'm barely wearing anything,' she says, looking down at her barely there attire.

'Interesting tactic,' I say. 'Anyway.' I lean in close. 'Been chatting to Ollie.'

'Oh him,' she says, her nose wrinkling on one side.

'You don't like him?'

'I just caught him trying to shoo Iggy away. Like, I swear he was about to kick her. There's something off about him.'

'Yeah,' I say. 'I know.' I tell her about our conversation, and Ollie telling me that Caitlin and James booked him for parties at their place in London.

'They don't have parties,' Kassie says.

'He said it was a business-related one.'

'But James won't let . . .'

'I know. That's exactly what I thought. Keep your eye on him. And Caitlin. And James for that matter. WhatsApp me privately if you find anything suss. I need to get something on her before the end of the night.'

'Oh, speaking of which . . . there's something dodgy going on with Steven too.'

'There always is,' I say.

'Yeah but this was different. It was Mrs Davies. Yesterday, I totally forgot to tell you, when we were in the kitchen and you were winding Brian up, eating the bread, well, I heard Steven and Mrs Davies arguing. She said something about Steven should be locked up for what he did.'

'What did he do?'

'That's just it. I've no idea. And she already knows about dodgy business dealings and bribes and stuff. This felt . . . different. We need to find out.'

'You don't think, what with James paying Ollie for something, that they might all be in it together?'

'Nah,' Kassie says. 'Not Steven's style. And Caitlin wouldn't have it. They're definitely in the game for themselves.'

I nod in agreement. She's right. After Steven took away the opportunity of us all having a fair share, there's no way Caitlin would let him in on her plans.

'We still have our deal, though?' Kassie asks.

'Of course,' I say, squeezing her shoulder before excusing myself to meet Naomi at the gates.

I feel bad lying to Kassie. But I know, deep down, that I might not be able to go through with it. I might have to break my promise to her.

Chapter 12

Kassie

Saturday

I sit on the edge of the grass in Caitlin's ridiculous costume, Iggy by my side chewing on neat green blades. I've got my freaky papier mâché horse's head on, which is obviously doing the trick given Paul's shocked expression just now.

I touch the tip of the headdress Caitlin placed in my hair. It just about pokes out above the horse's ears. The twisted wood is literally everywhere – I think even Paul and Steven have been handed some to decorate themselves, too, but I doubt Steven'll join in. Thicker, more sturdy pieces of wood create fairy-tale style structures – archways and furniture. I think I can count that as one of *my* gifts to the party, seeing as how a huge display of it sits next to the fireplace in my cottage and Caitlin has always loved the corkscrew nature of it. Nice to know I've finally inspired her in some way.

She was needlessly fucking rude about the pumpkins yesterday.

And anyway, since when did a party need a creative

director? Surely you just get a bunch of people together, stick some tunes on and let the booze flow?

It's only 2 p.m., but, as is the nature of summer parties, everyone wants to get going as soon as possible, so the early arrivals are trickling through the gates and being served drinks on the lawn by our hired help dressed all in beige. Poor kids. They all look about fourteen so they probably didn't dare say no when asked to dress as the weird naked people in the painting. Nude body stockings with carefully placed 'foliage' galore.

There's music playing through the speakers but it's not the DJ set quite yet. I think they've just arranged for some playlist of summer vibes to get everyone in the mood. Chilled-out Ibiza classics and lazy, bass-heavy trip hop beats.

With Caitlin's sinister aesthetics, my mushrooms and Paul's appetite for communal self-destruction, everyone will soon be off their faces and conjuring images of impossible buildings and walking trees with Cheshire-cat grins regardless of how they've been decorated.

A few of the faces filtering into the grounds are familiar. Regulars at our 'legendary' parties – as they have now become known – for better and for worse. I think they'll be disappointed that this one's going to end rather abruptly thanks to Monday's inspection and opening. We usually have a few party dregs passed out or carrying on into the new week.

Steven's currently hovering around the entrance as official meet and greet, no doubt spotting his potential victims. The ones whose business he wants to get his teeth into, or who he wants to extract cold hard cash from. He looks like he's dressed for a business meeting, and his body language matches his suit. I eye him as he shakes hands with a couple who have half-heartedly costumed up – slick matching suits and elaborate devils' horns. It's hard to tell, but I think it's Jake and Rhian. They have the medieval-inspired restaurant in town which they, like us, inherited from Rhian's parents – who used to cater for our medieval banquets when Mum and Dad were alive.

Steven's not overly keen on these parties but he sees the need for them and so encourages them. He'll wait for the booze to wash away his victims' business savvy, get what he wants, then he'll probably hide away in one of our private rooms playing snooker with James or something. I must keep my eyes peeled for that bistro investor guy – try to listen in on the conversation.

I stand and walk towards the cocktail bar area, squinting to protect my eyes from the sun that pushes its way through the eyeholes in my mask. We've had the big wooden bar installed especially for the party, and it has its own roof and backdrop, with the *Garden of Earthly Delights* triptych running the length of it. There are four people behind the bar, preparing the herbs and glasses ready for their first orders. One of them seems to be directing the others and is dressed in a shirt and waistcoat. He must be boiling hot. I remove my horse mask and approach him, Iggy following behind me on a leash.

'Hi,' I say. 'I'm Kassie. Are you David?'

'Yes,' he says smiling and making his way out of the bar area. 'So nice to meet you. You know we're adding your version of the spicy marg to our bar menu, don't you?'

'I did hear a rumour,' I say, beaming. 'You might have to add me to your list of suppliers, too?'

'The herbs? Yes! We may just do that,' he says. 'And who is this?'

'Ah this is Iggy Pop,' I say proudly, scruffing the fur on her head. 'My little sidekick.'

'Not just part of the costume then?' he asks, noticing the mask on my head.

'Oh no. She's as much a Morland as I am.'

He leans more closely to Iggy and smiles, but then his eyes flick intermittently to the bar behind her where his team are preparing things.

'I hope you don't think I'm treading on toes coming up with my own recipes,' I say. 'It's a little hobby. When you have a herb garden, you kind of want to experiment with your produce.'

David smiles. 'God, not at all. We were thrilled to be asked to provide the drinks.' He looks around. 'These parties are legendary. I've always wanted to see what goes on.'

I feel slightly uncomfortable at the thought that some of our guests and suppliers have clearly heard the rumours and are here with their eyes wide open ready to take mental notes.

'You'll probably be disappointed,' I say. 'The rumours are never as good as the reality.'

He smiles, but then glances back to the bar. I can tell he needs to get back. 'I better let you get on,' I say.

As I turn away, I spot my nemesis heading down the driveway and walk away from David and his team.

My nemesis is Dylan. He's looking ridiculously flash in his white jeans, low-cut T-shirt and huge sunglasses, a woman with her hair piled high on his arm who is gushing over him. You'd think drug dealers would want to remain low-key, but not Dylan. They're not even in costume.

They approach me and Dylan grins. 'Kassie.'

'Dylan,' I say. 'And here's me thinking staff weren't invited to the party.'

Dylan eyes Iggy suspiciously and his guest cowers slightly behind him. Iggy's tail is wagging, and I know it's not because she's pleased to see him.

'We both know there'd be no party without me,' Dylan says, trying to reassert himself even though it's clear he's terrified of a tiny goat. 'Those things you serve up are mere trifles.'

'Truffles, actually,' I say. 'So what have you come as then? A Fisher-Price drug dealer?'

Dylan removes his sunglasses and looks me up and down, ignoring my jibe. 'Well, you scrub up pretty well, don't you.' I notice the woman he is with looking away – presumably out of embarrassment.

I lean in closely to him. 'Dylan, babes,' I say mockingly, 'I might be the youngest Morland, but I can have you thrown off site faster than you can say MDMA.'

He lets a kind of snort escape from out of his nostrils, and I notice that Iggy has moved closer to him and started head-butting his legs. She's such a good girl. We definitely have the same taste in humans.

Dylan always arrives early. He wants to peddle as much of his shit as he can, squeeze as much money out of our party guests before kick-out time. I guess you can't blame him – it's a captive audience. They're always sweating buckets of cash and emitting a desperate desire for a kick of dopamine and, well, a whole other life for a few hours. I hate them all. But not as much as I hate him.

I feel a hand on my back. It's Paul. 'Dylan, mate. How you doing?'

I turn around to find Paul, bare-chested, twisted hazel in his head shaped like devil's horns and a kind of Viking vibe going on. Caitlin clearly picked that out for him. He does look good. I look him up and down and he gives me a sly *'well what can you do?'* shrug.

'Aye, aye,' Dylan says enthusiastically. 'Not bad at all, mate. Not bad at all.' They do the usual blokey slapping and hugging thing even though they're not remotely friends.

'Listen, mate, did you get the memo?' Paul asks, lowering his voice.

'No pills, sure. Powder only,' he says, desperately trying to push Iggy away from his legs without setting her off. He's been victim to Iggy's aggression before. I notice that she is now nipping at his trousers. I don't bother tightening the leash.

'Perfect, perfect,' Paul says. 'Need to finish up earlier for this one.'

'No problemo,' Dylan says, and I outwardly cringe. 'Short half-life only.'

Paul slaps him on the back appreciatively.

Great, so it's going to be booze, coke and shrooms then. What a delightful cocktail.

It's never made much sense to me that most of the people who want Dylan's coke have above-average levels of arrogance and narcissism in the first place – why do they need even more of it? That stuff'll be covering the grounds like a blanket of snow by sundown. I remember Mrs Davies freaking out a couple of parties ago – saying there was so much white powder it was clogging up the Dyson.

I spot the interior designer walking across the lawn, costumed up to the nines. I notice Paul's eyes light up.

'Got your eye on someone?' I say teasing.

'She's lush, isn't she? She's called Naomi. Isn't she just...' He lets out a guttural sound and I laugh.

'OK behave now, bro. She's approaching.'

Naomi's gone for the heavenly theme. She's in a gold angel costume with a short, feathered skirt and bodice and huge feathered wings. It's cool. Way better than my one-denier designer effort.

Paul and Naomi embrace and kiss cheeks, in a way that goes beyond a polite hello. I smile.

'Naomi,' Paul says. 'This is my sister Kassie. She's much nicer than Caitlin so you'll be in good hands with her.'

Naomi smiles at me and we quickly hug. 'Caitlin's not all bad,' Naomi says, looking again at Paul.

'Yeah. You don't need to pretend with us,' Paul says.

'Are you local?' I ask, wondering if there could be some potential romance here. Paul's always been one for the ladies. He's had many, many women, but I know deep down he wants more than a quick shag. And he looks at Naomi with more than lust. His eyes are literally dancing as she speaks.

'Newcastle,' Naomi says. 'Well, just north of Newcastle, really.' Iggy looks up at Naomi but stays pretty chilled and begins chewing at the grass again. It's a good sign.

'I can't believe you haven't worked with us before,' I say. 'What you've done here is just amazing. It's . . . otherworldly.'

'Certainly is,' Paul says, not taking his eyes off her.

'I love those dolls, and all the twisted hazel. It's like you've created an enchanted, I don't know, garden.'

'That was kind of the plan,' Paul says laughing. 'Garden of earthly delights, remember.'

'I know,' I say. 'Just trying to compliment. Honestly, Naomi. It's stunning,' I say, taking it all in again. 'It's just my vibe.'

'Kass has always had a dark edge to her. Nicest soul, darkest taste.'

Naomi smiles and then looks down to my side. 'So who is this delight?' Naomi asks, gesturing at Iggy. 'Can I . . . ?' She holds out her hand.

'Of course,' I say, confident that Iggy will behave herself. 'This is Iggy. She's one of the family.'

Naomi gently scruffs Iggy's head. 'Gosh she's simply gorgeous.' Naomi beams, standing back upright. 'How long have you had her?'

'Since she was a baby,' I say. 'She's a pretty rare breed – a Bagot. My father's gift to me just before he died.'

'Oh. I'm sorry.'

'No, no. It's been five years now. And, well, she's just a delight.'

'So sweet.' Naomi squeals, holding Iggy's face in her hands.

'Can I get you a drink?' Paul says.

I let them walk off and watch as he hovers his arm behind her back in a protective way. They are already leaning in closely together as they walk to the bar. I've high hopes there. You can just tell sometimes, can't you?

I scan the lawns, squinting in the sun, and take in the many different costumes that are starting to pop up. We've of course got angels and devils – goes without saying – but they've been put together with a twist. Devils in gimp masks, angels creeping into the realm of kinderwhore. There are also strange birds, fallen brides, black swans and an old-fashioned clown wielding a cleaver. It's a melting pot of steampunk, Victorian gothic and something else with a dark edge – like a warped Lemony Snicket. Hell is definitely winning over heaven, but, knowing some of the guests as I do, I can tell there's an underlying pattern here. The more reckless and obtuse guests are dressed in their own take on the heavenly theme, and the more staid ones are dressed for their place in hell.

I stand up in my ridiculous 'dress', lower my horse mask to cover my face, and move across the lawn with Iggy, feeling pleased that nobody is stopping to make excruciating small talk. It's only when I walk towards the main entrance that I see Caitlin, chatting animatedly with the DJ. She is laughing loudly and standing so close to him that their shoulders touch. She's always been a flirt. And James has never felt comfortable when Caitlin's been in the presence of other men. I think Paul's definitely onto something here.

I glance to the left and see James now, watching Caitlin from afar, a pained look on his face. He turns and walks away but then glances behind him again and his face contorts. It's practically a sneer.

Maybe she's gone too far this time. Maybe, this time, it's more than a flirtation?

Chapter 13

Paul

Saturday

Naomi excuses herself to chat to her friend, who is looking a little uncomfortable and out of place on her own. Kassie and Iggy catch me up and Kassie passes me a smoking cocktail from the bar, keeping one for herself.

'This one of your recipes?' I ask.

She nods her head as we both sip. It tastes of orange bitters and wood. I give the taste my approval with a nod. 'Mm. Delicious,' I say.

'I'd rather be behind the bar serving them than having to schmooze the guests,' Kassie says, as we look around us.

The lawns are buzzing with guests now, like a hive of enthusiastic insects crawling all over our manicured gardens.

'Have you seen our dear sister?' I ask.

'Yeah. Flirting with her DJ. You think . . . ?'

'I totally think,' I say. 'But there's more to it. Because of that fat roll of notes.'

Kassie swallows her drink and looks at me, her forehead crinkling. 'What could it be for?'

'Don't know. But there must have been thousands in there. There's something odd about it all. Like why bump my DJ for him? She's never meddled in my entertainment plans before.'

'James didn't look happy. I caught him watching them. She was doing that sickening fake laugh she does.'

I roll my eyes. 'Keep an eye on them. Maybe need to get some video footage or something. Have you got your phone on you?'

'Yes,' Kassie says.

'Good. Me too.'

Just then I spot Jack, my oldest mate, walking over to us. He gives Kass a gentle hug and a kiss then slaps me hard on my bare chest. My skin smarts.

'Great costume, mate.'

'You fucker,' I say, running a hand along one of the huge devil's horns spiralling from the top of my head. I'm pleased with how this costume's turned out, to be fair. It's conjuring bare-chested Viking vibes, with mud and blood all over my body, a waistcoat, black worn-in jeans with stitching and boots. It's kinda sexy. And Caitlin knows it.

I take in Jack's outfit. He's dressed as a scary white rabbit in a red coat with tails and a small pocket watch on display. His face is painted, blood dripping from his mouth, and he's got huge white ears protruding from his head. He must be roasting in that get-up.

'Where's Alice?' I ask.

'I was just wondering that. Have you seen your big sister?' Jack asks.

I dramatically roll my whole head. Jack and Caitlin used to

have a thing when we were teenagers, and he never really got over her. She probably only went for him because it gave her the same buzz as taking my toys off me as a child. Jack was my best mate, my wingman. Then all of a sudden, lost to her. The sexy big sister who couldn't be ignored. Still grates on me. But I know she liked to fuck him. I've heard the evidence of that, too. She's not a shy and retiring sort in the bedroom. So there's every chance Jack can work his magic with her. But then again, with Ollie here, I'm not sure we'll need him to meddle.

'Sh. Caitlin's heading over,' Kassie says. 'With James.'

'Deep joy,' I say.

Jack looks in the direction of the approaching Caitlin and James. 'I never did understand why she . . .'

'No,' I say, patting his arm. 'Neither did we.'

'Well, we kinda did,' Kassie says, rubbing her fingers together.

'How's my little Jack Rabbit?' Caitlin says, giving Jack a kiss on both cheeks followed by far too much tactile attention in front of James. And then it hits me why Jack's dressed like that. It's what she always used to call him. He's playing up to her. And she's delighted.

James shakes Jack's hand awkwardly. You can see the mismatch in grip between them. 'Jack rabbit then?' James asks nervously.

'Ah yes. It's what Caitlin used to call me,' Jack says, looking my sister in the eye.

'Cute,' James says, clearly irked and confused.

To be honest I don't know why Jack plays up to it at all. The name is pretty degrading really. She called him that when they first had sex as teenagers. Said he could replace her Jack Rabbit toy when the batteries were low, and it stuck. And he stuck to her like glue after that.

'How's the world of mental health treating you then?' I ask Jack. 'Oh, and sorry I missed the last trustees' meeting.'

Jack waves his hand. 'Don't mention it, mate.'

'You still playing at having a sound mind by day then, hm?' Caitlin asks.

Jack's light-hearted nature transforms in an instant, his smile dropping. 'Seriously, Caitlin?'

'I just always wonder how a mental health charity copes with having chaos at the helm.'

'It's contained chaos, though. Right, Jack?' I say. He nods but says nothing, clearly wanting to change the subject.

'It's go big or go home again tonight then, boys?' Caitlin asks, continuing to taunt Jack. 'Just try not to let those wheels fall off this time, hm?' She leans in more closely to Jack.

She's referring to his crash-landing from the cloud of intoxication. He was drink-driving down a Northumberland country lane a few years back. His family managed to keep him out of prison, of course. But it hit the news and he had to publicly commit to turning his life around – and he did that by investing family money in founding a mental health charity. His family were lucky that they caught sight of Dylan's TikTok post before it blew up and got it removed. To the public, Jack is renowned for going straight.

'Fuck off, Cait,' I say, shortening her name to rile her. 'It's not as if you won't be hoovering up the snow later on.' Her smile drops and she glances shiftily in James' direction. He's never so much as double dropped a paracetamol, never mind anything else.

'Can you two pack it in already?' Kassie says. We turn to look at her. I didn't even notice her move to sit down on the grass with Iggy. 'Party's hardly started yet.'

Caitlin lets out a wry smile. 'It's OK, sweetie. I'm just looking out for them both. Don't want them taking each other hostage again and going completely wild, do we, hm?'

'So, Caitlin, what did we pay the DJ you so unceremoniously dumped my booking for?'

'Hm? Ollie? Oh, five hundred pounds?'

'But that looked like a lot more than five hundred pounds you handed him, James?'

Caitlin shoots James a look, unable to mask her discomfort. 'James?' She looks genuinely puzzled.

'I just gave him a tip, that's all.'

'But didn't Dennis . . . ?' Caitlin is staring at James, her mouth agape. She doesn't finish her sentence. It's as though some kind of realisation is dawning on her. I'll grill her on it later.

'Excuse me a moment,' Caitlin says, a smile returning to her face. Her pupils are huge. She's mad as hell.

'I'll come with you,' I say, 'need to grab something from the living room.'

I follow Caitlin who is trying to throw me off by marching at warp speed over the grass, her barely there black dress flowing behind her.

'So what's going on?' I ask. 'Why is James paying huge amounts of cash to the DJ?'

'Oh, Paul, honestly. He'll have just tipped him.'

'Must have been a pretty hefty tip, Linny. Looked like thousands in that roll.'

She stops at the family entrance of the house and looks at me. 'Why are you always poking your nose in my business?'

'Because I was looking after the entertainment. You took over, and I want to know why.'

She rolls her eyes dramatically. 'Right. Bathroom. Line one up for me, won't you.'

I place my drink on the small table by the sofa and take the silver platter from the mantel above the fireplace. Kassie's told us all in no uncertain terms that substances – natural or otherwise – are not to be left at Iggy level if we want to live another day.

I remove the lid of our stash pot and place a decent amount of it in my personal powder bottle and slip it back into my pocket. Then I carve out a couple of chunky lines on the platter, making a mental note to return it to its Iggy-proofed shelf. I'm just hoovering said lines up my nose, using my thumb to tidy away any loose specks from my nostrils, when I feel a presence behind me.

'That mine?' Caitlin's returned. Perfect timing. I hand her the ornate silver straw. She holds it in one hand; then, with the other, she passes a palm over my bare arms and chest, pointing a manicured finger into my skin. 'Looks good on you,' she says.

'Thanks,' I say, rubbing better the flesh she's left a smarting indent in. 'So are you going to stop fobbing me off about this DJ business?'

She sighs, then swoops down to inhale a fat line. I watch her as her thinly veiled body bends over the silver plate, careful to hold her head at the right angle to avoid her twisted hazel headdress clattering amongst the powder. She is considered and calm and looking like some kind of black swan.

She straightens up, wipes her nose and sniffs aggressively. 'There's nothing going on, darling,' she says.

'Kassie said you were flirting outrageously with him earlier.'

'Oh come on, you know Kassie. She's the least flirtatious person we know. She thinks shaking someone's hand is flirtation.'

'You're fucking him, aren't you?'

Caitlin laughs. 'Who?'

'Well clearly not James,' I say.

'And what makes you think I'm fucking Ollie?' She scoffs, gesturing towards the now empty platter, a demand for me to carve out another one. I empty a little more powder out and slice it into a neat line with one of Steven's metal business cards. She leans back over the plate.

'Let me see. One, you're flirting with him. Two, you booked him when I already had someone. Three, James is handing money over to him . . . although I can't quite figure that bit out.'

Caitlin snorts and laughs again, straightening herself back up.

'How is this funny?' I say.

She laughs again, rolling her eyes and sighing inwardly. 'OK, so I think James might be buying me a bit of a birthday present. I mean, I don't know for sure. But I suggested a three-way, brought Ollie into the bedroom.'

'Ah – he's an escort?'

'A high-class escort. Very reasonable, too. You get plenty of value for money.' She looks up to the ceiling, a twinkle in her eye.

'Don't really want to know about your orgies, sis,' I say, snatching the straw back from her and diving back in for another go on the marching powder.

'Well you brought it up. Ollie might be a good decade or so younger than my husband but my God, he's got flair. Maybe it's being a DJ, I don't know. Like, the rhythm thing.

He has good rhythm, Paul. Like, seriously good. Fucked me to nirvana and back.'

She's chattering away at warp speed now. Coke's kicked in then. She always was greedy with it.

'I really don't want to hear about my sister's expensive orgasm, thanks,' I say. 'You're ruining my high.'

'I know you'll be desperate to knock one out the moment I leave the room.'

God, I hate her sometimes. 'You're a sick bitch, Linny,' I say. 'Besides. Doesn't explain why James is paying your horny fuck boy does it?'

'But I *already* explained it to you. He's obviously paying for his services. Thing is, what he doesn't know, is that I get it for free.'

I make a mental note of her indiscretion. She's sleeping with him behind James' back. Regardless of the three-way payment, he won't like that. 'Why don't you just divorce the man? Everyone knows you hate him. *He* knows you hate him.'

'Marriage is about more than love and sex. Everyone knows that.'

'Isn't it humiliating? Walking into a room with *him* on your arm,' I say, sneering.

'Not really.' She shrugs. 'Anyway,' Caitlin says. 'Naomi, hm?'

'Yeah, can you kindly stay out of that one, please.'

Caitlin cackles. 'Yeah. OK. I think she'd look better with Jack.'

'You don't have to push her and Jack together just to spite me.'

Caitlin laughs a big hearty laugh. It's real and laced with meanness. 'Don't fret, little brother,' she says. 'Besides, we need to get schmoozing. I want to track down that bistro guy – I don't trust Steven. Not one bit.'

Suddenly, we're in it together. Part of the same team again. And I can't help but let a smile slip out, as she links arms with me and we walk out back onto the lawn together, my back straight.

Chapter 14

Paul

Saturday

Of course Caitlin immediately breaks free of my arm, floating across the garden, black fabric gusting out behind her and squealing at people in that fake, nauseating voice. 'Darling. So glad you could make it.'

The sun is starting to go down and the whole place is sparkling with fairy lights and glowing woodland structures. Pairs of heels and shoes are removed from feet so people can plant their bare skin onto the grass, and I can see people perching on the edge of the fountain, seeing how quickly they can push their heads through the wall of water and into its dry inner sanctum. People are already well on the merry slide towards oblivion. Never takes them long.

The fountain, however, makes me shudder.

And the music needs to catch up. It's all laid-back trippy stuff and we need something more upbeat. Caitlin's DJ is still not at his decks. Oliver. Ollie.

Ol-i-verr.

I say his name slowly, letting the syllables roll around my mouth. My face screws up in disgust. I spot James and corner him, keen to see his reaction now I'm armed with more information.

'James. Have you seen Oliver?'

'You looking for him too?'

'Yeah,' I say. 'I mean, is he in charge of the music or not? Can't just leave this shite playing for hours on end; everyone'll be asleep.'

'Caitlin's idea,' James says, his sight focused on our DJ stand. 'She said he needed a big entrance.'

'And did she offer to provide it?'

'Hm? Sorry?' James says, taking a sip of his wine. Even his choice of drink is pedestrian.

'The big entrance.' The joke is lost on him. 'Never mind.' It's only when I look more closely that I can see Caitlin has indeed put *some* effort into her husband's costume. In a nude make-up, slight-enhancement kind of way. I think he's meant to be a dead businessman or something. It's not too far a stretch from James' everyday look, just with slightly darker circles around the eyes and a couple of rips in his clothes. This is so Caitlin. She's dressed him down and dowdy while she shines like a black star.

James is fidgeting, looking all around him. He has that lost puppy look whenever they're apart in the same space. Because she always does shake him off. You can't leash Caitlin.

'What did you want him for anyway?' I ask.

'Hm?' He rotates his head back around to face me. He's all chops. He's got that chopsy droopy inbred look about him. I notice it now more so than ever.

'The DJ. Oliver.'

'Oh. Oh *him*,' he says, almost theatrically, pausing no doubt to collect his thoughts and make something up. 'Just um . . . just to check what time he's going on. Like you said, the partygoers need a pick-me-up.' He cocks his head and shuts his eyes as he speaks, shaking it like a posh old prick with loose jowls. 'Some deep house bangers,' he says, exceedingly pleased with himself for attempting to use contemporary phrasing.

'Oh, James,' I say, patting him on the arm twice and shaking my head slowly, a smirk on my face, as I walk away in search of the elusive Oliver. If we're paying this Ollie kid he needs to inject a bit of rhythm into the atmosphere. Just because you've been paid to fuck one of the hosts doesn't mean you can slack off in the other department. Besides, most people know I'm usually in charge of the entertainment. It'll reflect badly on me.

I slip back into our wing of the building, walk through the living room and into the kitchen where I can see Kassie chatting with Brian, her horse's head mask discarded on the kitchen table. 'Cooking up a psychedelic storm, Bri?' I holler, slapping a huge grin on my face. They're standing in front of a batch of chocolate truffles.

'Shh,' Kassie says, looking around her. 'Mrs Davies was loitering earlier.'

'As if *you* could ever get in her bad books, sis,' I say.

'She'll know they've come from me,' she hisses.

'She already knows,' Brian says flatly, a small smile threatening to shatter his usual expressionless mask.

We both look at him astonished. He rarely speaks. He's one of those dark and brooding types. 'She does?' Kassie asks. 'How?'

'Uh-huh,' Brian says, the corners of his mouth still twitching.

'Well there you go, sis. You've been supplying our parties for the last two years and you're still teacher's pet. No harm done,' I say.

'Yeah well, it wasn't just the supply she wasn't happy with last time, was it?'

I throw her a baffled look.

'The vomit, Paul. The regurgitated canapés on the picnic blankets. This time, we're thinking ahead. We've added some ginger to the recipe. It's an antiemetic,' Kassie says.

I pick up one of the truffles and wolf it down. 'Ginger?' I ask through a mouthful of rich, dark chocolate. There are indeed hints of ginger. Hints of lime too. I throw Bri a thumbs up.

'Well that, my friend, is absolutely bloody lovely,' I say to Brian, adding a chef's kiss, before turning back to Kassie. 'An anti-what?'

'Emetic,' Brian says. 'Stops people puking.' Then he really does smile and I notice his stomach juddering beneath his white chef's jacket.

'Well, won't you look at that,' I say. 'Who knew?'

'Knew what?' Kassie asks.

'That Bri could actually smile.' We both turn to look at him and he starts sniggering and trying to cover his mouth. I join in but Kassie remains straight-faced.

'Have you been at the truffles, Brian?' Kassie asks, authoritatively, pointing at the platters then moving in more closely to inspect them. I can see her mentally counting them one by one.

'I couldn't let you serve something up I hadn't taste-tested,' he says. 'Chef's rules.'

'How many have you had?' Kassie presses him, glancing again between Brian and the neatly lined trays of truffles.

Brian, however, can no longer hold it in. His chest is shuddering, ready to break out. He covers his mouth to try to stifle it but, soon, he is laughing so hard tears fall down his face.

'Well I never. We'll make a jolly Father Christmas out of the big fella yet,' I say, laughing and picking up another truffle. Kassie slaps the back of my hand. 'Ow.' I flinch. I pop it in my mouth, chew it and stick my tongue out at her in defiance when it's gone. 'You seen Oliver?'

'Paul, you know I don't know half the stupid twatty guests currently invading our home and garden.'

'Have you not invited your old uni mates this time?' I ask. 'Thought you lot were quite the riot when you got together.'

'Hardly. Besides, we prefer the pub to all this pretentious bullshit,' Kassie says.

I think back to when Kassie came home from uni that holiday with three of her new mates. Something in her changed that summer. She was going through her Wednesday Addams phase – dying her hair even darker than it is, wearing all black and listening to emo. She was careful to keep her new mates away from the rest of us though – some kind of inverted snobbery. Mrs Davies offered to put on a drinks reception for them and all of us but Kassie were hellbent on taking them down the local in the village instead. I don't think she even wanted them to see the house but they'd all stayed at each other's places over the summer so she had to pass on the invite. I've never known anyone so uncomfortable in their own skin because of their wealth. It's so backward. But Kassie was. At least, she was when she went to uni and realised that we were a little more privileged than most people. Although, considering the fact she chose to study with the Eden project in Cornwall, she clearly already had designs to get as far away from Morland Hall as possible. And who can blame her?

'Anyway,' Kassie says. 'Ollie?'

'Yeah – he should be out there DJing.' I lick the sticky rich chocolate from my fingers. 'God that is nice,' I say, half to myself.

'He's down the hall I think. He was lost looking for the guest room.'

'I already showed him to the guest room.'

Kassie shrugs. 'He's pretty hot, bro. You might have some competition tonight. Better keep an eye on Naomi.'

'Why does everyone keep hinting that she's suited to every other man except me?' I say, moodily.

Brian lets out another laugh and quickly covers his mouth, turning away.

'I'm just teasing,' Kassie says. 'I can tell she likes you. She most definitely fancies you.'

'I quite like her as it happens.' I elbow Kassie's side and she grins. 'She's interesting. Hot as hell. And can hold her own out on the lawn with all those *stupid twatty guests*.' I imitate her words.

'Good,' Kassie says. 'You better go find her then. Before someone else does.'

I grab another truffle and leg it out of the kitchen before Kassie slaps me again.

As I walk down the hallway I almost trip on one of the old stone floor tiles. I look down and try to reposition it back into place, but it doesn't lie flush with the rest of the floor. I make a mental note to tell Dennis about it – he's compiling a list of maintenance jobs that need sorting before we open to the public on Monday. Obviously, we won't get this one sorted in time now, but then again, the public aren't allowed to wander in our wing so, if anyone does come in here and break their neck, they can't exactly sue us.

As I continue walking along the corridor and through the double stone archway, I turn left towards the guest room. I can hear music and voices behind the door. It's Caitlin with Ollie.

I stand still, straining to hear the conversation over the sounds of indie sleaze while looking up at the huge oil portrait of Granny. I shudder.

'I don't know what to do with it?' Ollie says from beyond the closed door.

'Keep it. Obviously,' Caitlin says confidently.

'But he told me . . .'

The song stops and a new riff starts. Take Me Out by Franz Ferdinand. I shudder. I hate that song with an unnatural passion. Still, I twist my head and push my ear closer to the door.

'I know what he told you. But you don't have to do it. I mean, how's he going to get it back off you? It's all in cash.'

I'm guessing they're discussing the payment for sexual services that Caitlin's expecting for her birthday. But then why would she tell him he didn't have to – because surely that means sleep with her – and surely that's exactly what she wants him to do?

'I guess we can still meet in secret,' Ollie says. 'Kind of fun.'

'It's always fun,' Caitlin drawls. 'And there's no way I'm letting you go.'

Then it goes quiet. I reach for my back pocket and take out my phone. I open the camera, switch it to record and position the phone in front of my face. Then I take a deep breath . . . and push the door open.

And there it is. In the frame of my iPhone. Caitlin naked. Ollie naked. Caitlin straddling Ollie, his head arching backwards, her lips wrapped around his cock. His hands grasping for her hair as her head moves up and down. He is groaning, pulling her head towards him. Faster. Deeper. His legs tense out and his torso judders violently. Then he turns his head. Opens his eyes. He sees me. His eyes wide. I place my phone behind my back. Ollie's legs start kicking frantically, almost knocking Caitlin.

'Ugh. Caitlin . . .'

She pulls her head up and swallows, then she, too, turns to look at me. Her lips are red and her skin shiny. She wipes her mouth with the back of her hand while not once breaking eye contact with me.

'Can I help you?' she asks, before breaking out into manic laughter. But she is still naked. And I have seen her naked before. She doesn't even flinch. She refuses to move. She just stares hard at me, her laughter dying back down, and she smiles.

I slam the door shut on them and place my hidden phone in my back pocket. I look down at my crotch.

Then I run to the bathroom. And I throw up.

Chapter 15

Kassie

Saturday

Paul marches into the kitchen with a right face on him. He stops at the cupboard, opens it up and removes the cheap blended whisky from the top shelf. He unscrews the top, lets it fall on the butcher block counter and takes huge swigs from the bottle that's usually reserved for Brian's cooking. 'Take it easy,' I say. Paul says nothing. He just looks at me defiantly and carries on. 'Paul,' I say. 'It's not even seven yet. We don't want a repeat of . . .'

'Why is our sister such a fucking bitch?'

'What's she done now?'

He ignores me and instead slams the bottle on the counter and grabs one of the full trays of truffles. 'Paul!' I say. 'Seriously. What the . . .' He picks the bottle back up and storms outside, tray in hand. I look to Brian for help but he isn't paying attention. Instead he has his back to me slicing limes on the other side of the kitchen, every so often holding the knife up and peering into it as if it's a distorted mirror at a fairground. Shit. A shroom trip gearing up in the mind of a knife-wielding bear-like chef, and a brother who, for some inexplicable reason, has charged through the kitchen like he's method acting the demon Viking costume he's wearing.

I glance back to Brian who is now staring at his own fingers, and decide to carefully slip in front of him and take the knife from his other hand. Thankfully, distracted by his seemingly interesting fingers, he releases the knife with little resistance. 'Why don't you knock off for the night, Bri? The cocktail guys have got the drinks covered. You can wander on back to your place?'

He just stands looking at me, a stupid smile once again spreading across his usually serious face as he lifts his feet up and places them back down again in turn as if they're sticking to the floor with treacle.

I weigh up my options. Who is more dangerous in this moment? I decide that the potential for fucking up monumentally lies mainly with my brother, so I head out of the kitchen, leaving Brian staring into space, and I hoof it across the lawn in search of Paul. God knows why he's so bothered. I wonder if it was something to do with the truffles? Have we put too much in? Can you even overdose on psilocybin when it's packaged into truffles that small?

I take Iggy back to her little place then head out onto the lawn where I spot Steven first, getting his glass topped up by one of the hired help in their stupid fig leaf Garden-of-Eden-style costumes. 'Have you seen Paul?' I ask, panting.

He nods at the young man to thank him for topping up his whisky, who then wanders back towards the drinks table to switch to champagne. Steven draws on his cigarette, affording me only a cursory glance. 'Why have you been hiding away in the wing? Shouldn't you be circulating? You're one of the hosts, after all,' he says, looking around at everyone but me. His costume is pretty underwhelming, but it works. It's a nod to Gomez Addams, which feels like a bit of a cop-out – you could probably buy a complete Gomez Addams costume from Temu. But of course, Steven's take includes wrecking a perfectly tailored designer suit that could have otherwise brought in a stack of cash for a charity shop. A style that takes little thought, but that perfectly complements his usual serious business attire.

'Nice costume,' I say.

'Caitlin,' he says, taking a sip of his drink and still refusing to give me his full attention.

'Looks a bit staid for Caitlin,' I say.

'Yeah. I refused to wear the costume she got me so our dear darling sister broke into my room and slashed my best suit.' He finally looks at me, his mouth pursed and his eyes narrowed. 'Isn't Cait just adorable?' He looks away again.

'Anyway, it's Paul I'm looking for,' I remind him.

'Forget Paul. Get circulating.'

'I am circulating,' I say. 'I'm circulating the grounds in the vain hope of tracking down my apparently possessed brother.'

'Oh great,' he says, now affording me his full attention. 'Not again.'

'I don't think he was off his face. Not yet, anyway. Bit drunk, maybe.' I don't want to give Steven too much ammunition by telling him about the several truffles Paul's washed down with whisky in the space of a few seconds. I need to remember whose side I'm on in that respect. But I do urgently need to find him. 'He seemed angry more than anything. I was worried maybe someone upset him.'

Just then James approaches. 'Kassie. Steven.' He nods his head at us formally.

'James. Have you spotted Miles yet? I could really do with that intro you promised me.' Steven places an arm around James and walks him off to the side. I can't understand why James would want to do Steven any favours given the family dynamics at the moment, but Steven does seem to get the upper hand with James. Most of the time, anyway.

I turn and look around me, hoping to spot Paul but instead I see Caitlin leading the DJ to his decks. He's now wearing a pure white fitted T-shirt with a slim chain around his neck, and, I have to say, he looks gorgeous. Not that I'll be going anywhere near him considering the vibes Caitlin's giving off around him. She's oozing the devil's oestrogen today.

Caitlin grabs a mic and I notice she's missing her hairpiece. 'OK, people. Apologies. Brief interruption to the proceedings.' There's a collective polite faux-sigh. 'I know, I know. I just didn't want to let this occasion get lost amongst the fun.' She waves the DJ over towards her and he smiles awkwardly as he stands next to her. She places a casual arm around him. I spot James to my left, looking down at his feet, while Steven watches our sister with a concentrated, strained look on his face, as if judging her performance.

'We're incredibly honoured to have Ollie Owens on the decks tonight all the way from Soho's Levelled Club. So, grab another cocktail and get yourself onto our outdoor dance floor.' Caitlin points towards the makeshift dance floor, marked out on the lawn by a living willow construction in the shape of a tall dome with a covered arched entrance, lit by even more fairy lights. It looks like some kind of enchanted fairy house. 'If you're not feeling the heavenly vibe, we've got dark trance pumping inside our devilish hall of hell for all you dark and deadly angels. See where you end up as the night goes on. But for now, let's hear it for Ollie!' Caitlin holds her hands up clapping theatrically and smiling at Ollie, who I have to say is looking a little unsteady already. Not a good sign at this point in the proceedings.

The garden is alive with whooping and the music starts up, a distant mournful voice reverberating over the top of muffled synth notes. I'd have rather had an indie band to be fair, but it'll do. It suits the slowly vanishing sun somehow and the whole place is aglow with twinkling lights and an orange-streaked sky.

James knocks the rest of his wine back in a one-er and stomps off towards the bar for another. Steven moves back to his original position next to me and leans in close. 'Trouble in paradise there, I reckon.'

'So lovely of you to finally involve me in a conversation,' I say with a fake smile. 'Shame you only speak to me when you're slagging the others off.'

'That's not true, actually. Because I want to discuss your future. I need you to charm Will.'

'Who?'

'The young Taylor-Banks boy. He's going to be pretty influential come Monday.'

'How so?'

'Really, Kassie. Do keep up. There's a Taylor-Banks on the inspection panel. They can make or break it for us.' He lights another cigarette, taking a deep drag and exhaling the smoke directly into my face. I waft it away with my hand and fake-cough. 'Not only that, I believe young Will has stakes in that new development in town.'

'And?'

'It's going to be a good place for doing business. It's attracting some promising tech start-ups as tenants.'

'You mean you want in with the tech bros? Jeez, Steven, how cliché.'

'It's where the money is. And I'd quite like to invest in the right business. Plus, that building has a rooftop bar and restaurant. I think you'd like it. Full of foliage. That's your thing, isn't it?'

'So can we use that place and stop having these god-awful parties at home then?' I ask.

Steven looks at me. 'Some people are starving. And you're complaining about having to live in a huge house and socialising with cocktails?'

'Yes. Precisely *because* some people are starving. I'd rather we used the ridiculous amount of money we spend on these things for something more . . . worthwhile.' We both look around us at what is fast becoming a bit of a mess as the sun has started going down. As expected. The volume of the crowd is way up, guests are becoming less and less bothered about littering the lawn and I swear there's a couple fucking underneath the monkey puzzle tree in the distance.

'You need to remember who you are, Kassie. Who you represent, anyway. Besides, this could be our last Morland bash. Your cottage could become the new clubhouse.'

'You're such a bastard,' I hiss at him. But my anger is overwhelmed by feelings of grief I know I will feel if I'm turfed out of my home.

Caitlin appears beside us. 'What are you two talking about then?'

'Kassie's feeling a little out of place,' Steven says and sips his drink again.

'He's basically asked me to prostitute myself to that Will TB guy.'

Caitlin looks towards Steven. 'Who? Will?' Steven nods. She turns her face back to me and breaks out into a beaming smile. 'Oh but, Kassie. He's simply divine. Of good stock too.'

'Oh. So *that's* what this is about. Trying to marry me off.'

'It's part of the tradition,' Steven says, chuckling to himself.

'Don't see *you* tying the knot,' I spit, pointing at Steven. He hasn't had a girlfriend – or indeed a boyfriend – in years. I don't even know if he has any interest in romance whatsoever. The only stiff things on him are his suit and his personality.

'Look, Kassie,' Caitlin says, her head tilted to one side in the most patronising pose possible. 'Just think of it as business. You don't have to stay faithful. You can still find your Prince Charming.' She leans in close to me. 'You'll just have to fuck him under the cover of darkness.'

'I'd rather not have my romantic life dictated by you . . .' I say this pointedly at Caitlin, but I doubt she even registers. If she does, she certainly doesn't care.

'You're just being petulant, Kassie,' Steven says now. 'If I hadn't asked you to schmooze him you'd have ended up doing so anyway. He's *so* your type.'

I frown, wondering how Steven could possibly know what my type is seeing as he doesn't even know how I take my coffee.

'Anyway,' Caitlin adds. 'The Taylor-Banks family aren't just wealthy. They're philanthropists. Ticks a big box for you, am I right?'

'To what causes?' I ask.

'To a more . . . productive society,' Steven says, finishing off his freshly poured whisky.

'You mean they're Tory donors,' I say. 'Or worse . . .'

'Oh don't be so cynical. Can't you try to be on the same page as us for once? Honestly, I question your loyalty sometimes,' Steven says. 'Seriously. Go get yourself a drink, chat Will up and at least *try* to look like you're having fun for a change. I've put a good word in for you.'

'Jeez. Thanks,' I say.

I roll my eyes, turn away and march off into the night. Not in search of Will, but rather in search of my less abrasive but far more worrisome middle brother.

I look all around me but can see no sign of him. Where the hell has he gone?

I head over to the fountain where a few partygoers are downing champagne and laughing uproariously. I place my Dr Marten boot on the edge of the fountain's base and stand tall on it, scanning the crowd. I'm about to step down and then something catches my eye, making me freeze.

Fucking hell.

A horse's head. *My* horse's head. Bobbing around on top of chef's whites. And he's holding a knife.

Chapter 16

Kassie

Saturday

I race across the lawn, keeping Brian – or rather, the horse's head – in my sightline. He is heading into the main hall. Those bloody truffles. And this will all be my fault if someone meets their maker at the hands of a deranged chef. But as I look around me I realise that nobody seems to be paying any attention to him. There is no parting of the sea as he makes his way through the crowds. They must think the knife's part of the costume.

Calm down, Kassie. Maybe it is. Maybe he's just joining in with the festivities?

Am I being overly anxious? I usually am at these parties. But it's Brian we're talking about. He barely speaks. He barely smiles. Except for today. Except for when he's inadvertently gotten off his face on shroom truffles. The idea of an erratic Brian is enough of a concern on its own, never mind with weapon in hand and that freaky fucking horse's head.

The hall is dark and hellish, with glowing orange lights only adding to the sense of unease. Orchestral synth plays over the top of a driving bass, and it feels like I've walked into some kind of bizarre sci-fi-cum-horror movie. Speared freaky dolls, Caitlin? Really? I can't believe she went for those. She used to tell me off for placing my lifelike dolls on the floor and taking a running jump at their bodies, watching their heads pop off and dart across the room. Still, it was probably just because she liked telling me off, rather than any kind of overt sympathy for the dolls. I don't think sympathy is an emotion Caitlin's ever experienced.

I spot the horse's head bobbing up and down among the crowd in the middle of the room, moving to the beat.

I manoeuvre myself through the gyrating bodies, some of which look as though they're convulsing violently. The dance floor is definitely being powered by pills and powder in here. Eyes are either popped and wide or half-closed and lost in some kind of gurning heaven. And Dylan promised he wasn't serving up pills tonight. I knew we couldn't trust him.

The white mane of the horse's head stands out against the darkness and I crane to keep track of it as it heads towards the back of the hall. The music is making me feel woozy as I try to wade through people and masks and freaky costumes, weird bird heads and pale painted faces looming in front of my eyes. I use my arms to push bodies to the side and create an opening, like a parting of the sea.

The head is almost out of view as we approach the back wall of the hall and I see it turn left towards the stairs. I push on more frantically, the heavy bass sounding like blood rushing in my ears and the synth dancing around my head like pins and needles. I realise I am anxious. It must be the adrenaline.

I get to the top of the stairs and Brian is nowhere to be seen. Then I turn to my left and head towards our apartment. Perhaps he's gone back into our wing? He has the keys, after all. I race along the corridor and can see the door to our apartment closing. I speed up and leap towards it, managing to slam my foot in the gap before it shuts. I pull it open, shut it frantically behind me and take stock of the situation. There's nobody around, which is to be expected during a party. But ahead of me I catch a knife being dragged along the wall and around the corner towards the living area. I pick up speed again and can hear my heart pounding in my chest as I notice the superficial cuts made in the wallpaper. What the hell is he doing? He must be completely out of his mind.

I dive into the living area but, there's nobody there. It's like he's completely vanished. Has he somehow managed to lose me and make his way to the kitchen?

I look all around me and am about to head towards the kitchen when I feel someone grab my backside.

'Brian!' I yelp, but when I turn around, it isn't him. It's some drunken party guest, his eyes half shut and an inane smile spread over his face. He looks fairly young, but it's hard to tell with all the white make-up and dark rings around his eyes. He is wearing a kind of shawl made of feathers. He reminds me of a haunted crow.

'Who the hell are you?' I yell. 'And what are you doing in here?'

He says nothing and just stands on the spot, his feet unmoving but his upper body swaying. At one point he sways forward towards me and the feathers brush my face.

'You need to leave,' I say, holding my hand in front of me to stop him invading my space any further.

He shakes his head silently. Then he lunges forward towards me, his face hitting mine, his skin clammy. His lips misalign with mine and there is a wetness around my mouth. I push him backwards and he wobbles but attempts to move towards me again, so I pick up my booted right foot, bring my knee to my chest, then I kick out hard and fast. He hurtles backwards, his arms flailing as he tries, unsuccessfully, to grab hold of the arm of the sofa. He lands in a heap and I dive for the door, pulling it open and grabbing the attention of one of our suited-up security staff, waving them over.

'Ms Morland?'

'There's a guy,' I say panting, struggling to get my words out. 'He's got into our apartment. Just tried to . . .' To what? To kiss me? To hurt me? To rape me? What was he doing? Everything is so confused and I'm in shock.

'Wait there,' the security guy says and I stand by the door, my back collapsing into the brick wall. Within seconds he is back out, the crow-man in his hands, his feet barely touching the floor as he is dragged along. He looks barely conscious.

'This him?'

I nod quickly. 'Yes,' I manage.

'We'll deal with him,' he says. 'Want me to call the police?'

I shake my head, unsure whether I want to escalate it or not. 'But maybe, get his photo or something?' The security guy nods and drags the creepy crow towards the gates with him.

I stand in our doorway looking out at the party. The sky is black now, the music is still pumping, and there is screeching and cackling from the guests. I move backwards beyond our door and into the apartment and slam the door shut on the crowd. I take a few moments to catch my breath then suddenly remember.

Brian!

I race around to the kitchen but it's completely empty. But it's there that I feel a breeze. The back door from the utility area is open. I race towards it ready to shut it and then something comes over me.

I give up. Brian's not my problem. Paul is not my problem. I've had it with this party.

I stomp back onto the lawns to the champagne bar and grab an entire bottle from one of the young waiters in his ridiculous flesh-and-fig-leaf outfit. I'm taking it back to the cottage and leaving my vile, ridiculous, out-of-control siblings and their shady guests to it.

I trudge over the grass, weaving through more prime examples of twattery and excess, and make my way along the dark gravel path to my cottage. I specifically asked for the lighting along the path to be turned off so nobody would accidentally find their way to my private sanctuary. I take a big swig from the bottle and wince as air forces its way down my throat alongside the champagne. I stop and burp. Loudly. But before I take any more steps I can hear rustling in the hedge, accompanied by heavy panting and rhythmic moans. I glance to my left to see outlines of bodies on the ground. Great.

'Give it a rest,' I shout into the darkening sky.

They ignore me, if anything they seem to get even louder, so I keep moving ahead, finally arriving at the little gate to my cottage. I push it open and stand outside my front door, placing the champagne bottle next to my doorstep, and take my key from my bra. God I can't wait to close the curtains and collapse onto my sofa in peace. I'll let Iggy come in with me tonight, too. She'll probably be sick of the noise in her place what with the gaps around the windows.

I turn to my left and towards Iggy's place, but the door isn't locked. It's only half shut. My heart plummets into my stomach. I push the door open and bend over to take my phone from inside my boots. I shine the torch into the room.

The empty room.

Iggy has gone.

Chapter 17

Saturday 23rd August

23.17

Bare legs and bare feet move and sway as the music plays. The camera travels in between them all, occasionally stopping and focusing on toes.

Beyond the collection of legs and feet there is an entrance to something made of wood. The camera pans upwards. A collection of leaves is silhouetted against the navy sky, stars twinkling amongst them calmly as banging music blasts loudly in the background.

Two people stagger past, giggling. A woman carrying her heels in one hand and a glass in the other. She stops and points her glass at the camera, swaying backwards on the heels of her feet. 'Is that goat real?'

The man stops too and looks towards the camera, peering in close and staring, the whites of his eyes creating light in the lens. He holds out a hand but it just floats around randomly in front of the lens. He starts laughing. 'No. *No!* It's not a goat. Is it?' He snorts.

'I think it is,' the woman says.

'Nah. It's a cat, Sian. Look, it's got a collar on.' A hand moves towards the camera and the view jerks backwards.

'That cat doesn't like you. You're a cat deterrent. Pussy deterrent. Hahaha. Hang on, no. That is a goat. It's a goat. It's an actual goat. I'm telling you.' The woman starts laughing uncontrollably now.

The man joins back in, snorting again. 'No. Is it?'

The palm of a hand edges slowly and cautiously towards the camera, fingers gently moving. The lens jerks backwards again and moves up and down.

'Fuck. Sian. It's like it's possessed or something.' The laughter stops.

'Goats, they're a sign, aren't they? Of something bad? I mean, even if it's not really there, the fact we've seen it, the fact our minds have created it, means something really bad's going to happen.'

The two people stand squinting into the frame, mouths gawping. Then, the camera moves away at speed, crossing the lawn where it passes bodies sitting on blankets in a blur of colour and sound. It nears the entrance to the wooden structure with fairy lights and people dancing. Two women sit on the edge of it, knees up, shoes off. They have a bottle placed on the ground between them.

'Yeah, genuinely. Can I take the rest of this?' One of the women picks up the bottle.

'Aye, why not,' the other says. 'You deserve some fun.'

'Just hope I can track him down. It's getting dark and there are so many people. I mean, have you ever been to a party this fucking big?'

'Nope. But you'll find him more quickly if you just go and stop fannying around.'

'Right,' the woman with the bottle says, a smile spreading over her face. 'Wish me luck.'

'Good luck. For a good fuck.'

The two women burst out laughing and the one with the bottle walks away into the distance, her movements wobbly.

The camera backs away and turns to the right, navigating around empty, tipped-over glasses and bottles, chatter emanating all around. It moves towards a door. The door opens from the other side.

Two legs in dark trousers. A woman's voice. 'Except it's not, is it? Not really.'

A man's voice. 'Not what?'

'Not. Oh. What's she doing in here? She's meant to be . . .'

'Right, Iggy, out. Now!'

'Don't you dare, Steven!'

'We can't have farmyard animals running riot in here. It's a . . . what's that?'

'What?'

'Oi. Who's there?'

The sound of a door opening. 'Sorry, I just needed to, er, freshen up. Is Caitlin around?'

'You're just the entertainment. You shouldn't be just wandering around the place uninvited . . .'

'Steven! He's staying in the guest room!' There's a brief pause. 'I'm sorry, Oliver. It is Oliver isn't it?'

'How long have you been stood there? What have you heard?'

'Nothing, I . . . sorry I wasn't listening in or anything. I just nipped in between tracks. I've left Caitlin on the decks, which might not go down well so . . .' The man laughs nervously then moves towards the door.

'Anything you heard you forget. Nothing is said to Caitlin. You got it?'

'Sure. Look, like I said. I didn't hear anything . . .'

'I mean it. Anything gets out about this and you'll regret you ever came here.'

The man opens the door and walks out, music suddenly loud with sounds of chatter and laughter. The door swings back almost into position.

'See, you just make yourself look suspicious. He wouldn't have had a clue what we were talking about anyway.'

'I'm gonna have to have another word with him. Make sure.'

'For God's sake, Steven. You're digging your own grave.'

The camera turns towards the door and moves outside quickly.

'Oh bloody hell. Iggy! Iggy!'

Chapter 18

Paul

Saturday

My heart is hammering so hard in my chest I feel as though it might escape. That Godawful song is stuck on a loop in my head, pierced only by Caitlin's taunting laugh. I take a deep breath and try to calm myself as I hide myself away in the cloisters, crouched to the floor on my haunches.

'Paul?'

I look around. It's Naomi. She appears seemingly from nowhere into one of the arches under the covered walkway. She's got a bottle of fizz in her hand and her angel wings look as though they're fluttering gently behind her back. I blink hard. Those truffles are kicking in then. Probably not the best time for this interaction. How many have I had?

'Naomi. Hi,' I say, standing up and moving towards her to give her a hug. She smells of perfume and champagne. She leans towards me and whispers in my ear, 'Fancy a party for two?'

I pause. Unsure what's going to come out of my mouth. Caitlin's sexual histrionics play on repeat in my head. I hold the butt of my palm to my forehead and wince.

'Paul?' Naomi nudges my arm playfully. She looks as though she has an aura around her. A halo. She's pure angel.

'Oh. Sorry.'

'You OK?'

'Yes,' I say, snapping myself back to the moment and smiling. 'Yes, of course.'

'Feel a bit stupid now,' she says, and it confuses me.

'Why?'

'Well, I just . . .' She looks into my eyes then lowers hers to the ground. 'Never mind.'

I place my fingers gently under her chin and lift her face back up in line with mine. She smiles. I smile. I lean in to kiss her. Slowly, closing my eyes. It is soft at first, becoming frantic. She lets out a sigh of pleasure. I grab her back, pulling her into me, her angel wings becoming loose. I open my eyes again. 'What the fuck?' Suddenly it is Caitlin's face up close to me. I jump backwards.

'Jesus. What is it?' Naomi says, her face morphing back into her own. Anger and confusion overwhelming her features.

I shake my head, close and open my eyes. She's there again. Caitlin is there again, touching my shoulder. I push her away. Opening my eyes. Naomi looks hurt; her angel wings drop. She pulls them away from her and chucks them to the floor. Then she looks at me once more, exasperated.

She takes a gulp of champagne straight from the bottle. Shakes her head. Then storms off.

Chapter 19

Kassie

Saturday

'Mrs Davies. Have you seen Iggy?' I am breathless having raced across the lawns. The idea of Iggy all on her own among this lot terrifies me. I don't trust any of them.

'Iggy? Yes, dear. But she just escaped.' She nods towards the door. 'I'm so sorry – there was a bit of a commotion.'

'I can't have her running round tonight,' I stress, my breathing shallow.

'She shouldn't be running round at all,' Steven chips in bluntly.

'She's less bother than Paul,' I say, immediately feeling guilty. Steven side-eyes me and storms off.

Mrs Davies shrugs her shoulders in sympathy then puffs up the huge patterned cushions on our L-shaped sofa. I collapse back into the corner of it, my legs kicking out in front of me and rest them on the pouffe. I look at my stupid sheer dress and the half-laced black Dr Martens on my feet that flop away from each other. I let out a sigh.

'You look tired, Kassie.'

'I am. I just . . .' A tear wobbles from my eye and my nose fizzes. There's something about Mrs Davies that allows my tears to flow.

She strokes my arm.

'I hate these stupid parties,' I say. 'What's wrong with a pint and a packet of cheese 'n' onion down the pub?'

Mrs Davies smiles at me as she picks the messy coke platter up and places it on the very top shelf of the cabinet. She has an eye for anything that's out of place. I sit upright. 'I mean it though. If Steven or Caitlin get hold of this place . . . honestly. It could be something so special. It could be a real gem.' I twist around to look at her. 'I do love the building, you know. I respect it. I just don't feel that we as a family do. It's all about the money.'

'Well, not long now.'

'That's what scares me. I could be made homeless. Or at the very least, Iggy could be made homeless.'

'It might not come to that. Try to remain hopeful.'

'I'm just so bored of them being so ruthless. Shallow. Being paraded around with Steven and Caitlin thinking they can palm me off on whatever young hottie they can get drunk enough to take me. And who is of *good stock*,' I say air-quoting the words.

'Nobody needs to be drunk for you, Kassie. And if they are, maybe they're not right for you. You're better than the others.'

'I was nearly attacked tonight,' I say, immediately regretting it. My mouth feels suddenly dry.

'Oh God, Kassie.' Mrs Davies walks over and perches on the arm of the sofa, rubbing my arm. 'What happened? Are you OK?'

'Some drunk got in here. No idea how. I was looking for Brian, then this awful guy lurched at me. I managed to kick him off. He landed pretty badly. And I got security to chuck him out. But . . .' I feel a shallow rasp in my chest and more tears threaten to spill. 'This is the worst party ever.' She squeezes my arm but then I suddenly remember and leap up from the chair.

'God. I need to find Iggy. I just don't trust the guests around her. What if she's escaped onto the road or . . . I don't know . . . worse?'

'You go,' Mrs Davies says, moving backwards and giving me space. 'I'll have a look for her too. I'll text you if I find her.'

'Thanks,' I say, sweeping down to check my phone is still tucked inside my boot. There was nowhere else to put it on this ridiculous piece of mesh after all. I walk towards the door and pause. 'Mrs Davies?'

'Yes?'

'You've not seen Brian, have you?'

'No. Why were you looking for him anyway? I thought he'd knocked off hours ago?'

'Yeah. Probably. Just wanted to ask him something.'

She walks over to me and places a hand on my shoulder. 'You know, whatever happens tonight. It's not your fault. Never, *never* think it's your fault.'

I nod and smile, confused by her words. There's something foreboding about her tone, but there's no time to enquire. I need to find Iggy.

I walk back out towards the lawns, stopping before the edge of the grass to think. Where will I find my Iggy Pop?

Dennis is walking towards our wing.

'Kassie, how's it all going?' he says, his gingery hair and stubbly beard even neater than usual, if that's possible.

'I can't find Iggy. Have you seen her?'

'No, sorry, love,' he says, and I turn as he heads into our apartment.

I decide to do a full lap of the exterior walkways under the covered arches. A methodical approach perhaps, starting on the outskirts then moving in towards the buzzing lawns and decorated makeshift dance area. The walkway is lit with old-fashioned hanging lanterns, adding a nice warming glow that separates the building from the lawn. I swerve around two women sitting on the floor smoking ciggies and using one of our margarita glasses as an ashtray. I watch my booted feet step over their delicate summer shoes. Heels and sandals and painted nails still just about visible under the darkened sky.

Then I spot a familiar face. Naomi. Except she's missing her angel wings. I stand and watch her briefly before I approach. She's standing in a circle with a woman and a man. Her hand is on his arm. Clearly not only interested in Paul then.

'Naomi, hi,' I say. 'Have you seen Paul?'

She allows a bit of distance between herself and the others and turns towards me. 'Saw him earlier. Why?'

'Was he OK?'

She shrugs, as if completely disinterested. 'I don't know. I mean, I don't know him, do I?'

She looks angry. He's obviously upset her.

'I'm a bit worried about him. He wasn't himself earlier,' I say.

'Look. There was a little spark of something when we met earlier. But, if I'm being honest, I don't want anything to do with him.'

'But what has he done?' I press.

'Look, I just don't enjoy someone coming on to me then blowing cold. No, not just cold – he was a bit weird, if I'm honest.'

'I'm sorry,' I say. I don't know Naomi well enough to push her. And I do know my brother well enough to know he's probably completely spannered right now. Whatever set him off earlier has clearly made him senseless.

Naomi shrugs one shoulder and is about to walk off.

She sighs, then points beyond the lawns and to the right of the building. 'Somewhere in that direction.'

'Thanks.'

I head towards the edge of the path and turn right beyond the east wing. The party crowd is less dense and there's the odd taxi arriving already to collect the more sensible guests and save them from inevitable oblivion. I walk towards the ice house. I know that's where he'll be.

Sure enough, that's when I hear Paul's voice.

The ice house is a place we've always gone to, since we were kids, to chat in private. *Somewhere only we know* as the song goes, but of course everyone *really* knew we went in there. And everyone else knows it's there too because it's on the public trail map. There were always various combinations of siblings getting together to bitch or plot against the others. I was always too young, in all honesty. But I'd sometimes sit in there alone with a book, just to get some peace from the others.

It's an empty stone building with a deep well behind a tall fence that our ancestors apparently used to store fresh food in – before electric refrigeration became a thing. Of course, these days we have a double-door Smeg and a walk-in wine cellar fridge. The open wine cellar underneath our rooms is simply a blank canvas for the public to wander around in and imagine what life might have been like before we all came along. They'd laugh if they could see our wing with its Steinway home cinema system, state-of-the-art gym room and said Smeg fridge.

I quietly wander over to where the ice house stands, a crude stone structure built into a grassy mound. I clamber over the small wall and up the grass, careful to avoid the ramp and open entrance where they'll no doubt spot me. I want to know what he's saying. I want to know why Paul was so visibly raging earlier. I sit on the grass, my knees up in front of me, to listen in. I look down at my shimmery dress. God, I hope there's a dry cleaner who can get grass stains out of this designer outfit.

As I concentrate on the silence I can hear Paul's sobs punctuate it. He doesn't sound right. Paul doesn't really cry. Not that I've heard, anyway. Then, Caitlin's voice pipes up.

'You're disturbed. You need therapy. Just like Jack.'

'Jack's only in that state because of you.'

'Oh please, he went off the rails long before we got together. I'm not responsible for you two and your warped emotions and chemical compulsions. Besides, we were kids. We were . . . Hey. Hey! Are you even listening to me? What the fuck are you even staring at?'

'Us.'

'What?'

'I'm looking . . . at us.'

'Jesus . . . fuck's sake, Paul. Turn away from that wall.'

Paul's sobs increase in volume. He sounds anguished. Then I hear him either kicking or hitting a wall. 'Cruel Caitlin. Cruella Caitlin.' He really doesn't sound right. He sounds almost . . . childlike. Chanting and chuntering stuff to himself.

'What?'

'Cruel, Cruella Caitlin.'

'You're fucking wasted. And why the fuck are you wearing those angel wings? Aren't they Naomi's?'

'You're just angry because you wanted to be the one to dress us all up. Like your weird fucking dolls. It's all about you. It's all Caitlin Caitlin Caitlin Caitlin Caitlin Caitlin.'

'All right, Paul, stop it with the weird muttering. You just can't handle me being happy, can you?' Caitlin snaps.

I hear stones scraping. He's kicking the ground again. 'But you're not happy. Not with him. Not with *James*,' he says his name slowly.

'And Ollie?'

There's silence, but I can hear his feet still shifting around on the ground. 'Ollie's a nobody. He's just another of your fucking boy toys. I don't know why you have to do it.'

'What?'

'Fuck everyone. You fuck everyone. But you take everyone from me.'

'Fuck's sake. Jesus. I'm sick of this. And stop with that weird hand shit. Go fuck Naomi. Go fuck Jack. Go hang out with our boring little sister.'

My stomach muscles lurch upwards and air catches in my throat. I feel like I want to be sick. I've always known I don't fit in. But this. It feels . . .

'She's ten times the person you'll ever be.' I feel my muscles relax again.

'Whatever. I need your phone, anyway.'

'Fuck off.'

'Ollie said you filmed us fucking.'

'Oh please. Why would I . . .'

'Turn you on, did it?'

I can't believe the line she's going down. But then again, if she knew the truth – if she knew we were gathering evidence against her, to force James to pull out of her plans, she'd go into panic mode and no doubt do something even worse to get back at us.

'Don't be sick.'

'I *know* you, Paul.'

I hear Paul kicking and sobbing again. An animalistic sound starts to come from him, like he's wailing and it gets louder and louder.

'Shh, shh,' Caitlin says. It sounds as though she's comforting him now. 'It's all going to be OK. We have our plan, remember? Me and you. James is . . . well he's just incidental. But you help me out with this, and, like I promised, you'll be fine. You'll be a partner. Just me and you, Paul.'

My legs almost buckle beneath me. He lied to me. He's been manipulating me all along.

through my chest and my eyes come alive again. I breathe out, fast. Short fast breaths. Lots of them. Ahhhhh. Good. That's good. That'll help. I shake my head and grin, ready to party once more.

Fuck Caitlin. Fuck Ollie. Fuck James.

Fuck.

Naomi! I need to find her.

I go to the bureau drawer and find our stash of cigarettes. I take a packet into the garden and light one, keeping my eyes peeled for Naomi. I've neglected her. I wonder if she fancies a moonlit garden trip?

'You all right there, mate?' a voice suddenly booms from nowhere. It hurts my ears.

'Yeah,' I say, covering my ears and wincing. Then, a face propels itself towards me like it's attached to a rubber neck. Like something out of *Beetlejuice*. I flinch.

'Need help lighting that ciggie, mate?' There's a laugh. Then lots of laughs. I look all around me as if trying to find a fly. Fast, canned laughter in surround sound getting louder and louder.

I look at my cigarette. It's not lit. Fuck's sake fucking shrooms. Why the hell did I eat more just now? I take my lighter out again and let the flame dance in front of my cigarette, puffing frantically until, finally it's lit. I inhale.

'Got it. Thanks,' I say, holding my cigarette up in front of me as hard evidence. The guy's huge moon face retreats away from me as he walks on by. It now looks as though his head is hovering on top of his body, like it has no connection, no neck. I laugh.

I head over to the fountain, weaving in and out between everyone, smiling, nodding and pretending to doff an imaginary hat. Then I hear voices behind the hedge. I peer through the leaves and can see that it is James shouting at Ollie. I turn around to look at the decks but Ollie is over there too. Which one is the real Oliver? Is that even James? I frown and peer in more closely but become distracted by the berries in the hawthorn, pulsing at me before exploding in front of my eyes and dripping with blood.

Fucking hell.

I scan over to the decks again but then, as my eyes move back over the lawns, I see versions of Ollie's face everywhere. On everyone at the party. On top of suits and bird costumes, angels and devils. Hovering above shoulders. No necks to be seen anywhere. I shake my head and Ollie vanishes again, giving everyone their own faces back.

The voices sound blurred, like they're under water. They're saying something about Caitlin.

'I paid you.'

'I know but . . .'

'It's not enough? Just name a price.'

'I've got to get back . . .'

'Please.'

I leave the voices drowning out behind me and walk over to the fountain.

'Watch it.' A voice hits me from nowhere.

'Shh. It's Paul. He's a Morland.'

'Oops.'

There's laughter. I ignore them. I can't make out who the voices belong to. Everybody's head seems to be attached to everyone else, like they're all moving in a Mexican wave of heads.

I get to the fountain. The sound of the water is overpowering. Loud, intense trickling and swooshing inside my head. Like there's a waterfall inside my skull. I take my shoes off and stand on the base of the fountain, bare feet in the water, and I stare into the middle of it. And I can see it. The memory of it.

I could see them in the distance. Hanging out, Caitlin giggling like a schoolgirl. She was putting that act on she always put on in front of the boys. Franz Ferdinand's 'Take Me Out' was booming from the Sonos. I was drunk and angry. She said I was jealous but I wasn't jealous. But she knew what she was doing. She was only seeing Jack so she could hijack my best mate. Now, he was always with her. Even missed my eighteenth cos she talked him into going to some lame festival down south.

As I got closer to the fountain I could see that Caitlin was lying on her side, naked, facing towards the water. She was still giggling a little but not as much now. Her pale gingery hair was flowing across her shoulders as if she was some kind of mermaid. Jack was fannying around on the ground, looking for something, scratting about. Then he . . . ohhh . . . the dirty bastards. Ha, the fucker was about to give her a booty bump. I could see him holding a glass and something in his hand. A jet injector. He was gonna give her a booty bump of coke wasn't he. I moved sideways to hide under the cover of a tree and watched from behind it as he peered into her backside. Parting her butt cheeks. She looked fucked though. She was barely moving. The words 'Take Me Out' were being sung out. The guitar riff repeating over and over, not giving in. Then, just as Jack was about to shoot the liquid coke up her butt, he keeled over to the side and started vomiting all over the grass, leaving my sister lying there, a spike-less syringe hanging from her arse.

Jack was completely fucking off it. He'd been banging on earlier in the week about getting some ayahuasca to try. That middle-class hippy shit they were all doing. Except it's usually in ceremonies in fucking rainforests or whatever. Caitlin and I decided to swerve it. But, she's definitely more than drunk.

'Caitlin,' I called. But she didn't answer.

'Caitlin!'

I was walking over then. She'd probably necked a ton of benzos with her booze. She had form for that shit. I got close to her and shook her but she only mumbled something. I shook her again and peered over her shoulders at her eyes. They were rolling backwards. Fuck.

I looked at her naked arse, the jet injector fell to the ground. Her breathing was so slow. Occasionally, it looked as though she was holding her breath. Then she'd breathe again, but only faintly. She was in trouble. Was she slipping away from me? Should I? I shook her once more then, realising she could literally fucking die if she didn't wake up, I pulled her butt cheeks apart. It felt . . . fucking hell. It felt so wrong. So weirdly wrong, and so right at the same time. I couldn't think like that. I shook it from my head. Then I shot that syringe and its cokey liquid straight up her arse. I could hardly get her to snort it. There was no needle to pierce the skin. It was the only way.

Within seconds, Caitlin gasped and shot bolt upright, rolling backwards onto her backside, the injector jabbing her flesh and making her yelp. She grabbed at her bum, grabbing the syringe, then she saw me next to her on the grass.

'What the actual fuck?' She leapt up onto her feet and grabbed her hoodie from the gravel that circled the

fountain. She chucked it over her head while continuing to shout: 'What the actual name in actual fuck have you just done?'

'You were out of it,' I said.

'Gives you free fucking entry to my arsehole, does it? Fuck's sake, I'm your fucking sister, you sick bastard.'

I sat there. Silent. Was she right? Should I not have done it? It did happen like that though, didn't it? She was in trouble. Wasn't she? Jack was in no state. But I couldn't find the words to defend what I'd done. To explain it. I was too fucked myself. And there was a strange feeling inside me that I couldn't explain but it felt like I wanted to puke myself up and stamp my rotten, regurgitated, liquid self into the earth.

'Where's Jack?' she spat.

I pointed over to where Jack was now rolling around in the foetal position, moaning.

She turned back to me. 'Sick fuck,' she spat again, grabbing her underwear and jersey shorts and chucking them on as quickly as she could.

She took one look at Jack, then back at me 'I'll never let you forget this. You're fucking ruined. Wait 'til everyone hears about this.'

But she never did tell anyone about it. Not even Jack. They just broke up.

Maybe it would have been better if it *had* come out, instead of festering inside me for fifteen rotten years.

I start to realise my foot hurts. I look down at my bare feet in the base of the fountain, water splashing down onto them. There is blood, a pool of it, growing bigger and bigger. The water in the basin is now blooming dark red.

I've stepped on glass. I pick it up and look at it, holding

it in front of my eyes. It has a million faces, like an old cut diamond. I throw it back down into the water. The glass multiplies and grows fur like a million little baby gremlins.

Then I look up into the fountain's water. The whole fountain is red. Blood is flowing down on me. And I put my hands in the air and open my mouth.

Chapter 21

Kassie

Sunday

A pain shoots through my neck as I twist my head around and open my eyes. I am propped up against the wall under the cloisters, an empty bottle of champagne by my feet and my ridiculous dress twisted around my body. I must have fallen asleep when I was looking for Iggy.

It is almost daylight, and the sky is streaked with orange and blue, the clouds like cotton wool, teased and stretched. I get to my feet, my mouth dry and my head fuzzy. A champagne headache pierces my forehead and I wince.

The ground is littered with bottles and glasses, random items of clothing strewn about the place. In the distance, sheltered underneath the rim of the fountain, I see human forms nestled beneath a suit jacket.

I straighten up and yawn, Paul and Caitlin's words from last night in the ice house ringing in my ears.

I need to find Iggy. I can't believe I let myself fall asleep before I had her home, safe and sound.

I walk towards the main entrance and into the hall, where a few more bodies are haphazardly littering the place. The music is silent now, and all I can hear are snores and breathing and the shifting of human forms on the tiled floor.

Then I see a little white face in the distance, by one of the columns. My heart dances. 'Oh!' I walk quickly towards her and she catches sight of me too and bounds towards me. 'Hello, baby girl!'

I grab Iggy's collar and pull her close to me. Her wiry coat brushes against my bare legs. My head flops forward onto her in relief.

The morning sun is shining its rays through the windows, casting pure light on debauchery. The dregs of hell are still passed out on the floor all around us and I can faintly hear people fucking lazily from the other side of the room.

I hold Iggy next to me, and she nuzzles her nose into my arm.

'God I was so worried about you,' I say. Her little tail wags quickly and relief floods me. As Iggy pulls her head back from me, I see red marks on my skin. I feel the blood drain from me once again. She's hurt. Somebody's hurt her.

I hold her little head in my hands and study her face. There's blood on it. In her whiskers, on her nose. Shit.

'Oh my God. What's happened to you?' I wipe her little nose with my fingertip. She doesn't flinch. Is it her blood? Maybe she isn't hurt.

I find a tissue in my pocket and wipe all the blood away from her. But I can't find a cut or a sore? Whose blood is it?

I look around the room. It's hard to tell if anyone's hurt as they're all so out of it. I tiptoe around quietly, Iggy following close behind, and try to look for signs of blood. But there's nothing.

Just then I notice Iggy making her own way to the back of the hall. I follow her, desperate not to let her out of my sight again as she stops at the top of the spiral stairs into the old cellar. She looks at me, and I am soon standing next to her. But then she races down the stairs and I follow in hot pursuit.

As I descend the winding steps, my hand is firmly on the rail – until suddenly it isn't. I almost fall, as the rail disappears beneath my hand, the shock of it almost making me lose my grip on the stairs.

I stand still and steady myself. It's broken. The wooden rail is snapped and broken, parts of it hanging off, sharp pieces of wood sticking out of the end.

I peer downstairs and can see a foot. A bare foot, covered in blood.

Oh my God. Jesus Christ. I move cautiously towards it.

A body. A man's body. Red-soaked T-shirt twisted up around its torso. Naked beneath.

I peer in more closely, curiously, at the mangled mess on the floor. The head is twisted to the side, almost face down. His limbs must be broken, bent at impossible angles. I scan up and down the contorted length of the body, and can see a compound fracture in one of the arms, the blood pooling out.

He must be dead.

I look up and down the body then back up the stairs. Was this a fall?

I shake my head, doubting what I'm seeing in front of my eyes. It's the first dead body I've seen since my newborn eyes opened. And *that* feeling of a dead body haunted my dreams for years. This feels . . . different. Like a curious cadaver, rather than a person. It's a stranger. It's a stranger right up until I look at their face. Maybe I shouldn't look? If I don't see it then . . . it's Schrödinger's body. Is it really dead?

I stand still for a moment, shock rooting me to the spot.

And then, carefully, I lean forward and place the dead man's head in my hands, sticky blood coating my skin. I pull the face towards me, letting the body follow and flop unceremoniously on its back.

'Oh my God,' I say to myself, on a sharp intake of breath.

It's the DJ. It's Ollie.

Chapter 22

Kassie

Sunday

'What's going on?'

I almost jump out of my skin at the sound of Steven's voice behind me. I turn to look at him, my face drained of blood and my hands covered in someone else's.

'Kassie. What have you done?' he says.

I look at my hands and then back at the body. At Ollie. 'It wasn't . . .'

'You're covered in blood,' he says, stating the obvious. 'Is that . . . ?'

'It's Ollie.'

'Kass, what the hell have you done to him?' he says, moving towards the body and standing over him.

'I-I haven't. Steven, I just found him here. Just now. Iggy had blood on her nose and . . .'

'You're actually trying to frame your goat? Well that's a new low . . .'

'Piss off, Steven!' I snap. 'I have no idea what's happened. I just found him. I honestly just . . .'

'You're protesting *a lot*, Kass.'

'We need to call the police,' I gasp desperately, my voice breaking.

'Um, no, we don't.'

'What do you mean we don't?'

'I mean look around you. We've still got people upstairs. We need to clear out, take stock. Then work out what to do.'

'But Steven. He's dead,' I gesture to poor Ollie on the floor.

'Yes. I know. And you're currently the one standing over the body covered in blood.'

'So what are we going to do? We can't just leave him . . .'

Steven picks his phone from his pocket and I notice he is already freshly showered and changed after last night. His hair is damp and I can smell minty shower gel. I can't help but wonder why he's up and about and showered this early.

'I'll message Mrs Davies,' he says. 'We need to start waking these bodies up and getting them away. I'll ask Dennis to sort some cars.'

He makes a call and wanders towards the wall, speaking quietly into his mobile while I stare dumbfounded at poor Ollie. Broken. Bleeding. Dead.

Mrs Davies soon appears, her voice forced but hushed. She looks at the body and I can see her inhale sharply. Then she composes herself and turns back to me. 'Kassie, do you want to take Iggy back to the paddock then help me wake the bodies up?' I shudder at the word 'bodies' but quickly nod my head, relieved to have a reason to vacate the cellar.

'And if I were you,' she leans in close to me. 'I'd wash that blood off your hands right away.'

I call for Iggy and take her out through the far cellar door. The space is empty, but for old wine storage areas. There is no furniture in there and everything is stony and cold.

When I head back to the cellar, I see Steven standing and guarding the body, on the phone again. He shoos me upstairs, so I race up the steps and see Mrs Davies shaking the partygoers – it's a routine we're all used to. 'Rise and shine,' Mrs Davies shouts. 'Wakey wakey. Time to go.'

There are groans and sighs and grumbles. But bodies begin slowly moving. There's audible yawning and shifting around until, gradually, people are standing, shuffling out towards the door, blankets around some of them. We let them take them.

The cars start pulling up outside and Dennis, oblivious to what we're hiding in the old cellar, is out on the front in his white shirt and trousers, looking fresh from the night before and directing people into cars. Mrs Davies and I also try to herd them.

I follow Mrs Davies back into the Hall, gathering up blankets while she uses a bin liner to remove the mess. We'll have others outside working in the gardens, but we can manage in here if we work quickly and methodically.

We move from one end of the hall to the other. All the remaining blankets are piled in a heap in the corner as Mrs Davies sweeps up the last few bottles and cigarette butts.

Then Steven appears and the three of us stand and stare at each other.

'So,' Mrs Davies says. 'You found him on the floor?'

I feel a sickly sensation in the pit of my stomach. Does

she suspect me as well? 'I did. I found Iggy. She had blood on her, then she led me down the stairs.'

Steven lets out a 'huh' and we both glare at him. 'What were you doing here so early anyway?' I snap.

'Doing a recce of the place. No need to snap at me, Kass. You're the one who had blood on her hands.'

'Yeah and you're the one freshly showered and dressed by 5.30 a.m. That's kind of suss too, don't you think?'

Mrs Davies' eyes flit from me to Steven and she stares hard at him. 'You were worried that Ollie overheard you last night.'

'No I wasn't.'

'Overheard what?' I ask.

'You practically threatened him to keep his mouth shut,' she says pointedly.

'Keep his mouth shut about what?' I ask again. But nobody fills me in.

'It's pretty clear what's happened. Kassie's pushed him—'

'I did not—' I say.

Steven holds his hands up in front of him. 'Pushed him or knocked into him. I'm not saying it was on purpose. But you were clearly here when it happened.'

'I wasn't. I told you,' I say, my eyes forming tears and my heart racing. Mrs Davies puts her arms around me.

'Good God, she can't do any wrong in your eyes can she,' Steven says of me.

'You're the one with motive, not Kass,' she says.

'Why don't we just call the police,' I say. 'They'll be able to tell, surely. Forensics and stuff. They'll be able to find out it wasn't me.'

'No!' Steven snaps. 'We can't have any trouble this weekend. We've got the inspection tomorrow.'

'Oh my God,' I say. 'I'd completely forgotten.'

'We just need to . . . get our house in order. Then we can call whoever we need to. It has to be a unanimous decision though,' he says. 'We need to speak to Caitlin and Paul.'

Steven walks off and I realise just how bad this looks.

Mrs Davies whispers to me: 'We need to get you properly cleaned up, Kassie. Your clothes . . . they need to go.'

'But. That's destroying . . .'

'We *must* get you cleaned up. Right away.'

Chapter 23

Kassie

Sunday

After the quickest and most rigorous shower ever, I head back to the main house and bang on Caitlin's bedroom door. 'Caitlin! Caitlin!'

I don't wait any longer for her to respond and instead fling the door open. She sits up, her eye mask on. 'What? What's going on?' She frantically pulls it from her face and swings her head around. 'Kassie. Jesus Christ. You nearly gave me a heart attack. What time is it? What's wrong?'

'There's something you need to see.'

Caitlin sighs heavily. 'What? What's so urgent?'

'Caitlin. We've found . . . we've found Ollie.'

'Right? In the guest room?'

'No.'

'So he's crashed out somewhere. Big deal. What's the problem?' She collapses her head back onto her pillow and starts to pull her mask back over her eyes.

'He's . . . he's dead.'

Caitlin sits back up, her face instantly grey. 'What? What do you . . . What, dead?'

'Yes.'

'But. He can't be. He was DJing. Here.' Her eyes are flitting from side to side as though she is recalling the events of last night.

'Why would I make it up?'

'But . . . but how?' Caitlin swings her legs out of bed and grabs her silk dressing gown, wrapping it tightly around her as she looks at me, daylight hitting hard behind her. 'What do we . . . do?'

'I don't know. Mrs Davies and Steven are with the . . . body. Where's Paul?'

'I don't know.'

'But you were with him.'

'We all were at some point. Anyway, forget Paul. What the hell are you telling me? Ollie is dead?' She places a hand over her chest.

'How many times do I have to say it?'

She stands staring, her mouth gaping. She takes a deep breath.

'Where's James?' I ask, suddenly suspicious.

'We had a row,' she says, sniffing loudly and standing up. She shakes her head as if to remove something from it. 'OK, show me.'

We leave Caitlin's room and walk through the living room, where Mrs Davies is speaking with Steven.

'What have you done to him, Caitlin?' Steven says.

'I haven't. Nothing. I . . .' Caitlin is lost for words. There's a first for everything I guess.

We follow Mrs Davies through the wing and into the

main hall and I feel sick. Everything feels surreal. Wrong, dark and utterly bizarre in the cold light of day.

As we all walk down the stairs, Caitlin is last to come face to face with Ollie's mangled body. 'Oh my God.' She gasps, her hand covering her mouth. Something lurches through her body, and I realise she is retching. Steven, meanwhile, stands silently. Stoically.

'Anyone got any idea how this happened?' Steven says firmly, looking at each of us one by one.

'Don't ask me,' Caitlin says. 'Last I saw of him he was on the decks. He was happy. Having the time of his life.' She is speaking through her hands that she holds over her nose. She looks white.

'Oh please,' Steven says. 'If there's one reason that DJ's half-naked . . .'

Oh my God, she's crying. I've never seen Caitlin cry. Not since she got that dodgy haircut when she was fifteen. 'He must have fallen,' she says, looking up to the stairs. 'The rail's . . . Steven, it's your fault, you were meant to ensure the building was safe!'

'But why would he have been coming down here?' Mrs Davies asks. 'Nobody comes down here during parties.'

'You think someone pushed him?' Caitlin asks. And I catch her wiping a tear from beneath her eye. Maybe there was more to Caitlin and Ollie than we all thought? 'Who found him?'

Steven shoots me a glare and I take a deep breath. 'I did. Well, Iggy did. And I followed Iggy.'

'What do you mean?' Caitlin asks, her eyes glassy.

'She had blood on her nose. Then she seemed keen for me to follow her down . . .'

Steven lets out a 'pah'. We all look at him.

'It's true,' I cry. 'I didn't hurt him. Honestly, Caitlin, you've got to believe me. I found him like this. I'd fallen asleep, outside. Then came in here. And found him. Like this.'

'Highly convenient that you were asleep,' Steven says.

'Steven, if anyone had reason . . .' Mrs Davies interjects, but Steven holds his hand up to her.

'If anyone had reason,' he says, 'it's Caitlin. You *were* fucking him, weren't you?'

Caitlin looks at him, her eyes growing wider. She doesn't speak.

'But you still haven't told us where James is,' I press.

'I don't know,' Caitlin snaps finally.

'Did he find out about you and Ollie?' Steven asks calmly.

'*Paul's* the one who was angry with him. With Ollie. Where's *he*? Hm?'

I think back to what they were discussing in the ice house. They kept mentioning Ollie. Paul was angry with him in there. That must be why he raced out of the kitchen in a rage then too? Did they fight?

'We need to find him,' I say. 'I was worried about him.'

'Worried about Paul? He was having the time of his life,' Steven says.

'He wasn't. He was tormented over something.' As soon as I've said the words I realise I'm implicating my brother. But then I remember what else was said in the ice house. Paul lied to me. I don't have his loyalty. Caitlin does. How could he be so cruel to me? How could he deceive me like that?

Scowls are exchanged among the group as Mrs Davies, Steven, Caitlin and I all continue to stand around the body.

The body – *Ollie's* body – doesn't seem real. He was the

fit DJ who got the whole place up and dancing. Infusing the party with rhythm and energy. And now, his is spent. For good.

'Well,' Steven says. 'One explanation could be that James was clearly incensed by you bringing one of your fuck boys to the party and parading him around like a prize. And now he's vanished – doesn't exactly look good, does it?'

'You just want that to be true,' Caitlin wails. 'You need him out of the picture.'

'Ollie? I do not . . .'

'James,' she snaps. 'You don't want James and I to take over the estate. And you know, full well, you know, we are the prime candidates.'

'You think?' he says, gesturing around him towards the dead body.

'But this has *nothing* to do with us. I mean, Paul's vanished. He was less than coherent when I last saw him.'

'Why were you arguing?' I ask. She looks at me confused. 'You and Paul. In the ice house.'

'We weren't.'

'I heard you.'

'Heard what? There was nothing to hear,' Caitlin says, but her eyes are full of fear. She's definitely hiding something.

'You were taunting him,' I say. I think back to the things she did to him when they were growing up. As teenagers, Caitlin had drawn Paul's blood under the pretence they were to be 'blood brothers'. Even though they already, literally, were. She just wanted permission to cut him. Then she disappeared saying she'd changed her mind. She didn't want his blood after all. Mrs Davies had to patch him up and have a stern word.

'You're such a bitch, Caitlin,' I cry. It's more a release

of the tension of being stood around a dead body than anything specifically related to Caitlin.

'*I'm* the one who's lost someone here!'

'Lost what, Cait?' Steven says. 'Who exactly was Ollie to you? Is this why James murdered him?'

'He did not,' Caitlin retorts.

'We need to find Paul,' Mrs Davies says interrupting. 'We need to know exactly where everyone is. We need to all stick together now.'

'He's probably with Jack somewhere,' Caitlin says, sniffing hard again, desperate to clear the emotion that's trespassing across her mask.

'Well, someone needs to find him. And we need to decide what we're doing with the body,' Mrs Davies says.

'Can you stop calling Ollie the body?' Caitlin snaps, before looking away, biting her lip and wincing.

'Dennis doesn't know about this, does he?' Steven asks Mrs Davies. She shakes her head.

'We need to call the police,' I say.

'No!' Steven snaps. 'Don't be ridiculous.'

'Well, what do *you* think we should do? Bury the body in Morland estate?' Mrs Davies says. 'Come on, Steven.'

'There's drugs all over the place. Our brother's missing. James is missing. We've no idea how this happened. Who was involved. We can't call the police. It'll ruin all of us.'

Are we really about to hide a dead body? What the hell is this – Miss Marple? The Thursday Murder Club? Shit happens – but shit like this doesn't happen.

Then I think about Brian. On that dance floor. Horse's head covering his face. Knife in hand. Shit. I'd almost forgotten.

'Brian!' I say suddenly, blurting out his name.

'You were looking for him last night?' Mrs Davies says.

'Yes. He . . .' I'm about to tell them that he'd sampled too many of the truffles – but that all comes back on me. So I just say, 'I think he got drunk. He was wearing my horse mask. I saw him with a knife. That's who I was looking for when . . .'

'When what?' Steven asks. But I decide now is not the time to reveal what happened in our living room with that guy. Everything feels as though it could lead to trouble, to suspicion. 'When I went into our living room,' I add, faintly.

Steven frowns at me. He knows I'm hiding something.

'Why was he walking around with a knife?' Caitlin asks.

I shake my head. But as we all look back towards Ollie, I realise there is no knife wound. At least, there doesn't appear to be. He could have used it to overpower him though. To push him. He might have had no reason to, but he wasn't in his right state of mind.

But Jesus Christ. Was *anyone* in their right state of mind? If the police find out just how much illegal stuff we had floating around the place . . . we'll never get Granny to hand over the estate.

'I still think he could have fallen,' I say.

'I'm just not so sure it was a fall,' Mrs Davies says, pointing to the broken banister on the stairs. 'That break looks pretty forceful. And the way he's landed . . .'

'You genuinely believe we've a murderer in the house?' Caitlin asks.

'We might have,' Mrs Davies says. 'And the press'll have a field day if there's even a whiff of that. Kill a tree round these parts and it goes global.'

'Whatever the reason,' Steven says, 'we can't have anyone find him. Not now. We need time to think, to figure out if anyone's had any involvement in this.' He looks at Caitlin again.

'For God's sake can you leave me out of it already?'

'*You* brought him here, you'll be first on the suspect list. I can see it now: *rich bitch murders lover to save her marriage.*' Steven moves his hand as if it's following a big headline.

'Purlease. I wouldn't put *that* much effort into saving my marriage,' Caitlin says, her usual personality starting to shine through again.

'Well, we better think fast and figure it out,' Mrs Davies urges. 'We need to call emergency services before the public turn up tomorrow morning . . .'

'No!' Steven snaps, raising his hand in front of her. 'I've already said no.'

'Excuse me.' I can tell by Mrs Davies' tone she is affronted.

'Because that's the whole point. We can't have *anyone* find him. We absolutely can't call emergency services.'

'Are you quite insane?' Mrs Davies snaps. 'If we don't call this in, we're all complicit.'

'But if we *do*, *one* of us, or even *some* of us, could be in serious trouble,' he says. 'And the downfall of one will be the downfall of all of us. We're all stuck with the Morland name. We can't have police crawling all over this house. The coke. Your fucking plants, Kass. Your affair, Caitlin.'

'That's hardly criminal.'

'It will be in Granny's eyes,' he says.

'But then why are you trying to keep that quiet? Surely it's in your best interest for that to come out? For you to get the estate. Unless . . .'

'Unless what?' Steven says.

'Unless *you* did this?'

'Don't be ridiculous. Why would I bother? And yeah, let's be honest, the reason I don't want the police round here is because of the driving range. The paper trail. There's evidence of council bribery that I need to dismantle.'

'Well trying to cover it up and being found out will only make things worse for all of us. Look at our former prince,' Mrs Davies says. 'And you, you're already breaking out in a sweat.' She points at Steven and he wipes his upper lip, frowning. It makes me wonder if there's more to Steven's involvement in this than he's letting on.

'Seriously,' Steven says. 'Some things need to be dealt with on the down-low. I know what I'm doing. We're telling no one.'

I begin to wonder how my brother can consider this 'business as usual' before Caitlin opens her mouth again. 'Right that's it. You've clearly had something to do with this otherwise you wouldn't be suggesting we keep it a secret,' she hisses.

'Oh, right.' Steven laughs sarcastically. 'OK, then. If you feel so confident that neither you nor your mysteriously disappearing husband have had anything to do with this . . . foul play . . . then let's do it. Let's call the police.'

'OK, *OK!*' Caitlin yells. 'You're right. It doesn't look good. You're absolutely right. We'll move him.'

'There's no need to yell at the rest of us,' I say.

'If there was ever a time to yell . . .'

'All right, all right!' Mrs Davies has had enough. It takes me back to when they were teenagers and I was a brat. 'Please. Just stop squabbling. If we absolutely must move him, I suggest the wine cellar.'

'What? But the public . . .' I say.

'No, not the *old* wine cellar. Your walk-in one. In the

wing. It's got a cooling function. It's got a solid door. It'll keep him . . . fresh.' She turns her nose up at her own words, then carries on. 'And nobody will accidentally wander in, so.'

'It'll ruin the wine,' Steven says.

'And that's really a priority right now? Because you won't be drinking a bottle of Leroy in your prison cell,' Mrs Davies says.

'OK. Fine. Wine cellar it is.'

'What are we going to do about this blood?' I say. 'Before the public arrive tomorrow? Get the Karcher on it?'

'But that won't remove all forensic evidence,' Steven says. 'It's the K7. If anything's going to work . . .'

'It'll do for now,' Mrs Davies says. 'I mean, what are the odds of a member of the public arriving with a CSI kit in the boot of their bloody Range Rover Evoque?'

We all stand in silence, staring at the mangled heap of man on the floor. I can't help but feel sorry for him. 'Poor Ollie,' I say, without realising I've said it aloud. I clear my throat. 'OK. Shall we, I don't know, chuck a sheet over him before we try to pick him up?'

'Plastic sheeting might be best. Like what Dennis gives to the decorators? And gloves, we need gloves. Old clothes, too – we should probably burn those after.' Mrs Davies snaps into operational management mode.

'Jesus. Mrs Davies,' Caitlin says. 'Have you got experience in this or something?'

'I've been cleaning up after you lot for long enough.'

'Remember who you're talking to, please,' Caitlin says, reasserting herself and throwing her hair back over her shoulder.

'I'm not sure moving a dead body is in the job description,

but by all means, sack me for using a slightly harsh tone of voice and we'll see what the tribunal has to say about it all. Meet back here in ten minutes, in clothes you don't mind destroying.'

Caitlin huffs then we all disperse while Mrs Davies gathers sheeting from Dennis' store cupboard. Well, tarpaulin, at least.

'I could hardly ask him where he keeps it all,' she snaps at Steven as he points out she has the wrong stuff. Then we all dress in our oldest clothes – jeans, joggers, vest tops and T-shirts – and regroup by the body. Mrs Davies takes charge, while Steven attempts to *look* as though he's taking charge. To be honest, he looks like he's going to puke. But that could be the whisky he's downed since being sent off to get dressed. He reeks of the stuff. His nerves are palpable, which makes me wonder . . .

Mrs Davies holds out a black and white shoebox-sized cardboard box full of black latex gloves. We all grab a pair and wrestle our hands into them.

'OK. If we lie the tarpaulin on the floor next to him, have two people standing on either end to pin it down, and then two of us move him onto it – one with the wrists, one with the legs.'

'But he's all . . . broken,' Caitlin says.

'Have you got a better idea?' Steven shouts, standing on the edge of the sheeting. Caitlin immediately jumps into the only other slightly less repulsive role and stands on the other edge of the sheeting to hold it in place.

'Guess it's me and you then, Kassie.' Mrs Davies sighs.

'Well, I'm not being funny or anything but . . . you *are* staff,' Caitlin mutters.

Mrs Davies shoots her a look and I roll my eyes. 'Just

admit you've got a weak constitution and we'll happily take the task off your hands,' I snipe.

'Ready then?' Mrs Davies says, moving to grab Ollie's ankles.

'It's so sad isn't it,' Caitlin says, holding a finger beneath her nose. 'I mean, his body, it was . . .'

'Not the time, Caitlin,' Steven snaps.

'But it's such a waste of a good man.'

I roll my eyes and go to grab Ollie's wrists. Even with the latex gloves between our skin, I can tell that something doesn't feel right. His skin just feels . . . off. 'I think rigor mortis has started,' I say, as we struggle to lift him even an inch from the stone floor. Mrs Davies is trying to wrangle his feet, too, but we're getting nowhere. 'He's all stiff.'

'He can't have been dead that long?' Caitlin says. 'I mean, I'm still feeling the after-effects of last night and Paul's clearly off somewhere, still going.'

We stop, take a breath and think. I look at Mrs Davies, who's staring down at poor Ollie, her finger on her mouth. 'The wheel,' she says, almost to herself.

'What?' Steven snaps impatiently, even though he's literally standing on some plastic sheeting doing fuck all.

'We roll him. That's what you mean, right?' I say.

She nods. We crouch down next to Ollie's lifeless body and kneel on the ground next to him. 'I think we need to tidy his limbs a bit, like, tuck them in?'

Mrs Davies nods in agreement.

'Oh please,' Caitlin says. 'He's . . . well, he's got blood pouring out of that arm. And it's all bent . . .'

'I don't think a fracture specialist can save him now, Cait,' I say, shortening her name on purpose. She huffs.

We tuck his limbs in and heave. And heave some more.

Eventually, he moves onto his side – albeit awkwardly – and we're able to topple him over onto the tarpaulin sheet, face down. We stand back and look at our work in progress. He is still slightly mangled, but at least he is more modest now, with only his bum cheeks on display. 'He'll be easier to slide along now,' I say and, finally, something goes to plan. I can hear Caitlin's breathing speed up as we push him further onto the sheet.

Eventually, we have him wrapped in the sheeting, his head sticking out the top. We stop and take a breath. We've done it.

'OK. So how are we going to get him up the bloody stairs, then?' Steven says.

Chapter 24

Kassie

Sunday

Man's greatest invention came in handy again. A wheelbarrow up the accessible ramp we had put in for the public proved an effective method of removing poor Ollie from the stone-cold floor of the old basement. We did, however, have to heave him up the final flight of stairs to our kitchen. Still, he's now languishing safely in our walk-in wine cellar refrigerator so it's all good.

Well, as good as can be under the circumstances.

A wave of guilt and shame rushes over me when I consider how I'm putting our successful removal of a dead body over the fact that a man has just lost his life. Can I really ever rid this place of our horrific past – which we're just making even worse by the second?

I shake my head to refocus on the tasks at hand. If I lose myself in guilt, we'll be in an even bigger mess. I still wish we could have called an ambulance and had him removed a little more . . . respectably.

There's still no sign of Paul or James. Mrs Davies and Dennis are currently out looking for them. Which, to be fair, is a regular occurrence after a party. They trawl the village for any intoxicated Morlands who have escaped the confines of the estate and bring us back in before we bring more shame on the family name. Damage limitation and all that.

James isn't answering to Caitlin either – which is *not* a regular occurrence and starting to smack of guilt. He's always at her beck and call, so this is really odd. And given how blatantly flirtatious Caitlin was with Ollie . . .

Then I remember. Paul saw James giving Ollie money. A big fat roll of cash, he'd said. There's definitely something going on there.

But Paul was raging too.

The realisation that the person responsible for this could be any one of my siblings reminds me that I was not born into a normal loving family. It's too much of a coincidence for something like this to happen the very weekend that the estate is being handed over. But I just can't trust any of them – not even Paul now. Whoever did this, they might see me as the obvious scapegoat. The one who found the body could easily have been the one who pushed him down the stairs and killed him. The one who will have evidence of blood on her belongings. The one who tried to clean herself up before even telling her sister what had happened. I've done myself no favours. And if they all stick together and try to set me up for this, I'll never be free of the Morland curse. I'll be languishing in prison for it and this place will continue to become more and more depraved, too.

I cling on to the hope that this could have been a stranger.

Or indeed, it *could* have been an accident. In which case, we've made everything ten times worse.

Brian has indeed turned up and is busy cooking us all a massive fry-up in the kitchen. I have to say, he doesn't exactly seem himself. He might not be laughing inanely anymore but he is kind of shifty and is refusing to look me in the eye, instead casting his gaze to the floor whenever I speak to him. I look at him curiously as he griddles tomatoes, his tattooed arm moving the pan quickly back and forth on the hob. Is it nervousness? Is he hiding something?

I'm not sure I can stomach anything to eat but, as Mrs Davies insisted, we have to carry on as normally as possible. We have to look as though nothing out of the ordinary has happened. We started this, so now we have to finish it. There's no other way. We've made our beds.

'Where did you end up last night?' I ask Brian. 'Did you . . . join in with the party?'

'Not really,' he says.

I try again. 'Didn't I catch you on the dance floor at one point?' I ask, desperate to get him talking.

'Me? I doubt it,' he says, frowning. And I know at that point that he's lying to me because I know full well I saw him.

Or did I? He was wearing that horse's mask. Could it have been someone else? But there were chef's whites? I'm sure of it.

Actually, I'm not sure of anything anymore.

I leave the kitchen still feeling suspicious. But, if it was him, I feel convinced it had to be an accident. There's no motive, no connection.

Is there?

Caitlin, Steven and I gather around the table in the dining

room for breakfast, Brian serving up the food. Everyone is uncharacteristically quiet, the only sound being knives and forks clanging on plates, and the slight thud of platters being placed back down on the tablecloth once we've retrieved our meat and eggs. At least, once Steven and I have.

Caitlin sits guzzling black coffee, back in her silk dressing gown, an empty plate in front of her, her foot up on her chair and her knee in front of her face. She is resting her cheek on her leg and sighing a lot.

'Not eating, Caitlin?' Steven asks. 'Something playing on your mind?'

She picks up the white packet of Davidoff cigarettes in front of her and lights one, slamming the packet back down ungraciously. 'Oh you know, just the dead body in the wine cellar,' she hisses in a stage whisper. 'Silly, really.' She downs the rest of her coffee, rests her burning, slim cigarette on her empty plate and immediately pours another cup from the cafetière. Just then, Mrs Davies rushes in and shuts the door behind her.

'We found Paul. He was in the Swan car park. With Jack. I've sent them to get some sleep.'

Steven drops his knife and fork dramatically and leans back in his seat folding his arms. 'Brilliant. I take it he was off his chops?'

Mrs Davies nods, but then the door opens behind her. It's Paul.

'Paul, you look dreadful,' Steven says flatly, pouring himself a coffee. Paul walks towards him, knocking into the table and causing Steven to spill coffee all over his arm. He freezes, the cafetière in mid-air and I wait with bated breath to see if Steven bites. He sighs and places the cafetière back down carefully.

Every move we make needs to be done carefully at the moment. Paul pulls out a chair and takes a seat.

'I thought you were going to sleep it off, Paul?' Mrs Davies says.

'Why don't you at least eat something?' I say, pushing the rack of toast towards him, my tone less friendly than it usually would be. I am still reeling at Paul and Caitlin's plans to stick together over the estate.

'Couldn't touch a bite,' he says, and I notice that he's chewing on the inside of his cheek and his legs are shaking violently under the table.

'This is all we need,' Steven mutters.

'What's that, Steven?' Paul says, rummaging around in his pocket. He removes a small bag, shoves a key inside it and sniffs a bump of powder deep into his nostrils. Steven slams his cutlery down on his plate. Paul looks at him, then repeats his action out of defiance, eyes fixed on Steven throughout.

'Where's Jack?' Caitlin asks.

'Who knows?' Paul says, his hair wild and his pupils huge. He stinks of booze and smoke.

'Fancy some diazepam, Paul?' Caitlin says.

'Not really,' he says.

Caitlin looks to me and Steven, concerned wrinkles spreading across her forehead. We don't have to say out loud what we're all thinking. We absolutely *have* to keep Paul under control.

'Paul,' Mrs Davies says, trying a new tack. 'Can you help me find Jack?'

'Is he here?' Paul says.

'Yes. He's come to see you,' Mrs Davies says, bending the truth because, let's face it, Paul hasn't a clue what's going on at the moment anyway. Paul stands and leaves the room with Mrs Davies closing the door behind him.

'You know, Paul was livid about me bringing Ollie on board,' Caitlin says.

'He was a bit pissed off; he wasn't *that* bothered,' I say, defending my brother out of habit. 'You really think he'd *kill* someone over music choice?'

Steven picks up a slice of toast and dips his knife in the butter tray. 'Funny, isn't it, that two of the three party casualties have had sexual entanglements with you, sis?'

Caitlin slams her cup on the table. 'This. Again? Seriously?'

'And yet your husband's nowhere to be seen.'

'This has nothing to do with James,' Caitlin yells.

Just then Mrs Davies walks back in. 'I've given them both a whisky. Made an executive decision to drop a couple of Valium in them. We need the pair of them to sleep. Although Jack's not *quite* as out of touch with reality as Paul. His family are sending a car to get him tomorrow after he's had a chance to sleep it off.'

'Good call,' Steven says. 'It didn't look like Paul was having fun anyway. He's way beyond that. Needs to come down.'

'Also,' Mrs Davies says, taking a deep breath and wiping her palms across each other, 'we've got something a little more . . . concerning to contend with.'

We all look at her expectantly. 'The body, yes we know, we need a plan. He can't stay in there forever,' Steven says, carefully placing his knife and fork back down in front of him. I notice a slight shake to his hands.

'On top of that. It's Lady Morland.'

A phone buzzes. Caitlin rummages around in her pocket and pulls her mobile out.

'It's her. It's Granny,' she says, looking at us all.

'Well you better answer it then,' Steven says.

Caitlin stares at the phone for another few moments then takes a deep breath and answers it. 'Granny hi how are . . . yes, yes, all good. No, it went really well. Will? I'm not sure . . . I hadn't heard. What? Now?' Caitlin looks up again, and mouths the word 'fuck' to us all. 'OK, OK. Sure. OK see you. Bye. Bye.'

'What is it? What's she on about?' Steven asks.

'She heard from Will Taylor-Banks that he left early and wasn't happy and wants to find out why?'

'What?' Steven says. 'Well, that seems petty.'

'Not petty enough,' Caitlin says. 'She's on her way. Here. Now.'

'Jesus. We're going to have to move him,' I say. 'Ollie, I mean.'

'Poor Ollie,' Caitlin says. 'So much for rest in peace.'

'Just because you can't be arsed to do the heavy lifting,' I snap. 'God forbid you break a nail.'

'Fuck you, Kassie.'

'Well . . .' Steven stands, slamming his palms on the tablecloth. 'We better come up with something fast.' He pauses in thought. 'What about the well in the ice house? We could cordon it off tomorrow – say there's maintenance or something going on?'

'You want to bury him in the ice house? The place our ancestors kept raw meat?' I say.

'Could work,' Caitlin says. 'If we cover him up once he's down there? Because we can't guarantee to keep everyone out with a simple barrier.'

I sigh. 'I guess we could use more tarpaulin,' I say. 'Maybe throw some mud down there.'

We all stand in unison and head out of the dining room and into the room off the kitchen where the chilled walk-in wine cellar is. Nobody opens the door, we just stand around it, bracing ourselves for the grim inevitability of seeing a dead body again.

Of seeing Ollie dead again.

'The wheelbarrow,' Mrs Davies says. 'I'll run and get it.'

'What about Brian? We can't have him . . .'

'I'll go keep him occupied,' Caitlin says.

'Oh trust you to avoid the dirty work again,' Steven says.

Caitlin shrugs her shoulders and saunters off into the kitchen in her flowing dressing gown, where Brian is clattering pots and pans, making a start on tidying up the cooking utensils. 'Brian, darling, did you enjoy last night?' Her voice fades into the distance as she closes the kitchen door behind her.

Mrs Davies scurries down the ramp for the wheelbarrow, and Steven and I take deep breaths. 'Go on then,' he says. 'Open the door.'

I hang my head to the side, pulling a face. Then I straighten up, inhale deeply, and open the door, allowing a blast of cool air to hit my face.

'What the . . .' Steven gasps.

We both stand gawping at the neat rows of bottles at the back of the walk-in wine cellar, lying neatly behind glass cabinet doors. And then we look down at the hollow, empty void straight in front of us.

'Where the hell is the body?' I say.

Chapter 25

Paul

Sunday

'Trip killer.'

I definitely read it somewhere. I know I did. I *know* I read it.

I keep googling, diving deeper into AI, its suggestions, asking the question in more and different ways. Deeper and deeper into source material. Analysing it. But the laptop is malfunctioning. The words keep floating and jumbling on the screen. And when I close my eyes, I can see all the words in my head. But they still don't make any sense, all mashed up together and dancing. Dancing in a train like some kind of evil fucking conga.

My brain is racing. I can't even keep up with the words in my head. But two words keep repeating over and over. And they're no longer inside my head. They are in the room.

'Trip killer.'

I jump. I turn around, face my bedroom door. But there's nobody there. Just a coat hanging on the back of the door.

'Jack?' I say, my voice barely a whisper. There is no answer. Of course there is no answer. He is not here.

I stare at the door for a time until it starts swaying from side to side. Then it stops again and everything is clear. Real. I take a breath. It's my mind playing tricks on me. I look back towards my laptop. Then, it happens again. Louder this time.

'Trip killer.'

I turn back around to see where the voice is coming from now. Still nobody. The coat on the door looks like it is moving slowly.

'Killer!' I still can't find the source of the voice. Who is it? Is it Jack? It doesn't sound like Jack.

'Killer!' It's become darker. Twisted. Angrier. Full of rage.

'KILLER!'

I grasp my head, pulling my hair between my fingers. My brain is fucking up again. It's fucking up.

'Trip killer.'

'Shut up, shut up, shut up, shut up, shut up, SHUT UP!' I hear the words leaving my mouth. There's a knock.

'Paul. Paul, you OK?'

Why won't they just leave me alone? Just. Leave. Me. Alone.

I'm going to have to get out of here without them seeing. I feel like a prisoner, under surveillance. Plucked from a pub car park like a criminal. And him . . . *he* should have known better. He has the knowledge. He knows the research. He's done this. Not me. Not me.

Not me!

I bite my top lip, desperate to silence my voice. My screams. They're going to come eventually though. I know they are. They always do.

Chapter 26

Kassie

Sunday

Time seems to stand still a moment. My brain starts asking questions of itself. Did this all actually happen? Is this real? 'What the hell is going on?' I say, turning to Steven, whose hands are now visibly shaking. 'I mean. What the . . . have we all just had some kind of collective bad trip?'

'I need a drink,' he says, his voice quiet and unsure.

'That can wait,' Mrs Davies snaps as she returns, Caitlin in hot pursuit.

Caitlin moves in front of the empty refrigerated cellar. 'What the . . .' Caitlin says. 'What have you done with him?'

'He's gone!' I gasp.

'Gone where?' Caitlin asks.

'One of you must have moved it,' Steven says.

'How do we know it wasn't you?' I say, pointing at him. 'You were first on the scene. I mean, how did you know?'

'I told you . . . Iggy.'

'Unless . . .' Caitlin says, interrupting.

'Unless what?' I ask.

She sighs. 'I still can't get hold of James.'

I look to Mrs Davies and Steven. All eyes are firmly on Caitlin who takes her phone from her pocket, checking for missed calls. She places it back in her gown pocket again.

'You look kind of chill about the fact your husband could be a murderer on the run,' I say.

'Well, what do you want me to do? Fall to my knees and wail? Jesus, Kass, I'm not like you.'

'What, an actual human being? Yeah. We know.'

'You know, as inferior as he appears in your shadow Cait, I do think the old boy could have it in him. I mean, living with you and your . . . ways . . .' Steven says.

'My "ways",' Caitlin says, dramatically air-quoting him.

'You're a seedy fucker,' Steven says. 'And James knows it.'

'Yeah, and he wishes he could have a bit,' Caitlin yells, suddenly realising that her words did her no favours. Steven lifts both his arms and shrugs in contentment. 'And there we have it.'

'Look,' Caitlin says. 'Sure, I get it. It looks suspect.'

'The money,' I say, suddenly remembering James' dodgy behaviour last night. 'Why was James giving Ollie money?'

'What's this?' Steven says.

'I don't know,' Caitlin says. 'Bonus for being the stand-in DJ, I guess.'

'Paul said it was a huge roll of notes. He said there were thousands in there.'

'Paul was floridly psychotic,' Caitlin says.

'This was before. He saw this before the guests even arrived,' I say.

'Well we can hardly trust him now can we?' Caitlin says. 'It will have just been payment for DJing. I mean, what else could it be?'

Steven, Mrs Davies and I stand there, our brains trying to work out the missing piece of the jigsaw. Why on earth would James pay Ollie so much money? And then disappear?

'You need to try harder than that to sound convincing,' Steven says. 'Dennis sorted all invoices and payments for the party. We know it wasn't that.'

Brian pops his head around the corner to see us all staring into the wine cellar. We instinctively move closer to protect it from him and close the door. Not that there's much to hide now. 'Is there a problem? Are we empty or something?' he asks in his low, quiet voice.

'You could say that yes,' Caitlin says.

Brian continues to look at us. 'Could I just check on the wine for later?' he asks.

'Like I said,' Caitlin says, her voice becoming snippy. 'It's empty.'

'There were hundreds of bottles in there,' Brian says, shifting on his feet. He looks at each of us in turn and I wonder if he was expecting us to find someone in there. But if he was expecting Ollie's body to be in there, then he couldn't have been the one to move it.

'Anyway. I'll um, place an order.' His stare lingers for a second or two longer, he's clearly suspicious – or concerned – but then he walks back into the kitchen and lets the door close behind him.

'Did any of you see Brian last night?' I whisper in his absence. 'You know he was off his chops on shrooms and free-ranging.' They all shake their heads uninterestedly.

'We're bloody lucky he didn't go in there while Ollie's

body was there,' Mrs Davies says, pointing to the now closed walk-in wine cellar door.

'He might well have for all we know,' I say in a whisper. 'He might have done it?'

'Brian? No. He's too . . . quiet,' Caitlin says.

'But off his face?' I say. 'And he was walking around with a knife.'

'What?' Caitlin says.

'I was trying to tell you!' I snap. 'Anyway, not only that, he could have looked in the wine cellar before we got here just now.'

'Why would he be accessing the wine cellar in the morning?' Steven asks.

'He just said he needs wine for later. Oh God – that's cos Granny's coming isn't it,' I say, starting to feel the panic rising in me.

'Well, at least one of you is responsible for moving him,' Mrs Davies says. 'And if James isn't here then it can't have been him.'

'When did you last see him, Cait?' Steven says.

Even in the midst of all this she remembers to narrow her eyes at him. She looks up as if trying to pull her memories from the ceiling. 'He didn't come to bed. I don't really know before that. I wasn't paying much attention to him to be honest.'

'Figures,' Steven says.

'I think it's clear now that any thought of it being one of the guests is old news,' Mrs Davies says. 'Ollie's body was moved after the party had been cleared out. And you'd only do that if you were guilty.'

We all look at each other. She's right. It had to be one of us. Or James – if he's still on site somewhere. Paul, maybe?

We think he's asleep but what if he's not . . . But he was in the Swan car park when we first found the body. What if Paul and Jack did this, and that's why they fled? Questions are racing around my mind and I've no idea who I can trust anymore.

'Problem is,' Mrs Davies says, 'now we've lost the body we have no way of working out which part of the building to keep Lady Morland from wandering into. I suggest one of you is tasked with keeping an eye on her at all times. And Paul and Jack, too – we can't risk them wandering into the village again. The locals will have a field day.'

'I'll take Granny,' Caitlin says, which surprises nobody, seeing as she'll be wanting to whisper manipulative somethings into her ear the entire time. Something she's done pretty much her entire life. She's always had one eye on the prize.

'Can you take Paul, Kassie?' Mrs Davies says. 'And I'll watch out for Jack.'

After overhearing Paul and Caitlin last night I am tempted to say no, to get angry. But maybe I can still work on him. Maybe there is an explanation for him betraying me like that? Maybe it's all part of the plan. Either way, I need to find out. 'Fine. I'll take Paul,' I say. I'm keen to check in on him anyway.

'And we need to make a start on scouring the house now. There's a body on the loose,' Mrs Davies adds, looking at each of us individually. 'So why are you all still standing here?' she snaps.

We all abruptly turn on our heels and start a methodical sweep of the house. And not just our wing, but the entire house. The full estate.

Thankfully, all traces of our party have been expertly removed. Glasses have been boxed up ready to go away for glass washing. Litter pickers have tidied the lawns and paths in record time. The only things left that can tell tales on our party are the freaky dolls and birds that still adorn the place. I assume Naomi will need to come back for those at some point.

We have no more than two hours before Granny is due to arrive and a dead body lost somewhere within the estate. It was always going to be stressful, Granny turning up, our fate in her mean old hands. But now . . .

'I suggest you search each other's rooms,' Mrs Davies says, as we regroup in the dining room. 'We can't trust each other right now.'

'That's a good point,' Steven says. 'We haven't discussed the fact that it could have been you.'

'And why on earth would I want to hurt that poor young man? *I* don't have motive.'

'What's this?' Caitlin asks.

Mrs Davies and Steven look at each other. 'Nothing,' Steven says.

'But—' Caitlin pushes.

'We need to get on with this,' Mrs Davies says. 'Caitlin, you can take Steven's room. Kassie, you take Caitlin's room. Steven, you take the cottage.'

'Are you serious? I don't want anyone looking around my room . . .' Steven says.

'And what about me?' Caitlin says. 'Besides, I need to find James.'

'You've probably hidden *his* body too,' Steven says.

James definitely has motive. I saw his face when Caitlin was gushing all over Ollie at the decks. But the money doesn't add up. Unless this is something Caitlin and James are in cahoots on?

'For Christ's sake,' Caitlin says, her voice trembling. 'I've just lost—' She stops suddenly, cutting herself short.

'Just lost what, Cait?' Steven says.

She says nothing and merely shakes her head.

We finally agree to the plan. Although I can't see anyone hiding a body they killed in their own bedroom. But I guess that's not the issue here. I guess nobody expected us to find anything in our siblings' rooms; we just needed to give each area of the building the absolute all-clear before the public and – worse than that – Granny descends. We just need to be absolutely sure they are 'clean'.

As I walk into Caitlin's room I realise that this is probably the first time I've been unsupervised in here since that time I broke into her make-up drawer as an eight-year-old. To make me pay for it, she painted my face in the most awful make-up imaginable, shoved me in front of the mirror and made me say Candy Man five times like something from a horror movie. I can still see my own frightening face staring back at me like it was wearing a hideous mask.

I close the door behind me and look around. Last night's black barely there dress is strewn over the back of the chair that sits in front of her dresser. Her wardrobe door is open, the dressing gown she was just wearing hanging over the top corner of it from where she quickly changed before allowing me to nosey through her room. Her bed is unmade and there's a half-empty wine glass on the table next to it. I pick it up by the stem and study it. No lipstick mark. Must have been James' glass. Besides, Caitlin was on the cocktails most of last night.

I shake my head and laugh to myself. What am I trying to be, some sort of amateur detective? Having the half-empty glass by the bed doesn't necessarily mean James actually got *into* bed, does it? He might have been drinking it before the guests arrived. It might even have been Caitlin's before she put her make-up on.

I decide to linger a few more minutes before checking on Paul, peeking inside drawers, getting a sense of who my sister really is these days. Of course, there can be no body hidden inside a small drawer but . . . well . . . there could be a finger, maybe.

Or at least some kind of clue.

As I pull the top drawer of the bedside table open, the one where the wine sits, I see a mobile phone. It's in a dark red leather-backed phone case. It's not Caitlin's. And I don't think it's James'. I don't think I've ever seen this before. I pick it up and flip it over. It says 'Aspinal of London' and, underneath are what I can only assume are two initials: *O.O.*

Ollie. Ollie Owens.

Shit. I drop the phone and close the drawer quickly. Why on earth would Ollie's mobile phone be in here? He must have been in here. Would Caitlin really have fucked him in this room? With James around?

Or might that be James' bedside drawer? Did *he* put it there?

I open the drawer again. My brain desperately tries to come up with reasons, a rationale. An explanation for this. Did James disappear and then Caitlin brought Ollie in here afterwards? If we can work it out, we can make sure they take the fall for this. We can cover our own backs. And they'll finally be out of the picture.

But did Ollie even come into Caitlin's room at all? And, if not, why would only his phone be in here? Especially when Caitlin had put him up in one of the guest rooms. Did they take his phone after one of them pushed him?

Caitlin or James must know what happened to Ollie. They simply must. There's too much motive.

We regroup once again in the dining room exhausted and with nothing to show for our efforts. At least, nothing I'm ready to share yet. I have to digest what I've just seen. Do I confront Caitlin? Or does that give her prior warning to come up with an explanation? Has she even seen it?

'So what now?' Caitlin asks. 'I mean he can't just have vanished into thin air. Bodies don't just move of their own accord.'

We've searched the entire estate. At least, we can't think of anywhere else to look. And nothing. No sign of Ollie – bar his mobile phone. I think about the fact that I've picked it up. That I was the one searching Caitlin's room. My fingerprints are all over it. And they all know I've been in there.

'I'm thinking one of the guests might have been responsible. It's ludicrous to think that one of us has done this. I mean, seriously,' Caitlin says laughing to herself. 'We should look at the guest list, see who was here, who might have had an issue with him.' Her words are beginning to convince me that she does indeed know about the phone. And, possibly, the whereabouts of his body.

'But that's the problem,' Steven says. 'The only people who might have had an issue with him are here. Aside from James, of course. And we were the only people here when the body was moved, so . . .'

We hear a crash from one of the rooms along the hall.

'What the hell . . .' Steven says.

'Paul?'

'He was asleep last time I checked,' Mrs Davies says.

'I'll go check,' I say, leaving the table and racing down

the hall towards Paul's room. I still don't know if I can forgive him for his disloyalty, but I need to know he's OK. And whether or not he might have had anything to do with Ollie's death.

When I get to his room, the door is already ajar. I push it open and immediately see gaping holes in his tallboy chest where the drawers should be. I look down on the floor and can see he's pulled out two drawers at such speed they've landed on the carpet spilling out all their contents. There are books and papers and receipts everywhere. As well as toiletries, socks and condoms. This must have been what caused the bang we heard.

But Paul is sitting on his bed cross-legged with his laptop in front of him, frantically typing away. Shit – he's not putting stuff out on social media, is he? He's in no fit state. He can't have slept more than a few hours since Mrs Davies and Dennis rounded him up and got him safely back into the confines of the estate. Although, I don't think he knows about Ollie. Not unless he had something to do with it.

'Hey, Paul. How you doing?' I say, trying to be as light-hearted as possible. He looks up at me, his eyes wide. Then he looks back down and carries on bashing away at the keyboard.

'What are you doing?' I ask, trying to get a look. He pulls the laptop screen closer to his body, shielding it from me.

'Research,' he says. 'It was never confirmed.'

'What wasn't?'

He closes his laptop and looks back up at me. 'Doesn't matter. What do you think of Jack? Think he's OK?'

'Yeah, I mean. Mrs Davies said he's sleeping it off in one of the guest rooms.'

'I don't mean that. I mean, can I trust him?'

My heart sinks. This isn't right. Paul has never, never doubted Jack. Even during the Jack and Caitlin months, from what I heard. Apparently it was a little awkward, but nothing comes between Paul and Jack. Thick as thieves since they were kids, apparently. But then again, I thought Paul and I were, too.

'Why do you think you can't trust him all of a sudden?'

He looks at me, locking eyes, a pained expression on his face. Then he looks away again and reopens his laptop. There's a darkness to Paul today. You might call it hangxiety, I guess, but Paul usually copes well with whatever he's done the night before. Well, aside from that one time. 'But are you feeling OK?' I press.

'I'm scared, Kass. I feel OK sometimes, but then everything shifts again. I can see the devil. Something demonic. It's everywhere.'

He's clearly still hallucinating. I obviously can't talk to him about what we've just discovered. About Granny being here. It will have to wait until he's back to his normal self. However long that might take. This feels like one hell of a bender.

'I've got to get on,' he says, turning his head back to his laptop. His face suddenly serious and full of concern.

'But, Paul. I'm worried about you.'

He pulls a face, shaking his head as if trying to erase something from his brain. Then he dismisses me with the back of his hand as if I'm an annoying child. I decide I'm not going to get much sense out of him and leave him to it. He's clearly consumed by whatever 'research' he's doing so I can't see him leaving the house anytime soon. I go back to the dining room.

'It was just a couple of drawers he's pulled out. He's not

quite right, but he's deep in some "research".' I air-quote the word. 'Whatever that means anyway – so I don't think he's planning to go anywhere for some time. He's definitely not right though. Seems really paranoid about Jack.'

'This has happened before,' Caitlin says. 'Doc called it . . . what was it . . . ?'

'Substance-induced psychosis,' Mrs Davies says. 'And if I remember rightly, the last time this happened he needed antipsychotics and a lot of supervision. It lasted a couple of weeks. I'll get the doctor over. Better safe than sorry.'

'I don't remember that?' I say. 'You mean, from that time when he ended up naked at the bus stop?'

'No,' Steven says. 'It was when you were really young. Partied too hard with Caitlin and Jack. Didn't come back down for days.'

I look at Caitlin who turns away, biting her nails. 'Always been the same,' she mutters. 'Always been a fucking nightmare. You can't trust him. I mean, given the state he's in, it's Paul we need to be looking into. James isn't the only one who disappeared during the party.'

She's trying to set him up for this. I just know she is.

Chapter 27

Kassie

Sunday

'Thank you, dear. No, not you. No don't take that! I already told you. It's this. Oh, for heaven's sake do I need to do everything myself?'

I can hear her entering the hall, talking down to everyone.

I walk into the living room where they are all gathered as if waiting for an execution. Granny, Steven and Caitlin. Dennis is there too – standing formally beside the sofa she is sitting on.

We're always on edge in Granny's presence. But today's anxiety is on another level. There's that small matter of the missing dead body for starters. And of course, because of that, we haven't had time to change into our best clothes for her visit – a hangover from our childhood but one that has seemingly saved us years of sour looks and mean comments given her reaction to us today. We decided that we'd have to make do and just butter her up as best we can.

'Caitlin, *really*, this isn't like you? This isn't like you at *all*,' Granny says, gesturing towards Caitlin's clothes – jeans and T-shirt – and shaking her head. She hugs her nonetheless, but what is a hug if you don't physically embrace? It's like an air kiss but an air hug. A slow choreographed dance move towards one another that's designed purely for show.

Caitlin smiles at our angry relative. 'But, Granny, this T-shirt's Prada.'

'Doesn't matter what label's inside it. Smacks of couldn't-give-a-monkey's your grandmother was on her way to see you.'

Caitlin simply smiles back at her and argues her enthusiasm. 'But, Granny, I always love to see you – you know that.' It's like an inter-generational flirtation – but the end point isn't romance, it's money. I guess in Caitlin's eyes, that is romantic.

Steven, however, has somehow managed to quickly change for Granny's arrival. He is now wearing a crisp white shirt and chinos. The creep.

He's trying to reassert himself as the patriarch now he knows Granny could well be going for something a little more matriarchal in Caitlin as main beneficiary.

The air is laced with a manic energy that buzzes around us. I don't know about anyone else, but I feel as though I can't sit still and that I constantly need to pee.

Every time I catch a glimpse of something out of the corner of my eye I flinch, seeing Ollie's limbs in the folds of the curtains or his face in the paintings on the wall. They're not real – but his dead body, us moving it, that's all true.

'Will you please sit down. Honestly,' Granny says impatiently.

We take a seat like a reverse Mexican wave. Caitlin, as

awkward and uncomfortable as she clearly feels right now wearing jeans and trainers in front of the family matriarch, dives straight in next to her anyway, a satisfied smile sneaking across her face.

We all look at Granny expectantly.

'What? You honestly don't think I'm here to pre-announce my decision do you? Because that is absolutely not what my visit is about.'

'So, what is this visit about?' Caitlin asks.

'As if you don't know. Frankly, I'm disappointed that you could put your inheritance at risk for the sake of a party.'

We all glance at one another, wondering just what she knows. The terrifying anticipation of Granny having somehow found out about what we've just done hangs in the air. Caitlin's pupils are wide, and Steven keeps looking at the floor, as if he's trying to conjure some kind of explanation for any scenario Granny might hit us with. Meanwhile, my chest flutters with palpitations that feel as though they're stealing the air from my throat.

'Is anyone at least going to offer me a slice of cake?' Granny says, prolonging the agony.

'Mrs Davies!' Steven shouts. Mrs Davies appears almost instantly.

'What can I get you, Lady Morland?' she asks.

'Have you any of that cake I like?'

'The Bakewell?'

'Good Lord, no. Your chef completely destroyed that last one. You know, the lattice thing. With the syrupy stuff?' She points her finger downwards, shaking it as if it will magic the words 'treacle tart' from her mind.

'I'm afraid I . . .' Mrs Davies pauses when she notices Granny looking at her, her top lip curling slightly. She changes tack. 'I'll ask Brian to rustle some up for you. In the meantime, biscuits, perhaps?'

'That'll do,' Granny says, waggling the backs of her fingers in Mrs Davies' direction. She leaves and closes the door.

'Where's your brother?' she says, looking around the room as if he might just be hiding behind the drinks cabinet or the flatscreen TV.

'He's got food poisoning,' I say, at exactly the same time that Steven says: 'He's come down with that summer cold.' We look at each other in horror.

'Well which is it?' Granny says. 'Food poisoning, that summer cold, or . . .' she leans forward in her seat '. . . is it a bad case of too many illegal substances this weekend?' She glances at all of us one by one. Steven and I say nothing, but Caitlin, as typical Caitlin, tries to lower Granny's opinion of our missing brother.

'Oh God, you heard?'

'Heard what, dear?' Granny says.

'Oh, sorry. I thought you meant . . . nothing. It's nothing.'

Caitlin thinks she's being clever. *Accidentally* dropping Paul in it and putting on a fake panic as if we're really going to believe it was a genuine accident. She's all theatrics.

Suddenly, Granny stands, and so do all of us. My heart is in my mouth at the thought of her bumping into a mangled, broken limb or slipping in a bloody puddle. We know we can't let her wander around the estate on her own. 'What on earth is up with you all today?' she says, shaking her head and tutting.

'Do you need something?' Caitlin asks.

'I'm not useless, you know,' she says, batting Caitlin's fussing hands away. 'I can manage quite sufficiently thank you.' She makes her way to the door. Caitlin shoots us both looks, pinching her brows as if to ask what to do now. As Granny's back disappears to the right of the door, Steven shoos Caitlin with his hand, urging her to follow and keep an eye on our wandering grandmother – and our unpredictable brother and his house guest.

Caitlin leaves the room and we can hear Granny's irritated tones from the corridor. 'What now, hm? I'm trying to go to the bathroom, for heaven's sake. I don't need a chaperone.'

'Sorry, Granny, I know. I just wanted to . . . I just needed to get something from my room.'

Caitlin's acting skills are frankly terrible.

'She's going to drop us all in it, if she's not careful,' I say to Steven.

'It's Paul I'm most worried about right now,' he says. 'We think he doesn't know what's happened here, but what if . . .' Steven leans forward in my direction and looks over both shoulders. 'What if it was him?'

'But he was off his face,' I say.

'Exactly.'

'No I mean. He wasn't *menacing*. He wasn't like Brian.'

'Brian?' Steven sits up straight. 'Brian has no motive,' he says, shrugging off my alternative explanation.

'But why the knife?'

'I don't know. I guess it's possible. I guess . . .' Steven looks up to the chandelier. 'I guess if we had been quicker on our feet we could have framed him either way. Then none of us would be in this mess.'

'You're the one who said not to call the ambulance.'

'Yes but we couldn't have called it before having concocted a plan. And, Jesus, Kass, it's not all down to me you know. You could have come up with the idea. Caitlin could have. It's clear you all look to me to lead this place.' He turns his head and mutters, 'Seriously, nobody else should even be in the running.'

'Change the record, Steven.'

Mrs Davies returns to the room with the biscuits, Granny and Caitlin right behind her.

Granny sits back down in her spot and carefully studies the selection of biscuits in front of her before picking one.

'Right,' Granny says, her gaze directed solely at me this time. 'We need to discuss what happened with the young Taylor-Banks boy.'

'Who?' I ask, genuinely confused.

'Will Taylor-Banks. Kassie, what on earth were you thinking? Creating tension between our two families. Our relationship with the Taylor-Bankses has always been good. Up until now. And, frankly, it has reflected terribly on me.'

I rack my brains but I simply can't figure out what she's talking about. 'I'm sorry, Granny, I . . .'

'You've caused serious harm to our family relations. You need to think before you act, darling.'

I think back. I remember Steven and Caitlin talking about Will. The guy 'of good stock'. But I never went to speak to him. 'I don't think I've met him,' I say. 'I'm sorry, Granny, I'm not sure . . .'

'Not met him? You assaulted him. Had him escorted off the property. Of all the people you could have picked a fight with.'

Oh shit, Will Taylor-Banks must have been the guy who attacked me. Who tried to grope me – assault me – right here in our living room, when I was looking for Brian.

He's the bloody grandson of Granny's best friend, Fiona. Wonderful. Just. Fucking. Wonderful. I decide to make an appeal to her – albeit rather shallow – feminism.

'He actually assaulted *me*,' I say. 'He grabbed me from behind.'

'Kassie, dear. I'd give anything to be grabbed from behind. Especially by a young man like Will.'

I should have known that getting groped by a guy of 'good stock' wasn't going to cut it. I didn't count on her being so 'ick' about a guy two generations younger than her though. Gross. Why is this family so debauched? Honestly!

'If you're going to have any sort of hand in the estate, darling, you need to know how to move in the circles.'

'But, Granny. He *groped* me . . . He tried to force himself onto me.' I am exasperated now and I can't hold it in. Why does this family not care about harm coming your way so long as there's a monetary prospect at the end of it?

'I don't want to know,' she says, holding up her hand. 'I mean, if you were *that* put out couldn't you have had a quiet word with him? Save everyone the embarrassment? Save me having to swerve next week's dinner because my own granddaughter can't keep her fists to herself.'

'But . . . I didn't hit him. I just pushed him off me. It was self-defence.'

'All I'm saying, Kassie, darling,' Granny continues, throwing me a stern look, 'is that if you want to play a key role in the estate when I hand over the rights, then you need to understand how the social system works. We just don't want to have to keep you out of the transfer of rights, dear,' she says. 'And if you carry on the way you're going – with goats running riot and slap-happy fists – then I'm going to struggle to place any faith in you. And you'll be on regular pocket money allowances from your siblings in perpetuity. *If* they choose to continue to give you that charity.'

I inhale, look around the room and catch Steven's expression as he lets out an undeniable smirk.

I stand up. 'Excuse me,' I say, as if asking for permission. 'I need to use the bathroom.'

I leave the room and close the door behind me. My heart is pounding. Has Granny basically informed me that I am not in the running? That the estate will go to either Steven or Caitlin? Or Paul? But given that he's not here, he's not exactly looking like a prime candidate.

I head down the hallway to check on my still-inebriated brother. Hopefully he'll be sleeping it off. The doctor went in to see him just before Granny got here and I'm sure will have given him some sedatives. That's what they do isn't it? If you're rich enough they'll arrive within minutes and give you whatever you need.

Paul's door is firmly shut this time. I turn the handle and push it open as quietly as possible – the last thing I want to do is wake him now. I walk over to his bed to check on him, noting the acrid smell of booze hanging heavily in the air. But when I get closer, I realise there's no sign of him. Just a pillow underneath a duvet. He's vanished.

Chapter 28

Kassie

Sunday

I made an excuse about tending to Iggy and left the main house to check the grounds for Paul. I was convinced he'd be sleeping soundly with a stomach full of diazepam by now. My breathing is shallow and fast as I march across the lawn in my trainers. Why am I literally always looking for people? People and animals. It's too hot to be racing around all the time.

As I get closer to the cottage I can see the greenhouse in the distance. The door looks like it's open.

I walk into the greenhouse. The afternoon sun has already created a sauna inside and I can feel the heat land on my face like a warm blanket. Along the little paved path down the middle I see Paul sitting at the other end of the building, facing away from me. He's still and seems to be staring out of the window.

'Paul?'

He turns his head slowly and looks at me as I approach

him. His appearance startles me. His eyes are completely vacant, dead. Like he's looking at me, but he doesn't recognise me. His hair is in his face and some of it sticks to his damp forehead. He's sitting in nothing but an unbuttoned white shirt and his pants. At least he's out of that Viking demon costume he was wearing at the party. What he must've looked like in the pub car park Sunday morning when the staff were arriving for their shift, all bare-chested with fake blood and mud covering his torso. It would be funny, if he'd recovered. But the Paul I see in front of me now is seriously troubled.

He has a half-empty bottle of cooking whisky in front of him. I doubt it's the same one from Saturday night. He'll have downed that one a long while back.

'I thought you were sleeping?' I say. 'Since the doctor came. Didn't he give you something to chill out?'

I walk closer towards him and he grabs the bottle, wrapping it tight into his body like it's his baby or something. 'I'm not stupid,' he says, his voice shaky and fast. 'I'm not taking that shit. I know what it does. This'll do just fine.' He takes another drink of it.

'But you're not yourself, Paul.' I hold out my hand. 'Come on, at least if you're going to drink that stuff, you might as well do it somewhere less . . . airless.' I look around me and feel how close the air is. A trickle of sweat runs down my spine.

'Thought you adored this place?' Paul says, a hint of my real brother suddenly seeping into his words and his tone.

'I do. But it's possibly not the right environment for you right now.'

Suddenly, Paul leaps backwards, stumbling and almost falling before sticking to the wall as if he's on a rotor ride. His knuckles are pushing on his cheeks, pulling his lower eyelids down. It's an expression of sheer terror. He is looking behind me, beyond me. I turn around and see Iggy, standing at the window, her little tail wagging. She hops in delight when she sees me and gets closer to the window. Paul's knuckles are now gripping the brick wall behind him, stretched and white.

'Paul. Paul!' I shout when he doesn't respond. He still refuses to look at me. I walk towards him but he's almost frozen. Catatonic with fear.

I put my arm out towards him. 'It's just Iggy, Paul.' He jerks away from me but I put my hand back out towards him more slowly this time. He lets me gently squeeze his arm. 'Paul, it's just Iggy. Sweet Iggy Pop,' I say. He eventually turns to look at me, his hands relaxing away from the brick and the muscles releasing in his cheeks. He shakes his head. Then he looks back towards Iggy and his eyes seem to be his own again.

'Jesus. Kassie. I don't know what's happening. I'm fucking losing it again.'

'It's OK,' I say trying to comfort him. 'You're having some kind of . . . prolonged reaction to the drugs you took. The doc's been, you've got some sedatives and stuff to bring you round. It'll all be OK. Promise.'

He collapses back down to the ground and perches on his haunches, wrapping his arms tight around his bent legs. The shirt stretches across his back and I can see the transparent patches where it sticks to him with sweat. He's shaking now, almost rocking. 'I'm not falling for it,' he says. 'Not again. Not again.'

'Come on, Paul,' I say. 'You'll neck almost anything usually. Couple of sleeping pills'll do you the world of good.' He looks at me, doubtfully. 'Please,' I say. 'Look. If you won't go back to the house, at least come back to the cottage with me. You can sleep it off on the sofa.'

He's still trembling but thankfully not as violently as he was just moments ago. 'Honestly, Paul. We've been here before. It's transient. It's the end of a bad trip. It'll all be over soon.' I hold out my hand again and this time he takes it.

I lead Paul back to the cottage as though I'm leading Iggy. He's just like a vulnerable young kid right now. I open the door and make him comfortable in the living room, leaving him with a blanket, a pint of water filled with electrolytes and the sofa to crash out on before heading back to the house to see Granny. After all *one must keep up appearances*, as Granny would say. And I want to make sure Caitlin isn't doing too much damage to the rest of us. She's never been one for lifting up others to make herself feel better. She gets her kicks by literally stamping us into the dirt.

Chapter 29

Kassie

Sunday

When I get back to our wing, I straighten my top up and fluff my sweaty hair out before walking through the door. I walk past the living room and into the kitchen where Mrs Davies and Brian are preparing dinner. I'm still not convinced about Brian's innocence.

'Kassie. How's Paul?' Mrs Davies looks genuinely concerned as she gathers the crockery and silverware needed for dinner. She raises her eyebrows, which I know now is code for 'any news on the body?' We simply can't discuss it but it's on all our minds constantly. The energy in the house is even more restless and edgy than usual.

Brian, meanwhile, is throwing veggies up into the air from a sizzling wok over a hob. His face is more standard Brian now – his mouth a straight line across his face and his eyes concentrating on the task in hand.

'He's . . .' I exhale, puffing out my lips. 'Ah well, he's

not good. Actually, he's fucking terrible. He needs sedating. Have you got his pills?'

'He was given some not long ago?'

'Yes. But he's not taken them. He doesn't trust anyone. Thinks everyone's out to harm him. Even little Iggy.'

'Iggy?'

'Yeah he saw her outside the greenhouse and, honestly, Mrs Davies, the sheer look of terror on his face. It was disturbing.'

'OK, stay there. I'll go and grab those pills. A sleep might be all he needs.'

Mrs Davies leaves and I eye Brian suspiciously. I'm not sure I can completely rule him out of the equation when it comes to Ollie.

I couldn't care less if people are snorting coke or brewing up psilocybin mushrooms or getting wasted on cooking whisky. *I* enjoy it on occasion – the coke and booze, anyway. And 'occasion' being times when I am literally nowhere near my siblings, of course. I can't let my hair down in their presence. It's dangerous.

Mrs Davies reappears and hands me a prescription bag. 'There you go. He's to take no more than two a day.'

'Thanks,' I say, taking the paper bag. Then I spy a pastry case on the sideboard.

'Did you end up making the treacle tart for Her Majesty?' I ask. Brian keeps his head down and Mrs Davies' eyes widen. I sense a presence behind me and turn, only to be met with Granny's imposing figure in the doorway.

'I'll take that as a compliment rather than sarcasm, if you don't mind,' she says.

'I . . .' I stutter and she jumps back in, cutting me off.

'We need to talk about your goat, dear.'

I swallow. This isn't going to be good. She hates Iggy. 'Yes?' I say.

'I don't believe you should have a pet goat running about the house. I mean . . .' She wafts her hand in front of her and crinkles up her nose. 'They probably have all manner of diseases.'

'She's a clean animal,' I say, thinking that my promiscuous siblings are far more likely to be spreading disease than poor Iggy.

'She's an animal, though.'

'But you'd have a dog in the house,' I say. 'I don't really see the difference.'

'Frankly, dear, I really don't think you're taking estate life seriously.'

Then my brain jumps into survival mode. 'But imagine the PR, Granny? If I were to inherit, if we were to work with the National Trust, imagine the number of families who would want to bring their kids during the holidays to see Iggy. We'd have the Morland heritage tales for the parents, and Iggy could be a main attraction for the children. She'd be amazing.'

Granny raises an eyebrow at me and I know I've impressed her somewhat. It might not be enough, but if I can keep chipping away while she's here, I might just stand a chance.

Chapter 30

Sunday 24th August

15.23

Black wispy hair hangs down into the top and sides of the frame as the camera zooms in on blades of grass before being swooped upwards and onto a log. The hair blows gently, fluttering in a breeze before a gentle *thud, thud* announces its return to lower ground. Twigs and tree branches obscure the lens and sounds of snapping and more gentle thudding start up, increasing in tempo as the picture moves towards the Hall in the distance. The sky is bright blue and the sun's rays keep catching on the lens, creating trails of circles that momentarily bleach the image.

The camera makes its way around the back of the building, trotting – up and down, up and down – along the gravel path, stopping every so often to zone in on the small open holes in the foundations of the building, covered with grates, short sprigs of grass poking up around them.

As it stands still by a grate, there's a banging, clanging

sound coming from below. Then scratching. The sound of quiet whimpering.

The camera moves on and stops again, two pairs of legs come into view ahead. Beige men's sandals on sockless feet, a pair of chino trousers resting on top of them. A pair of black cropped linen trousers, flat black shoes positioned neatly together. The camera lowers itself towards the ground, lush neat grass coming into view. Snuffling and slurping.

'Why are you so convinced it was me?'

'You know why.' It's a woman's voice. Loud sniffing sounds take over and the conversations weave in and out of the audio, as if being carried by the wind.

'I was a child! You can't have one rule for Kassie and one . . .'

'*She* wasn't even . . .' The voices become distorted as the wind pipes up again, muffled sounds that get louder as the black fur blows wildly in the frame. '. . . *You* were fourteen.'

'Yes, a child.'

'A child who knew right from wrong. A child who . . . was full of *hate*.'

'Hate's a strong word, Mrs Davies. Oh for fuck's sake, Iggy. Shoo.' The back of a hand moves towards the camera lens and there's a harsh clapping sound. The camera moves backwards slightly and the angle changes a few degrees.

'See? You can't even show compassion for an innocent animal. And besides, if it was anything less than hate that . . . then I despise you even more. If that's even . . .' The wind blows wildly again, the hairs lying flat against the camera lens, the sound shooting up in volume, a noise like paper being ripped. Crackling overwhelming everything. It quietens again . . .

The male voice jumps back in: '. . . destroyed our family.'

'And *you* destroyed . . . unless you've forgotten the basic facts of . . . didn't do it alone.'

'*She* didn't know what she was doing.'

'You know that, do you? You could read your mother's troubled . . . you were too young to take responsibility for what happened?'

'It was an accident.'

'If it was, then that's one hell of a coincidence . . . happening so suddenly after you found out about it all.'

'So what do you want me to do? You . . . relinquish everything I've built? Because that's the fact of the . . . the one who built this place up after he left it in ruins.'

'No, you *pay* people to do stuff. Christ, you pay people to tell others what to do. You delegate the delegation, Steven. Kassie, meanwhile . . .'

'Oh, here we go . . .'

'Kassie . . . sleeves up and looks after this place.'

'Yeah, she does the menial work. The work anyone could do.'

'That's the problem with people like you.'

'What?'

'You haven't got a clue. You think doling out money to people more intelligent and more hardworking than you makes you . . . aspirational figure.'

'Isn't that what everyone strives for?'

'Frankly no, Steven. It's dull.'

'Well I'm not about to . . . without a fight.'

'Of course you're not. Besides . . . wouldn't *look* right. Because the way you've treated her. Her entire life. You *and* Caitlin.'

'What about Paul . . . saint all of a sudden?'

'Clearly not. But he destroys himself. Not other people.'

'You weren't saying that when he almost ended up all over social media . . .'

'Yes well. That wasn't his fault. You should ask your other sister how that all came to light.'

'What?'

'Ask Caitlin. Kassie deserves more . . . peace.'

'*I've* never found peace. Why should she . . .'

'Only because you can't live with yourself.'

'For fuck's sake. I was fourteen. I was a kid. It won't even hold up.'

'Don't be so naive, Steven. I've got the evidence.'

'OK, so what? So what if I agree to this crazy plan? I've still got to convince Granny that Morland needs to go . . . beneficiary. And given what she was just saying to her before, I can't see it happening.'

'All that nonsense about Will Taylor-Banks? But that was outrageous.'

'Doesn't matter. It's up to Granny at the end of the day.'

'Which is outrageous . . . Your father should have sorted all this out before . . .'

'Well he didn't, did he? He just listened to what that mad old cow wanted.'

'Steven! Really!'

'Please. It's what we all think . . . it's going to sound strange, ridiculous . . . see me fighting for Kassie's rights.'

'I'm sure you'll find a way, Steven. You always do.'

Chapter 31

Paul

Monday morning

It's 3.15 a.m. I told Kassie I would sleep on her sofa but I haven't closed my eyes once. I can't. My brain is racing and I have a hidden baggie of coke stashed in my pocket. If they're trying to quieten and slow me, I'll just make myself louder and faster. I'll get the truth out.

I pull my key from my pocket, dip it into my bag, and inhale sharply. I shake my head and let it trickle inside the back of my throat, waking up every cell it hits on its way down. My teeth coil like a spring.

Kassie ran over to the house earlier to get the pills they're trying to silence me with from Mrs Davies. But, after showing Kass my empty mouth, I threw them back up when she wasn't around. I can't trust them. Pills that are prescribed are on a mission. They have an agenda. The prescriber's agenda. And it's never what you think it's going to be. It's never for you; it's always for them.

Fuck that shit.

I've been sitting in the dark since Kassie went to bed. Hours ago. Trying to work it all out. They keep telling me it's substance-induced psychosis. Sure. It might be. I know it's happened before. But there's a part of your brain that wakes up, isn't there? With hallucinogenics. A part of your brain that sees things, true things, that your everyday brain can't. The clever, perceptive, elevated part of your brain. Who are they to say my perception's all wrong? What's their reference point? They can't see what I can, because their brains are fast-a-fucking-sleep. Dormant. Redundant. Unseeing.

Their matter is grey while mine is dancing in light. Rays of it are bouncing around the room, alive and knowing. Knowing stuff they don't.

I stand up and pick the blanket up that Kassie insisted on putting over me. It is morphing into the blackness around me, an all-consuming blanket trying to wrap me up in its black claws. I am comforted and scared and suffocating all at once. I shake the blanket out to remove its spell and fold it neatly four times to shapeshift it back into what it is meant to be. I place it back down on the sofa. I stand still for a moment in the room. I can hear the fridge humming. It's so loud I don't understand how Kassie is sleeping. It gets louder and louder and I have to block my ears. I walk quietly to the front door, my head still in my hands, careful not to make a sound. I open the Yale, let it creak open, step out and close it gently behind me, so that I don't wake Kassie. I am desperate for the light.

I walk down the path and can hear shuffling around. It's Iggy. Or rather, whoever she is now. I keep my distance, my heart thudding. She can sense it too. She knows too. She knows that something in this place is completely off. There's something coming for us.

I traipse across the gardens and the moon is close to full. The blackness still surrounds us but as I cross it peels away from me and I can see through it. I have night-vision goggles built into my eyes. The moon is shining on me and through me and out of my eyes while the blackness encapsulates everyone else. I can see laser-like beams marking out my route.

I look down at my feet. I forgot to put on my shoes. Or did I never have them at Kassie's in the first place? My feet connect with the earth as I stride towards our wing.

I open the front door with my key, scooping it back into the bag while I have it out in front of me. I hold it to my nose and sniff hard. It's lighting me up. Keeping me going like a battery being recharged. I let the door close softly behind me. I walk towards my room so I can get back to my MacBook and pick up on the research I began.

Trip killer.
Trip killer.

It's coming now in different voices. Male, female. Scared, angry. From behind me, in front of me, below me. I trip over that damn loose tile again. It shrieks loudly as it scrapes loosely across the stone floor and I steady myself on the wall. I stop, stock-still, and kneel down slowly, listening for the sounds of my relatives stirring. I can't hear anyone getting up. Thank God. But wait. I can hear . . .

What *is* that? A scratching sound. Shuffling.

Trip killer.
Trip killer.

I look all around me but there is nobody there. The voices must be coming from me like the light is. It's still dark in the house, but I can see in front of me. And I can hear everything. I stand and focus on the sound of the huge old grandfather clock. I close my eyes and can still see the pendulum swinging from side to side, knocking into the sides of my skull over and over again. It sounds as though it's getting faster and faster, cracking at bone, so I open my eyes and shake my head and look down at the loose tile in front of me. It's a puzzle part that's asking to be solved. I grip my fingernails around it and find enough of a wedge to lever it out of place completely. It snaps in half. I place it quickly to the side. I put my ear to the floor in the place of the tile. More shuffling. Echoey shuffling. There's something beneath the floorboards.

There's some*one* beneath the floorboards.

I pick out another tile, and another. Yanking them, snapping them. The sound is getting louder. Then, in place of the stone floor a piece of wood comes into view. I keep taking more tiles. More and more tiles. Stacking them, shattering them. A tile-shaped Jenga game. Then, the full form of the wood appears in front of me. It's a trapdoor. It's a wooden trapdoor with a brass ring pull. Jesus. I knew there was a reason for this. For this puzzle of tiles.

Then I hear padding on the floor getting louder and closer behind me.

'Paul! Paul!' Caitlin is standing there now.

'Why are you speaking like that?' I turn to look at her. She is in her short floral pyjama set, bare-footed. The flowers on her pyjamas move forward in 3D design like a stereogram coming into view.

'Like what? And what the actual fuck are you doing? You're going to wake Granny.'

'Like that . . . that sound. That's not your voice. Go back to bed,' I say.

'*You* need to go back to bed,' she says, her voice becoming louder and louder, like a hissing snake.

'I haven't been. There's something under the floor. There's a trapdoor.'

'Don't be ridiculous,' she says. And when I look at her, her head is undulating on her neck like a snake's. She is laughing at me. 'Look,' she says, hissing. 'It's gone three. Can't you just do whatever you think you need to do tomorrow?'

I cover my ears with my hands. 'Jesus, Caitlin. Can you please stop making that noise.'

'What are you on about?'

'The hissing. Just stop with the hissing. It hurts my ears.'

'I'm not hissing. Jesus fucking Christ.' She *is* hissing.

'Just. Just look,' I say, removing one of my hands and pointing towards the wooden door in the floor.

Caitlin moves closer. 'Fucking hell. What the hell is that?' she asks.

'Exactly. You all think I'm crazy but I'm not.'

'Well, that's still a point of debate right now. But I've never seen that before. Does it open?'

'Shh!' I say, pointing my finger in the air. 'Hear that?'

We both stand quietly in the dark.

'I can't hear anything, Paul.'

'Just. Listen . . .'

There's a loud shuffle. And a thud.

'Oh my God. There's somebody down there. Under the floor.'

Chapter 32

Kassie

Monday morning

I wake and sit bolt upright in bed. The sound of the front door slamming repeats over and over in my ears. I shake my head and become conscious of my eyes being open and my mind waking up. I was asleep. Did I really hear that? Then I remember, Paul is in my living room.

I jump out of bed and grab my dressing gown, wrapping it around me. Everything is silent. Perhaps he's sleeping and it was just the dregs of a dream waking me up? But when I make my way from my bedroom to the living room the sofa is empty. Perhaps predictably, Paul has vanished, leaving nothing but a folded blanket on the sofa.

I stuff my feet in my Docs, leaving them unlaced, knot the cord of my bright orange hooded dressing gown around me and race across the grounds in search of him. The air is quiet and still, with just the occasional sound of an owl high up in the trees somewhere and a gentle rustling from the bushes.

As I get closer, I can see a light on in the downstairs area of the wing. There's movement, too, an outline of someone who appears to be bobbing up and down in front of the window.

'Paul?' I whisper. Is it him? What the hell is he doing at this time? If he's woken Granny up she'll be furious.

As I get closer to our wing I crouch beside the window and peer in. Paul and Caitlin are looking down, towards the floor. Weird. At least he's not on his own. I get closer still and try to listen to their conversation but it's difficult to hear. I stand on tiptoes and direct my eyes to the floor. Paul is leaning down, pulling something up. And Caitlin is shining her phone torch towards it. It's too difficult to see out here so I stand back up, walk towards the door and push it open.

'What are you . . .'

'Shh!' They both turn around shushing me in unison. Paul's eyes are still wild and vacant, but Caitlin looks pretty level.

'What's going on?' I whisper.

'We've found a secret basement,' Paul says. I look over to Caitlin, expecting an eye roll, but she just looks at me wide-eyed and nods.

'How can we have a secret basement? How is that possible?' Are they both high right now?

'One of the floor tiles was broken,' Paul says. 'It was a sign.'

I glance to Caitlin and this time she does roll her eyes. 'I think the only thing that tile was trying to tell us was that it was time for a new floor. That's Steven all over that is. Too bloody stingy,' she says.

'More important things than a broken tile right now,' Paul says.

'Well, yes. Seeing as you've smashed about fifteen of them.'

'Look,' I say. 'Sign or no sign. I take it that is actually a thing. Down there,' I say, jabbing the air in front of what looks like a wooden trapdoor. Paul leans back in and loops his finger through the brass hook. He carefully lifts the door up – it's attached to the floor by a hinge on one side. It takes a couple of yanks but eventually it opens, forcing Paul to topple backwards a few steps. He regains his balance. Caitlin gets her torch back out.

'Yes, Kassie. Paul might be impressively off his chops right now but he's right about this.'

We all peer in, and, as Caitlin's torchlight illuminates the blank space below, we can see a set of concrete steps heading into oblivion, and what looks like rolls of old carpet or rugs, and a couple of tins of paint.

'Is it like a storage room or something?' I ask. 'Those tins can't be that old, surely?'

'Look. Is that a shadow . . .' Paul says.

'Well it's all shadowy down there,' Caitlin says. 'It's dark. And spooky.'

'But it moved,' Paul says, pointing downwards.

'Everything is moving before your eyes right now, Paul.'

'No, seriously, Caitlin. Just watch.'

I squint, not noticing anything. My vision starts to make sense of things. Old paint pots. A rolled-up rug. Cardboard boxes stacked on top of each other. And then something shifts in the dark.

Chapter 33

Kassie

Monday morning

I gasp, jerking backwards.

'What was that?'

'There's something down there,' Paul says, eyes wide, feet shuffling frantically. 'Some*thing*. You all think I'm mad. I'm not, I'm telling you . . .'

'Sh!' I say, and we all lean back in. 'Caitlin, angle the torch over there. The right-hand side. There.' She follows my lead and there, in the dark below us, is something even Paul's ravenous appetite for hallucinogenics couldn't conjure. In a corner, in our new secret basement, there's a grubby, dirty, naked body. A human form folded into the shape of an angular, bony foetus.

'Oh my God.' Caitlin gasps. '*Ollie*.' She rushes forward but Paul instinctively grabs her and pulls her back.

'He's alive,' I say. 'He's shaking. He has to be alive.'

Then I turn and my building nausea explodes as I projectile vomit all over the broken tiles.

'Jesus, Kassie, really?' Caitlin says. 'There's enough already to deal with here, don't you think.'

I wipe my mouth with the back of my hand and take a breath.

'No, no, no, no, no, no, no . . .' Paul collapses into a crouch, his arms wrapping around his knees. He is gasping. Sobbing. Rocking. Caitlin and I both turn to look at him. Tears are streaming and his eyes are even darker and more vacuous than before.

We both turn to look into the basement. 'We've got to go in there,' I say. 'He's still alive.'

'Barely,' Caitlin says, wiping her eye. She's traumatised. She's never traumatised. 'I mean, look at him, he's all . . . mangled. Broken.'

'Ollie,' I say, trying to get his attention. But nothing. I can feel my skin pricking with cold and nausea builds in my throat. 'What's wrong with him?' I say. 'How did he even get in there? He was dead. I mean, he was, wasn't he? We all saw him. We all carried him. This is fucking impossible.'

Meanwhile Paul continues rocking and crying. 'No. No. No. NO!' He suddenly screams the word, and I hear a door open and slam shut.

'Who's there?' It's Mrs Davies. She's taken the guest room to help keep an eye on Granny what with dead bodies being on the loose. Although we seem to have found it – dead or not.

'It's us,' I say, crouching down to where Paul is to try to keep him quiet. I try to still him and can feel him trembling beneath my hands. Then I remember. He didn't know about Ollie. He didn't know about the body. He must be really traumatised. Unless he's guilty. Unless it's just triggered some kind of flashback.

'What's going on?' Mrs Davies asks, her face contorted in confusion at the gaping hole in the floor and the stack of broken tiles. 'What have you done?'

'It's Ollie,' I say, pointing to the hole in the floor.

'What on earth is going on? You've found Ollie's body? Down there?' Mrs Davies says.

'It moved,' Caitlin says. 'Ollie's body is either possessed – or he was never dead in the first place.'

'I think he's moved himself? Or, maybe, maybe someone kidnapped him and kept him there?' I splutter.

'But, he was dead. We all saw him.' Even Mrs Davies is losing her cool now, which makes me feel even more sick and on edge. She's always the sensible one.

Paul is still sobbing and rocking on his haunches. He appears to be in his own world. His eyes are distant and staring at nothing. 'I was trying to help him,' he says. 'I was only trying to help.'

'What do you mean?' Mrs Davies asks.

Paul is shaking his head. 'He was freaking out. Really, really, really bad. Completely freaking out. He needed a trip killer.'

'He'd had the truffles?' I ask.

Paul nods his head quickly and urgently, wiping the snot from under his nose with the back of his hand. 'OK,' I say. 'So he had the truffles. Then what?'

'He was so bad, so *so* bad.'

We're all urging Paul to finish what he's saying but the state he's in none of us want to push him over the edge. We let him gather himself before he speaks again.

'Jack said . . .'

'Jack said what?' I say.

Steven appears behind us. 'What the hell is going on?' he

asks, then he peers into the hole and his face loses all trace of composure. 'What the . . .'

'Secret basement,' I say. 'With a half-dead DJ inside.' Steven stands still, staring down into it.

'What the hell . . . ?'

'Ollie. He's down there,' Caitlin says. 'And he's alive. Well, almost. I mean, he's not responding. He's undead, at least.'

Steven moves towards the steps.

'What are you doing?' Caitlin snaps.

'This can't be right. It'll be the dark, playing tricks. It's probably Iggy,' he says.

I know that's not what we saw. I know it's dirty, naked, human flesh down there, all skin and bone. All angled and impossible.

'I'm going down there,' Steven says. 'Give us your phone.' Caitlin reluctantly hands it over and Steven cautiously makes his way down the steps, his head eventually disappearing into the darkness. We can see him moving the torchlight around.

'Ollie,' he says. 'Ollie, can you hear me?' No answer.

'What do you mean when you say he needed a trip killer?' Mrs Davies asks Paul.

'Clora-clora – clora-something.'

'But what was it meant to be?' Mrs Davies asks.

'Jack said it would kill his bad trip. Bring him round. But it didn't. I think he had too much. It's overloaded him. Overflowed. Like the blood.'

'What blood?' Caitlin asks.

'The fountain blood,' Paul says. Caitlin looks at me and we are both completely confused. Paul is making sense one minute, and then saying something completely bizarre the next. Can he really be going in and out of reality like this?

'Where'd you get it?' I ask. 'The trip killer.'

'Jack. Said he's used it before, in situations like . . . this.' He gestures to the hole in the floor. 'But it must have been too much. He must have drunk, like, loads of it.'

'Oh dear God,' Mrs Davies says. 'Poor Ollie.'

Then we hear a sound. Like a thud. We all peer down into the black hole below.

'What was that?' I say, directing my voice into the void.

Steven calls up from down below. 'I just checked him. He's not alive. I mean, he's cold and rigid and unresponsive.'

'He was making sounds before,' Caitlin says.

'Well what can I say, sister? He isn't now. Maybe you were tripping?'

'Fuck off, Steven.'

'What do we do?' I ask, knowing that nobody is going to do the sensible thing. I say it anyway. 'Should we call . . .'

'No!' Steven says firmly. 'Paul'll go down for this. I mean, for all we know, this whole psychosis thing, it might be rather convenient, don't you think?'

Paul starts wailing again. 'How did he end up down there though?' As he says it he seems genuinely perplexed. But then again, everything about Paul is genuinely perplexed at the moment. He could have done all this while in a complete state and not have the recall. And they say, don't they, when you're high or whatever, you can find an impossible strength.

'But did you actually give it to him?' I ask Paul. 'Do you know how much he had? Do you even know if it was the right thing?'

I can see that I'm distressing Paul further still.

'It doesn't matter,' Steven says firmly. 'We found him almost twenty-four hours ago. We never called an ambulance. James is still missing. Paul's . . . logic is still missing. It's a disaster waiting to happen.' Steven swipes his hands together, removing the dust.

'It already has happened,' Mrs Davies says firmly. 'Why did I listen to you in the first place? If we had just called the police there and then, he might have been saved.'

Paul looks up at us all, squinting in confusion.

'But he . . . he was dead. I mean, we rolled him up, put him in the bloody wine fridge. How is this even possible?'

We all look back to the hole in the floor where Steven is now half visible, his head popping up from out of the darkness.

'What do you mean you rolled him up?' Paul says, still sobbing. 'What's happening? What's going on? Is it them? Iggy?'

I rub Paul's shoulders but decide there's no time to indulge in whatever chaos his mind is serving up right now. So strange that he's focused on Iggy. He loves that goat.

'Steven, check his pulse,' Mrs Davies says. 'Check his wrists, check his neck.'

'He was definitely alive before. He moaned,' I say. 'At least, I think he did. Unless there was someone else . . .'

'Don't be ridiculous,' Steven says, heading back down under the floorboards. We all stand stock still, focusing on the floor. Aside from Paul, who is now muttering something to himself.

Steven calls up. 'He's definitely dead this time,' he says. 'And he's rigid as steel.'

'But how?'

'He can't have . . . ?'

'I don't understand.'

We are all talking over one another. Has Paul done this? He is still shaking and crying.

I look into his eyes and there is a genuine fear. And I see him, the real him. And knowing Paul, regardless of how wasted he might have been, he won't have tried to hurt anyone. It's not in his nature.

If he did, he certainly never meant to. There was no malice. He was obviously trying to help him. But it would still be manslaughter, wouldn't it? At the very least. And we are all implicated now.

Paul locks his focus on me, just for a moment. And it's like he's finally back in the room. His eyes look desperate. And I wonder if what I heard in the ice house, maybe he wasn't being disloyal. Because I know Paul. Out of everyone I know him. Maybe it was part of a bigger plan? Maybe Caitlin has been manipulating him?

'What's going on?' A haughty voice suddenly breaks my thought pattern and the usual rush of dread associated with its tone floods me.

Mrs Davies quickly races towards Granny, who is standing in her dressing gown. 'Oh, Lady Morland. Really nothing for you to worry about. There's a problem with the drains.'

'That's right,' Caitlin says, moving towards them and trying to obscure what's happening in the background. 'We're just calling maintenance. Honestly, you go back to bed.' Meanwhile we are all stood stock-still, me hugging Paul tight in the desperate hope that he doesn't start wailing again.

I can hear Granny moan and mutter something as she shuffles back to her room. We wait, still silent, until we hear her door shut behind her. Everyone let's out a collective sigh of relief.

But it hits me then that whoever moved the body couldn't have been Paul. Paul wasn't here between us putting it in the walk-in wine cellar and it disappearing and making its way down there. So if Paul did have something to do with Ollie's death in the first place, someone else must be involved. Caitlin, maybe? If she's really in cahoots with him over the inheritance?

'OK. We need to move fast,' Steven says. 'Kassie, get that wheelbarrow. Mrs Davies, have you got Paul's pills?'

'I've got them,' I say, rummaging around in my pocket. 'Here. Paul. I think you could do to take a couple of these.'

He pushes his head backwards, his chin into his chest. 'No. I'm not having them.'

'Paul, please. You're really not well,' I plead. 'You need to rest. You have to get some sleep.' I feel desperate but he's having none of it. Then Caitlin snatches the packet off me and leans in close to Paul.

'Paul, darling. Trust me. I really need you to take these now.'

He looks up at her, lifting his chin slowly back away from his chest. 'But what are they?'

'Just to knock you out. Get some sleep. I mean, you can't really want to be conscious with all this crap going on, hm?' She takes two pills from the blister pack and holds them in her palm. 'Please Paul. Do it for *me*.' He eventually takes the tablets from Caitlin's hand and swallows them down.

'Can I see?' she says. And he obediently opens his mouth. How has she done that? He doesn't even like her. I thought it was Paul and I who were close. But then all that stuff in the ice house. What's with these two?

'I'll take him to his room,' Mrs Davies says in a loud whisper. 'You lot – get this cleaned up. And fast. Before she gets up again.'

Chapter 34

Kassie

Monday morning

I check my phone. It's gone 5 a.m. Barely night anymore. We've literally five hours until the public are being let into the grounds, and we are currently wheeling a dead body across the lawns in a wheelbarrow.

We covered Ollie's punctured, broken body back up with a blanket. The tarpaulin was nowhere to be seen. It wasn't left in the fridge, and it wasn't in the basement according to Steven. Although it was dark down there.

I imagine us being caught on camera doing this. Three Morland siblings lugging a heavy wheelbarrow across the lawns in the early hours of the morning. This can't look normal no matter how you try to justify it.

I look up to the sky to check there are no planes or helicopters in the distance. Not that I'd see them before I heard them, of course. But it all feels so . . . exposed. Committing a crime as the morning light creeps in, in open grounds.

Steven stops every few feet for a breath and to wipe his brow. He's wearing wellies, which I'm not convinced were the best choice of footwear for the task in hand but this is where we're at. I'm grateful of the little pauses, as the morning air is still close and stuffy, and I feel increasingly clammy.

I glance back towards the main house and notice that all the curtains are still closed. Although it looks as though Paul's curtains are twitching, slightly. Flashes of light keep escaping from behind the fabric. His state of mind seems to be getting worse and worse. And we know full well that if he has the chance, he'll spill all. He's so racked with guilt and trauma over whatever he gave Ollie. It wasn't his fault, but in us moving the body like this, we've made the situation ten times worse for him. He could have got off with a misdemeanour or whatever you call it.

We're approaching the lake, which is to be the final resting place for Ollie. Steven manoeuvres the wheelbarrow so it sits directly in front of the water. He stands back and takes a deep breath in, hands moving to his hips as he surveys the scene. Everything is silent but for the leaves rustling gently in the trees. The sky is calm, as if it has no idea what is happening in full view of it.

'Go on then,' Caitlin says, her head turning away from the contents of the wheelbarrow.

'What just, drop him in?' I say. 'Just like that?'

'What do you want?' Caitlin whispers loudly. 'A fucking funeral service? Shall we sing a song?' She poses dramatically, arms out, and breaks into chorus. '*Amazing grace, how sweet the sound . . .*'

'Fucking hell, Caitlin, keep it together, will you,' I snap.

'You're the one who said me *not* reacting to the situation was weird.'

'Yeah, but I didn't want you to belt out a funeral banger at the top of your lungs when we're trying to . . .'

'Shh!' Steven commands. 'We need to do it fast. And quietly.' He looks at Caitlin. 'We need to do this, calmly and quietly, and get back inside before Granny sees.'

'Are we quite sure this is the best place though? Shouldn't we be walking along the lakeside for a bit, get him further away from the house?' I ask. 'You know, off the beaten path and all that.'

'Oh for God's sake,' Caitlin snaps. 'Steven, just do it already.'

'But what if he floats?' I say. 'What if some cute little family are walking along by the lakeside, eating ice cream, and then Ollie's body suddenly pops up to the surface?'

'We've done what we can. The scuba belt should keep him down,' Caitlin says. 'Besides, he's not as big as Steven.'

We'd already attached Steven's Scubapro weight belt around him – well, Steven did, anyway – before we set off from the house.

'But is it enough?' I say.

'It'll have to be,' Steven says. 'Look, we've got no choice. We're more at risk if we don't do it quickly. Sun's coming up. We've just got to do it.'

Caitlin and I watch as Steven picks up the wheelbarrow handles and wrestles one end of it up into the air, but Ollie doesn't move. Steven is standing, panting for breath, his arms shaking with the weight of it. 'Jesus. Can you two give me a hand, please.'

'What the hell do you want us to do?' Caitlin says.

'Oh I don't know. Help to slide him from the barrow, perhaps?' Steven says, a look of incredulity on his face. Caitlin and I reluctantly make our way towards the front of the barrow where Ollie's lifeless and marbling head is dangling over the edge. We push more of the blanket underneath the body so we don't have to directly touch the cold, grey skin and bone.

'Hunch his head up onto the side and angle his shoulders,' I say, and – protecting our skin with the material – we manoeuvre Ollie's head and shoulder over the lip of the wheelbarrow. He slumps downwards but then stops.

'His other shoulder!' Steven calls, and we lift that up and over too. Eventually, the body flops, awkwardly, loudly, into the lake, making a huge splash that catches my eyes. I wipe them clean, pulling a face, wondering whether I now have a dead person's DNA welding itself onto the juices of my eyeball.

'Well,' Caitlin says. 'If ever a fling were short and sweet.'

Steven and I turn our heads to look at her, but she simply nods, turns on her heel, and storms back towards the house. We both stand, silently, and stare into the murky water.

Chapter 35

Monday 25th August

10.19

'Look at that goat, Mummy.'

'Yes, very cute. OK, now, keep back. Katie! Katie! What did I just say?'

'Can I have an ice cream?'

The little girl runs towards the coffee shop, her T-shirt billowing out behind her, making her legs look even skinnier. Her ponytail swishes as she leaves two women standing, one resting on a pushchair, cropped jeans and flip-flops. She speaks: 'Honestly, you did right. Summer holidays are a fucking mare.'

The women begin walking away from the camera in the direction of the little girl. The camera follows them.

'I think we have a friend,' the other woman says, laughing.

The two heads turn back around to the camera and peer into it for a moment. 'Cute. It's probably spoilt though. Like them.'

'The family?'

'Aye. The landlady in the local told me all about them when we moved in. Called them a Frankenstein family. Said they were positively monstrous.'

'No?!'

'Oh aye. And that's not all. The middle son, Paul I think. He was caught flashing school kids last year. At the bus stop. Stark bullock naked and off his face. Oh. Hang on . . . What is it, darling? . . . It's in my bag. I'll get you a . . . in a minute. Just wait for Mummy.'

'Seriously?'

'One of the locals got it on camera. Well, actually, he was sent it. From someone inside the house, I think. I'm guessing the staff all hate them. Probably some downtrodden servant.'

'What happened with it?'

'Family found out so . . . he was paid off, of course. It's the way they work, isn't it. Keep it all quiet.'

'Privileged fuckers.'

'Oh aye I knaa. Oh and . . . you'll never guess . . . in a minute, sweetheart . . . yes, I'm just coming . . . just run along . . . you know they don't even own the place.'

'No?'

'No! It's in trust or something. Some relative has final say-so. So they're like fighting between them over who should have it.'

'Can't they just share it?'

'Something to do with the old gardener. Well, not old, I mean. The last gardener, before the current one. Eeh, Josie, honestly, rumour has it he looked like Cillian Murphy.'

'No!?'

'I know! But anyway, there's some story about him. The gardener. Died though. Suspicious circumstances. I bet they don't have *that* in their visitor guide.'

Chapter 36

Kassie

Monday morning

We're all sitting around anxiously in the living room as we wait on the results of the inspection. Jack has joined us too. He's had a couple of hours of sleep but still looks slightly vacant. He's pacing the room as he waits for his lift home.

I dangle my feet over the edge of the sofa, Iggy curled up on the rug and a horror movie on TV in a bid to distract myself. It's not working. Steven is sitting with his reading glasses on, poring over accounts on his iPad Pro, and Caitlin is watching Jack like a hawk. He is aware of her fixed gaze and keeps his eyes lowered.

Meanwhile, we currently have a very stern-looking man and woman being escorted around the estate by Dennis, checking on the outstanding issues from last time.

Paul, of course, is currently MIA in the grounds, and Mrs Davies is desperately trying to track him down before he puts his foot in it.

Steven says we should lock him in his room but we can't do that. Human rights and all that. It's not like it's our call to make as to whether or not he's got capacity. Although, he clearly hasn't. But it still doesn't feel right.

Caitlin stands and walks over to Jack. 'How are you feeling, Jack Rabbit?' she says, rubbing her hands up and down his arm. I notice Steven look over to her with disdain.

'Yeah. Not bad. Just need a good sleep,' Jack says, his hand shaking as he picks up the pint of water from the bureau. It's cloudy and clearly has some kind of painkiller or vitamin or something mixed into it.

'I'm worried about Paul,' Caitlin says. 'He's not been this bad in—'

'I know. Think he just really let loose because of the impending inheritance stuff, I guess.' Jack takes another gulp of his cloudy drink. He is much quieter than usual.

'Any idea what "trip killer" means?' Caitlin asks.

Jack's head suddenly jerks to attention. 'How do you mean?'

'Paul keeps saying it. We're trying to work out what he means.'

Jack shifts on his feet and puts his drink back down on the bureau. I notice him glance at the shake in his hand. He places it in his pocket. 'It's an antidote to hallucinogenics. In an off-label kind of way, anyway.'

'Antidote?' I ask.

'They're actually antipsychotics. But sometimes, if someone's having a bad trip, it can help bring them round.'

'Right,' Caitlin says. 'So did Paul have one?'

'No. That DJ. Ollie.'

My eyes suddenly widen. 'So what exactly is it?' I ask. 'What's its official name?'

'Chlorpromazine. It's a syrup, rather than a pill,' he says.

'Paul could do with some of that himself,' Steven says, uncrossing and crossing his legs, disparagement emanating from him.

Just then Mrs Davies walks in. 'Your car's here, Jack.' He nods, downs the rest of his drink, places the empty glass down and goes to leave. He turns at the last minute and addresses Caitlin. 'Let me know how he is will you?' he says. She nods and smiles.

Once Jack's left the room I grab my phone, type in 'chlorpromazine' and hit search. I try to work out which results will be the most reliable. I click on one of the links. 'Ah. Right. So yes, it can come in syrup form and . . . hang on.' I scroll down the page to read the warnings. 'It says here, if you overdose, it can cause a thing called catalepsy.'

'What's that?' Caitlin asks. 'What like catatonia?'

'Not quite,' I say reading on. 'But. Oh shit. Fuck no.' My throat tightens at the realisation of what may have happened to Ollie.

'What?' Caitlin gasps. 'What is it?'

'Catalepsy can make you appear as though you're dead. Like, people have actually presumed people dead when they really weren't. It apparently causes people to become stiff and rigid – as per rigor mortis. Except they're not actually in rigor mortis. They just look and feel as though they are.' My heart hammers when I think about the fact we might have been able to save him. If we weren't so hellbent on covering our own tracks, he might still be alive.

'So what are we thinking?' Steven says. 'That Ollie, desperate to escape his hellish psilocybin trip, downed a bit too much of the antidote, his body went into some weird state, he fell down the stairs and ended up a literal stiff. And being mistaken for a stiff. And being manhandled like a stiff.'

Caitlin shoots him daggers. 'What if Ollie wasn't dead at all? Oh my God. We put him in the wine fridge. Did we . . .'

'No,' I say. 'We can't have. Because he got out of the fridge. He was in the secret basement. What if . . . what if he had that . . .' I check the wording on the phone screen '. . . catalepsy. And, I don't know, came round or something.'

'It's possible,' Steven says. 'I guess.'

'Can't be the case,' Caitlin says. 'That's crazy. We didn't know there was a secret basement down there. How the hell would Ollie know?'

I think about that poor man. If this is indeed what happened, it's not Paul's fault. Jack, well, if he knew what it was for he should have known better. But surely they would have classed it as a misadventure. An unfortunate accident. They were genuinely trying to help him.

Shit. They were trying to help him reduce the effects of the truffles that I provided the hallucinogens for. I could still be done for manslaughter if all this comes out. Because that was the root cause of all this at the end of the day.

I shudder at the mess we're in. I shudder at the nature of what we've done. The hideousness of a man approaching his deathbed apparently wandering around the halls in the middle of the night and somehow ending up in a basement we didn't even know we had. He must have still been tripping. And cataleptic. Or whatever it is.

But how can he go from being in that state, all rigid and stiff, to being able to move again? It still doesn't make any sense to me. Paul was simply not in the house when the body moved – or was moved.

'Did James know?' Steven says, lighting up a cigarette. 'About the basement?'

'If *we* didn't know, how the fuck was James meant to

know? Besides, it was tiled over. So how is it even possible?' Caitlin says.

'Well someone got him in there,' I say. 'And something's traumatised Paul. I'm going to go look for him again.' I pull my Doc Martens back on my feet and head out of the house.

I try the ice house first of all. It's already open to the public, but I'm not even sure he'd notice. Which is a particularly worrying thought. I can't understand how nothing's knocking him out. He looked as though he was taking the pills. But maybe he's been shovelling coke up his nostrils the whole time to combat it? He's uncontrollable at the minute. And out of all of them the last one I want anything bad to happen to.

I wander into the ice house, which is completely empty. Although, a frightening thought strikes me as I glance over towards the fenced-off well at the back of it. What if Paul's fallen?

I walk over to it tentatively and take a deep breath. I look down, bracing myself. Imagining my brother all twisted and mangled like Ollie was.

There's no Paul. Thank God. But there is something.

I peer more closely. Angel wings. Naomi's angel wings lying in the pit.

I leave the ice house and head back into the main house, a million different scenarios and explanations running through my mind. I WhatsApp the Morland Twats group.

> Paul's not in the ice house.
> Think we need to try main house.
> Public are coming in.

We rarely go in the main house beyond our apartment –

other than for our own parties or formal public occasions we need to be present for. Hence me looking everywhere else first. But, given Paul's fractured state of mind at present, it was definitely worth a look. He certainly hasn't been going about business as usual. He might have even left the estate. Gone to the police to confess all. Who knows?

I walk in through the main entrance. The hall itself is currently empty but I can see and hear people walking around on the balconies above me. It's not overly busy yet, thankfully, but a few early birds have trickled in. I walk through the main hall and up the first flight of stairs on the left-hand side. Then I spot a couple standing at the entrance to the collections store, looking into one of the rooms from just inside the doorway. They have their backs to me so I hover close by to listen in.

'Think we should tell someone?'

'Well, I guess. I mean, this stuff's got to be worth a fortune . . .'

'Not just that, it might have significance. It's probably stolen from some other country . . .'

'Is everything OK?' I ask brightly, interrupting them and catching them off guard. They both jump slightly and turn to me, their faces pinched with concern.

'Oh, do you . . . do you work here?' the man asks, clearly suspicious and looking me up and down for some kind of identifying badge.

'I do, yes. Is there a problem?'

'I think that guy's trying to steal from the display cases,' the woman says, leaning in my direction and whispering. 'But he's doing it in full view. I'm not sure if something's wrong with him?'

I peer in and see Paul sitting on the floor cross-legged

in front of an open cabinet. I feel relieved. He's OK. But he won't be if I don't get him out of here with as little fuss as possible. 'OK. I'll deal with it,' I say.

'Do you need us to call backup? From one of the volunteers downstairs?' the woman asks.

'I mean, I can wait around, help you out, if . . .' the man says.

'Oh that's so kind of you but no, honestly, you both carry on with your tour. I'll be absolutely fine. He's, um, he's a regular visitor. We know each other.'

They walk off, and I can feel their eyes on me and hear quiet whispers. 'How can she handle that on her own?' the woman says. 'Patricia, I did offer,' the man says defensively.

I take a deep breath and walk into the room.

'Paul, what on earth?' God knows how he's got into the cabinet in here; they're under lock and key. It's the collections room for god's sake. It's where all the valuables are displayed. And some of the items that are centuries old. I mean, we could *ask* for the key, it's our family's stuff after all, but nobody mentioned anything to any of us about a wandering middle brother requesting keys to the family jewels.

He ignores me so I walk a little closer. 'Paul. What's going on?' I say as gently and calmly as I can. He has a rucksack on the floor next to him and is taking the two gilt bottles from the display case. I look inside the rucksack and can see he's got the freaky 1940s puppet in there too. We might all hate that fucking puppet, but it's got a backstory; it's worth a fortune and it's especially delicate.

I'm about to crouch next to him to try and talk him round when a voice makes me jump.

'What's going on in here?' It's Granny.

'Oh, nothing, just . . .' I try to play down my concern.

She takes one look at him and can tell the state he's in. He looks as though he simply isn't present. Like he's in another dimension. 'He should not be out in public. Get him back to your quarters,' she barks.

Paul still says nothing. He's completely silent. He's definitely not just high. Oh God, I hope he hasn't had any of that trip killer or whatever the hell it is too. I can't deal with Paul ending up like Ollie.

I glance towards the door and can see that we now have a volunteer stationed there to direct the public away. They won't be happy though. Regular visitors love the collections rooms. 'I'll take Paul back to the wing,' I say.

'I suggest you knock him out with something too, darling. We can't risk this happening again.'

I stand up to leave, pulling Paul to his feet. He barely resists but he's so heavy – and his eyes remain fixed on the gilt bottle he's still holding.

'And if you can return those items to Dennis,' Granny adds, 'he'll get them checked over before we put them back.' I nod and walk towards the door, dragging a reluctant Paul behind me.

We get back to the wing and I chuck a blanket over him. I'm just trying to keep everything calm when Steven bursts in, phone in hand.

'Paul!' he shouts.

'Sh!' I say.

'Have you seen what he's done?'

'The collections, I know. Granny said . . .'

Steven holds his phone out in front of me. I take it from him and study the moving picture on the screen. 'It's Paul,' I say, as I watch footage of my brother, leaning on a car bonnet and drinking from a bottle in the pub car park.

'Yeah. All over Instagram. I can't believe he's done this again.'

'Can you stop talking about me like I'm not here?' Paul mumbles.

'Oh look who's back in the room. I swear you're putting it on,' Steven snaps.

'He's not putting it on, Steven. He's not well,' I say. But then I do have to wonder. Could he be exaggerating it? If he knows he's done something to Ollie, could he be ramping up his poor state of mind to show diminished responsibility or something?

'Please,' Steven says. 'He partied too hard. Again. As per fucking standard. Can we stop making excuses for him?'

'What about the excuses you make?' Paul asks, eyeing Steven.

'What's that supposed to mean?'

Paul looks at Steven and I swear there is fear in his eyes. Perhaps he's coming round to reality more quickly than I thought.

'Yes, yes,' Steven says. 'And fountains flow with blood and goats speak to the devil, blah, blah, blah-de-fucking-blah. Nobody can believe a word that comes out of your mouth. Not even you.'

'You fucking hypocrite,' Paul suddenly yells. 'You fucking hypocrite.' He leaps off the sofa and goes to run from the room. I try to stop him but he's too fast.

'Nice one, Steven. He'll end up on all the bloody socials now.'

Chapter 37

Paul

Monday

Shadows race around me, getting closer and closer. I can almost feel them on me, itching at my skin. A fucked-up merry-go-round with shadows of goats and dolls and Caitlin moving in and out, back and forth.

I feel sick. I move towards the barrier and look into the depths of the ice house. Naomi's angel wings.

Oh my God. She's down there. Naomi's down there.

Paul
Paul

I jump onto the wooden barrier and swing my leg over, almost missing the ladder on the other side. I push my foot onto the rung, and swing my other leg over to join it. My hands are shaking as I grip hard and descend into the pit.

Paul
Paul
Paul.

I move at pace, my feet finally hitting the floor. I grab

Naomi's wings, move them to one side, kneel on the ground and dig with my hands. Grabbing dirt and mud and stones and dust.

Paul

Paul

Paul

She's down there. I put her there. Just like I put Ollie down. Will she come back too?

Chapter 38

Kassie

Monday

Caitlin is in the kitchen on her own, her phone to her ear. She's pacing frantically. I pause at the door. She's angry. She holds the phone out in front of her and says, 'Bye to you too,' then presses the screen and turns to look at me.

'Kassie, darling. How are you doing? Has Paul been recovered yet?'

She talks about my brother as though he's a simple liability. 'He was, but then Steven kicked off, giving him grief about all sorts and he flipped out again. Honestly, if Paul's the bomb, Steven's the . . .' I lose my word and click my fingers in front of me, trying to find it.

'Detonator?' Caitlin says.

'Exactly. Detonator. He's undoing everything we're trying to do. *He's* the biggest liability.'

Caitlin puts her phone in her trouser pocket and it reminds me of what I found in her bedside drawer. 'Problems in paradise?' I say. She frowns at me. 'You sounded pissed off? On the phone?'

'James,' she says.

'James. You've heard from him?'

Just then Steven walks into the kitchen.

'Yeah. I mean, nothing to do with Ollie,' Caitlin says, looking over to Steven. 'Well, everything to do with Ollie but nothing to do with, you know. What happened,' she says the last two words in an exaggerated whisper.

I shake my head. 'Remind me not to get married,' I say light-heartedly, even though I suspect there's far more to it. The phone in her room, for starters.

'Was that James? On the phone?' Steven asks. 'What happened to him? Why did he leave so suddenly?'

'I think just having Ollie in such close proximity sent him over the edge.' She leans in close to me. 'But he won't have had anything to do with . . . you know.'

'Cait,' Steven says, 'there's a dead body in our bloody lake and your husband, who clearly had issues with him, hasn't been seen since. If you've just spoken to him, you must know where he is.'

'Honestly, *Steve*,' she says trying to goad him. 'He didn't say. He's just pissed off about Ollie having been here . . .'

'So he's clearly a suspect.'

'Not now we know Paul's . . .'

'Maybe he talked Paul into it?' I offer.

'Look. We know what Paul said. There's a rational explanation, Paul explained it to us, so we know what happened.'

'I don't think we can take what Paul says seriously,' I say.

'Um, yeah. Because it makes sense. It stacks up,' Caitlin says.

'No, I'm sorry. But in my mind, it doesn't rule out James. Or you,' Steven says pointing towards Caitlin. 'Motive is a powerful thing. And betrayal is a powerful reason for motive to kill.'

'Caitlin,' I say, realising that if I don't start to ask the question I'll never ask it. 'Why was Ollie's phone in your bedside drawer?'

Her smile drops and her face pales. I can't decide if it's out of shock, or being caught out. James could have put it there after all.

'What's this?' Steven snaps.

She opens her mouth, about to say something, when Granny enters the kitchen, followed by Mrs Davies and Dennis.

'Unbelievably,' Granny says, 'you've passed the inspection.' I feel the air release from my body. 'However,' she continues firmly, 'your father would be mortified at your behaviour this weekend,' she says, looking at each of us in turn. We all hang our heads like naughty children. It's like a knee-jerk reaction to her. 'Turning in his grave. And that stunt you pulled,' she says pointing at me, 'that could have scuppered the inspection. Thank God for James.'

I frown. Steven frowns too. And Caitlin looks just as shocked.

'I'm sorry? James?' Steven says.

'Yes. He's used his influence. Smoothed things over. With the Taylor-Banks family. You could do with taking a leaf out of his book, Steven.'

Steven shifts uncomfortably on his feet. 'To be fair on us all, we are managing the estate well. If I had known about Kassie's behaviour when it happened I would have smoothed it over myself.'

'*My* behaviour?' I say, shocked.

'But you didn't, did you?' Granny says. 'And you're the one who refused to allow the estate to be split four ways. So, I wouldn't get so defensive.'

'You know I can't be responsible for Kassie and Paul's behaviour.'

I am livid. I cock my head at him and my jaw drops slightly but no words come out of my mouth.

'As the eldest, you should be leading the way,' Granny says harshly. 'You're letting the others run riot. These bloody parties. Networking you say?' She narrows her eyes in Steven's direction. 'Out of all of you, I don't know who's the worst.' She sighs and eyes us in turn. 'If I have to sign over to young Kassie and her goat it'll be a terrible day.'

I suddenly feel all eyes burning into me. That's got to be the worst thing she could have said to Steven and Caitlin. And of course the worst thing she could say to me. She's clearly already ruled me out. And now she's using me as some kind of worst-case scenario.

'But, Granny,' Caitlin says, 'I thought we . . .' She leans in close to Granny. 'I thought we had an understanding.'

Steven leans closer. 'Pray tell.'

'Your sister is referring to the fact that she has been doing the hard sell on me for some time. Not that it makes much difference given the state of her relationship right now. James is terribly upset over your indiscretion with that disc jockey, Caitlin,' Granny says. 'If he can't forgive you, well . . .'

Steven and I both start paying even more attention now.

'It's all fine,' Caitlin says. 'He just called me. I literally just spoke to him.'

'But I thought he just hung up on you?' I say.

'Stop stirring the pot, Kassie,' Caitlin says.

'That's rich.'

'Can you please be quiet,' Granny continues. 'You are all just proving my point. It seems to me that none of you are, frankly, capable. Except, perhaps for James – and his link to this family is hanging in the balance. In fact, in terms of vision, Kassie's the only one showing any degree of sensibility, but she still has much to learn.' Granny turns to me. 'You're too liberal, dear. You don't get by in life by being generous, you know.'

'But Kassie isn't like us . . .' Steven says, desperately.

'Thank God,' I mutter. He shoots me a look.

'Exactly,' Granny says. 'She's sensible. But she's not ready either.' She looks at me and plasters a sickening, patronising smile across her face. 'There's no place for rich little socialists in today's world. You'll be rejected by absolutely everyone, darling.' Granny sits back up and looks around the room. 'And this place. Honestly. There's smashed tiles in the corridor. Your brother's high on drugs and running around like a crazed headless chicken on opening day. You threw a party that, frankly, I have no idea how you managed to remove the evidence of given the reports of vomit and bodies lying around everywhere that I heard from Dennis.'

We all remain silent. Unsure what to say that could make the situation any better.

'And now,' Granny continues. 'Now your brother's going to be all over social media. Again. Another blow to this family's reputation. I've seen and heard enough. I'm leaving. And I honestly, honestly do not know how I'm going to come up with my answer by tomorrow morning.'

Steven looks like his face might explode. 'I have to say, as the eldest—' he interjects.

'*You* should be doing better!' Granny snaps, standing up out of her chair. She walks over to the window and signals to her driver that she's ready to leave. We can see him, leaning on the bonnet of the car. He catches her eyes, places his phone back in his pocket and stands to attention.

She commands so much authority it's terrifying.

But money is power and power can be dangerous in the wrong hands. You see, we're in the thick of it. We're all concerned about how this is going to affect us. But our family's money has far-reaching consequences. We can say, without any legal intervention because, frankly, who would dare challenge the Morlands, whenever we want a leaseholder off our land. We can chuck a member of the public off our property. We can give to charity and take it away again with no warning. We can throw parties and silence the gossips.

We can even hide dead bodies.

For now, at least.

I think back to Ollie. It's been quiet on that front. Nobody's been looking for him; the police haven't called. But it's only been a matter of hours. So of course nobody will be missing him yet. He probably won't have another gig until the weekend – maybe Thursday at the earliest. We have a few more hours' grace, I'm sure. But what happens after bank holiday weekend is over? What happens when his mum or girlfriend or boss or whoever are missing him? We might have taken care of the body, although that's perhaps a strange way of describing what we did, but we haven't taken care of the narrative. Of our story. We haven't decided who saw him last, where he 'went' – all of that stuff. And no doubt somebody will have him on video at the decks. There will definitely be questions asked.

We say our goodbyes to Granny, who steps out onto the path and makes her way across the gravel. Dennis helps her into the back seat of the black Jaguar XJ. We stand at the door and we watch as the tyres crackle over the stones, turning the car around. We can make out the outline of Granny sitting upright in the back seat, knowing that she won't look behind her to wave at us but doing our duty nonetheless.

The car makes its way through the mouth of the estate, pausing, indicating and turning left onto the B road. Steven then turns on his heel and storms past me, knocking my shoulder with his. I follow him inside the house.

He storms into the dining room, removes a glass from the cabinet and decants an especially large whisky. Caitlin and I follow him. He downs the whole drink, then fills it back up.

'There's no way *you're* getting your hands on this place,' he shouts, slamming his empty glass back down on the table. 'You're not like us.'

'She was winding you up,' I say, knowing full well it will take more than an idea about using Iggy as a main attraction to get her to take me seriously. But she did focus most of her wrath on Steven today.

'Ignore him, Kassie. He's just in a bad mood,' Caitlin says.

Steven gives her a glare and defiantly pours another whisky while not taking his eyes off her once.

'Oh this is going to be fun,' Caitlin says. 'Paul's on some kind of paranoid, hallucinogenic everlasting bad trip, and you're going to be slurring and dribbling all over the public.'

'Not my problem. If you were listening, it sounds as though Kassie should be in charge. So she can deal with it.'

'Oh don't listen to the old woman,' Caitlin says. 'Like Kassie says, she was winding you up. Besides, she changes her mind on a whim. She just says whatever she wants to toy with us. Keep us being nice to her. Keep us in line.'

'You know what though,' Steven says, puffing his chest out and standing taller now. 'I'm actually not going to let it happen. I don't care what that poisonous old cow says. You . . .' He points at me with his glass, a smirk creeping over his face. 'You don't get to lay a hand on our father's estate.'

'It wasn't my fault,' I cry. 'It wasn't my fault. How could it be? I wasn't even born.'

Steven almost spits out his drink. 'It's the very fact you were born . . .'

'But why? What do you mean?'

'Steven, really. This is getting us nowhere,' Caitlin says. 'We're better sticking together in this. Acting as one.'

I eye Caitlin suspiciously knowing full well she's been sidling up to Granny with her own views on how she can run this place. And now she's got to get James back onside as, clearly, that's what Granny's after. That's the ultimate outcome she wants.

'No!' Steven shouts. 'She's not one of us. No fucking way is she getting her hands on this place. Fucking hell, Cait, I'd even rather you got it.' He storms out just as Mrs Davies walks in, almost knocking her sideways into the doorframe.

Mrs Davies sighs. 'Right. I've had enough of this,' she says furiously, and turns back around.

Chapter 39

Kassie

Monday

I follow Mrs Davies out of the room and into the hallway.

I can hear the conversation flowing in the kitchen. If indeed 'flowing' is the right word for it. It's angry, impatient and kind of staccato.

'But she's not one of us.'

I storm in, my heart hammering in my chest. 'Yeah, so what? Just because I'm not as self-centred and fucking arrogant as you.' I feel angry but also wounded. Like I've been kicked in the chest.

He shakes his head and smirks. 'Ever wonder why? Ever wonder why you're not like us?'

'That's enough, Steven,' Mrs Davies snaps. Steven's on a roll though, downing yet another drink. This time it's red wine. He doesn't care.

'You know, in some ways, it serves our mother right,' he says. 'You, killing her.'

I gasp. So does Mrs Davies. 'I was a baby,' I say, tears

forming. 'No, in fact, I wasn't *even* born. They pulled me fully out just after she stopped breathing. That's what I was told.' I look to Mrs Davies for backup.

'None of this is your fault, Kassie,' she says, placing her hand gently on my shoulder.

'You would say that,' Steven snaps.

'Behave yourself, Steven. Before you say something that could bite you on your arse.'

'I don't understand all these secret chats you've both been having. What's going on?'

'Secret chats?' Mrs Davies says.

'Yes, I've heard you.' I realise I can't fully explain how I've heard all those secret chats without giving myself away, but I think back to a time when I was right there in the room. 'You were stood outside this door.' I point towards the utility room and the door that leads outside from it. 'You were saying something about our inheritance then.'

'*Our*,' Steven says, making theatrical air quotes as he does.

'Well, yes. It is ours,' I say. 'Even if one of us gets handed the overall running of the place, we'll still all have a stake in it. We'll still all have an allowance from it.'

'Not if the old cow has her way,' Steven spits.

'The thing is . . .' Mrs Davies says, pointing a finger at Steven. 'Kassie isn't the only person who has heard us chatting, is she?'

'Not this again.'

'What?' I ask.

'Nothing. It was nothing. Business. And now she's trying to make out I had something to do with Ollie's death. I mean, there's some pretty significant motives swirling around this place and mine's negligible. James, Caitlin – all had reason. And Paul, well, he's practically admitted it. In fact, if he carries on causing us reputational issues we might be better off seeing him incarcerated.'

'No!' I shout. 'Leave him be. He's ill.'

'He's a waster, Kass. Besides, what would you know? The genes you come from.'

'What?'

'Steven, I'm warning you. Don't do it,' Mrs Davies says.

'Don't do what?' I say. 'Will someone just tell me what the hell you're both talking about? Just because I'm the youngest doesn't mean I'm a kid, for Christ's sake.' I look at Mrs Davies who is looking pleadingly at Steven.

'Steven, no.'

'She should know,' he shouts.

'Know what?' I can feel my heart hammering and my mouth has gone dry. But they stay quiet. 'Know what?' I shout, stamping a foot.

'Our mother was having an affair. And not just any affair. She was having an affair with one of the staff.'

I shrug my shoulders. 'Right. So? People have affairs.' This was news to me but, given the weird dynamics and quirks of our family it didn't feel particularly far-fetched. 'Caitlin's always . . .'

Steven interrupts me. 'Jesus Christ are you stupid? It's simple fucking mathematics. Our mother was having an affair. And then you came along.'

Mrs Davies slams her hands down on the table but says nothing. She stands stock-still.

I feel like I've been stung by a thousand nettles. Confusion, clarity, pain and shock ripple through me, smarting me all over my body. I go to speak but nothing comes out.

'Bingo. Penny's dropped. She finally gets it,' Steven says.

'But I was closer to Dad than any of you.'

'On the outside, maybe. Because he made a point. It wasn't natural though, Kass. It was an effort. He was making a point. He'd made a promise to our slut of a mother.'

'Ignore him, Kassie,' Mrs Davies says, turning back around to face us. 'He's drunk. And your grandmother knows he's not fit for the job. Too self-obsessed.'

'She's as blind as everyone else,' he snaps, waving his arm at Mrs Davies. 'Hasn't a clue. Hasn't a clue that her dear, dear son was a total mug. And our dad, bringing up someone else's kid as his own. You're . . .' He looks at me, the corner of his mouth turning down and his nose turning up. 'You're a fucking peasant.'

I feel my chest shudder and a tear starts to form in my eye. I try but I can't hold it in. It swells over my lower lid and balls down my cheek. Mrs Davies walks over to me and puts her arm around me.

'See what you've done? Do you think, whatever your mother did, whatever your father did, whatever he did, that any of this, any of it, is her fault?'

'She reminds me of it all. She looks just like her. When she cries. And she was always crying, our mother, Kassie. But not over our father.'

'That's your problem. Not Kassie's,' says Mrs Davies. 'That's unfair, Steven. Totally unfair.'

'*Life's* unfair.'

I wipe my cheek. 'So who is . . . who is my . . .' I can't bring myself to say it out loud. To make it real. To make it a part of my reality rather than keeping it as part of Steven's angry ramblings.

Steven shifts around uncomfortably and looks out of the

window. A smirk spreads over his face. I hate him more than ever.

'He was the gardener,' Mrs Davies says. Her words cement it as fact. Her words remove all previous knowledge of who I was.

'But. Dad,' I say, more tears falling.

My father. The man I looked up to, ran to. The man I shared my school grades with. Who put a plaster on my hands and knees when I tripped over the fallen branch in the woodland. The man who taught me how to play guitar – to a point.

'Mr Morland was still your dad.' Mrs Davies stands to the side of me and puts her arms on me, squeezing me close. 'He just, you weren't . . .'

'He was never your father,' Steven snaps and strides towards the door. 'And your real one didn't stick around either.'

'You just remember why,' Mrs Davies yells. 'You remember why he never got chance to stick around.'

Steven slams the door behind him and his footsteps thud along the hallway.

'Where is he?' I ask. 'My dad?'

'Oh, Kassie,' Mrs Davies says. 'He was pushed out of having anything to do with you. And then . . . he died.'

Chapter 40

Kassie

Monday

I run back to the cottage, tears streaming down my face. I slow down and walk, quickly, in and around members of the public. I notice strange, concerned looks and try to keep my head down. But my chest wants to roar and sob and scream it all out. I don't want this to be real.

Around me are happy activities in the sunshine. Children eating ice-creams, parents wiping their kids' dirty faces, couples pointing to a map and to the splitting pathways in front of them. It looks like a scene from a National Trust visitor guide. But inside I am dark. I feel like a tree made only of splintered bark, all hollow inside. No idea who I am. And ready to peel and crack into a thousand pieces.

I knew they were different. But I never once imagined this.

There's something that sort of clicks into place and yet, at the same time, makes me feel robbed. Everything about my father was a lie. I was sure he loved me.

But then I think – how could he have? Surely, every time he looked at me he saw the child who killed his wife. The child who only existed because she fucked . . . who? The gardener? Is that all I know? Who even was the gardener?

But a gardener. It all makes sense. That's part of who I am.

I unlock the front door to the cottage and race to the green Welsh dresser. I crouch down and swing the lower cupboard doors open, pulling frantically at the contents. Books and photo albums fall out.

Where the hell is it?

I know I've seen it somewhere. An old, blue velvet photo album that's packed full of newspaper cuttings. There was something about the gardens. Something from the Eighties or Nineties. I remember, in the local press. Before I was born, we'd had some special open day for the public one Christmas, a night-time trail of the gardens, all lit up, guiding a starlit walk for the public, mulled wine gripped in woolly gloved hands. I read all about it. The gardener was quoted. I know he was.

I just can't remember his name. I need to know his name.

When I looked at that cutting, he wasn't important. His name wasn't important. The Morland name, the estate, that was all we cooed over. That was all we got told about. We were always proud of the things other people did – and we took them for ourselves. Because that's what the Morlands did.

But am I even a Morland?

My mother was a Morland only by marriage. So really, who am I?

Kassie who?

I pull everything out but it isn't here. Did I take it back

to the house? I think back. Did I flip through it with Dad? With . . . he's still my dad. He brought me up. He has made me who I am even if I don't look like him.

And I don't, do I? I don't look like the others. My hair is darker. My skin is darker. Paul and Caitlin are all strawberry blonde and freckles. Steven is a pale brunette.

I collapse back on the floor, my legs spread, bordering the mass of books and photo albums I've haphazardly pulled out from the cupboard. I think back to the gardeners we had. The one from my earliest memory was a woman. Then there was, oh, what was his name? Ned, that's it. But he came later. And he was twenty-seven when I was five. He couldn't have had anything to do with my mum. She was so much older. Not that that's a crime, of course. But he came to us later in the proceedings. After I was born, I'm sure of it. And he had an accent. Cornish. That was it. He was from way down south. It wasn't him.

Who was it?

I think about the fact that my father was a gardener.

And now I do it . . . I garden. It's in my soul.

It's in my blood.

It's always felt like home, being out in nature. Potting and pruning and cultivating and harvesting. I wonder if he had a love for animals too. I was the only one of my siblings who spent any time at all with the hens we used to have. I'd pick them up, hold them close. Chat to them. And I brought in many a stray bird as a kid – feeding them scrambled eggs and worms. Caitlin thought it was disgusting and dirty.

Did he love The Cardigans and Belle and Sebastian like I do? Did he dress in black like I do? Did he eat crunchy peanut butter and Marmite like I do? Did he read books about the Romanovs, about London's Victorian streets, about fairies and pixies and enchanted forests?

I've got to find out who he is.

If the scrapbook of newspaper cuttings isn't in my cottage, there's only one other place it will be. My father's old study.

Chapter 41

Kassie

Monday

I close the door quietly behind me and sit on my knees in my father's old study, the mahogany cupboard doors open in front of me, sorting through my father's – the person I thought was my father – belongings. Nothing in this room is in any real order, which I guess is symptomatic of the state of my father's mind in his last few years. Well, in any of his years, if I'm honest. His chaotic way of working was Granny's justification for always sticking her beak into estate business.

But I need to find that scrapbook. Mrs Davies put the book together for us. Nobody else was all that bothered about local newspaper stories. They were above all that 'local community bollocks'. But I liked it. I loved reading about the Christmas opening events and medieval banquets and summer garden parties that used to be held when my mother was alive. She drove all that stuff. She was sociable and, from what I gather, the locals really loved her. It hurts that I was never able to see it with my own eyes. To get to know her for who she really was, rather than the stories my brothers and sisters tell me.

Because of me, her life was cut short.

Because of me. And because of whoever the gardener was back in 1996. And I'm here to find out who he is. And who that makes *me*.

All around me I have stacks of old folders and ring binders full of paperwork, as well as old estate brochures and visitor guides. We really have no need for any of this in today's digital age, but when you live in a historic building the potential for everything you do to have future historical significance is never overlooked. We hoard literally everything relating to this place and who we are. Personally, I think the world would be better off forgetting about us.

I pull out more old books and files until I see a familiar flash of a blue cover. I reach out my hand and can feel the velvety fabric of it. This is it. It's the scrapbook.

My pulse firing at speed, I start to turn the pages of the book. I move through them quickly and impatiently.

There are cuttings showing my mother and father – my *step*father – in front of a huge Christmas tree, a significant number shouting out in the headline to inform the local community just how much they gave to charity that year. Let's be honest, it was more like sponsorship than philanthropy. I look more closely at the picture, the image becoming fuzzy, a collection of dots. But I *can* see that my mother's smile doesn't reach her eyes. They appear vacant. Not like Paul's do at the moment. Just, dull, perhaps. Even though she is wearing lipstick and flashing her white teeth, that smile is definitely forced. My father – *step*father – was not a bad man, but I know it must have been hard for her here.

I continue turning the pages until I come to one with a

black and white image of kids dressed in a white T-shirt and black shorts taking part in an egg and spoon race, our imposing house looming in the background, reminding readers who allowed the frivolities to take place in the first place. I think it was maybe the local school's sports day. They've since had their sports field redone. I know I've seen a cutting on that somewhere too. I think that was a Morland donation.

And then, as I turn to the next page, I am met with a picture that is familiar and new all at once. Huge rhododendrons towering behind a photo of my mother standing next to our gardener.

It hits me like a familiar shock.

He is a handsome man. Dark-haired, just like me. Arched eyebrows, slightly overlapping front teeth. He's good-looking in an imperfect sense. An antidote to this prim and fake world we all strive for perfection in.

He is my father. My blood father.

And my mother's smile reaches her eyes.

I begin reading the paragraphs just as the door opens behind me. I jump and slam the book shut, keeping my hand inside to bookmark the right page. I turn around and see Mrs Davies.

'Kassie, love—'

Her mouth drops open as she looks at what I'm holding in my hands.

Underneath the photo the caption says:

Mrs Jayne Morland in front of her family's legendary rhododendrons. Accompanied by Morland Estate gardener, Mr Jamie Davies.

Chapter 42

Kassie

Monday

I look between the newspaper cutting and Mrs Davies and back again. Then I rest my eyes on her face and I feel as though I'm seeing my reflection for the first time.

'Jamie Davies?' I say.

I can see a lump move up and down in her throat. 'He was . . .'

'Your son,' I say. 'My father, my *real* father . . .'

'Yes.'

'But . . . didn't he . . . wasn't there a fire?'

'Yes,' she says, her eyes glassing over. 'Yes, he died. Before you were born.'

I sit, staring at the photo.

'But that makes you . . .'

'Your grandmother, Kassie. Yes.'

She kneels in front of me and leans forward, taking me in her arms. She holds me tight, close to her, and everything in my core physically sighs in relief. And I sob. And Mrs

Davies – my grandmother – sobs. I feel her back shuddering beneath my arms. It's like relief. And it's as though I've finally found my home.

'Have you always known?' I ask. I feel her chin nodding in the crook of my neck. 'But why didn't you tell me? I've always felt alone. I've always felt like I didn't fit. I could have had family. Real family.'

She pulls away from me and looks at me, her eyes flitting quickly from side to side as the bond between us comes into focus for the first time.

'Your father, your stepdad, I guess, Tony, he truly loved you. He always knew and he always truly loved you. He had his faults – he was as snobby as they come – but deep down, he was a good man. Luckily, your granny's narcissistic tendencies appear to have skipped a generation.'

I let out a laugh and wipe the back of my hand under my snotty nose. Mrs Davies pulls out a pack of tissues from her pocket and offers them to me. I pull out a fresh tissue and wipe my nose again.

'He saw you as his own,' she continues. 'He brought you up; he moulded you as much as my Jamie's genes have. But part of the deal of him raising you was for Jamie to never meet you. Oh, Kassie. I wish he could have seen you. He'd have been so proud.' She places her right palm underneath her chin and squeezes her eyes tight shut.

When she opens her eyes again she sniffs, takes a breath, and speaks again. 'When Mr Morland was dying, he confided in me. He told me he wanted you to have an equal share. To be treated exactly the same as everyone else when it comes to the estate. Because you deserved it. And because I grieved so terribly for Jamie for years.' She looks away, sadness overwhelming her eyes and turns back to face me.

'I've never stopped to be honest. I think about him every single day. But seeing you blossom every day. Seeing the difference in you – and seeing my son in you – that's what's got me through all these years. You have kept me going. You've kept Jamie alive.'

I feel disloyal to both of my fathers now. It all makes sense, but I have no idea how to position them in my mind. In my heart. Can they both co-exist within me? I notice that I am ripping the tissue to shreds within my hand. I try to hold it still.

Thinking about the man who brought me up I feel awed that he took me as his own. And yet I feel confused as to why he would want a portion of the estate, his family's estate – his bloodline – to go to me. The product of an affair. The result of his wife cheating on him.

'I don't understand why he was so kind to me. Surely I reminded him . . .'

Mrs Davies – my grandmother – sighs. 'Because your mother was suffocating. He never blamed her because Lady Morland – your granny – bullied her incessantly. She couldn't breathe in this huge house. She had no agency. On paper, it looked like she had everything. In every newspaper article, she gushed. In every photo, she beamed. But behind the smiles she was crippled with depression. Crippled by Lady Morland's emotional abuse of her.' She looks up to the ceiling and lets out a smile. 'You know, when it all started with Jamie, she began smiling again. Properly smiling.'

'Does Granny know?'

'No. Absolutely not.'

'What happened? To Jamie? He was younger than my . . . than Tony, wasn't he?'

She takes both of my hands in hers and holds them

firmly before whispering close to me. 'You need to listen carefully, Kassie. You need to listen and you mustn't, under any circumstances, react. Keep quiet, Kassie.'

I look deep into her eyes and can see my reflection in them. I have no idea what's coming. But whatever it is, surely nothing can shock me now. This weekend has numbed me to the very worst of humankind. I nod my head.

'Your father. Your real father. Is dead. Because . . .' She takes a breath and I can hear the jerks of her diaphragm singing out through it. She looks towards the ceiling and I can see water forming on her eyes.

'It was the fire, wasn't it? I heard about a fire, about one of the staff dying. Staff, God, I'm sorry, I mean . . .'

She takes another deep breath. 'Remember, do not react. Not now. Save it for later.'

I nod again, quickly, desperate for her to continue.

'He is dead, my boy, your father is dead . . .' she is sobbing now '. . . because Steven killed him.'

Chapter 43

Paul

Monday

Iggy is staring at me. Her eyes are not her own. She has the devil inside her. Smoke is coming from her nose. Dark grey smoke curling into monochrome fractals, spinning and dancing like the devil.

Iggy races out of the ice house, screaming. But the screaming remains, bouncing off the roof of the ice house and hitting me hard in the chest.

I look back at the angel wings. I remember dragging them in here from the lawn. To protect us.

They're a sign. I have to help. I have to save them before it comes for us all.

Chapter 44

Kassie

Monday

Steven killed my father.

The fire. This cottage. It was here. Right here where he died. Is that why I was so drawn to it from the off? Even when it was a ramshackle mess, I wanted to be in here. I needed to be in here.

Closer to my father.

And as far away from his murderer as possible.

And if Steven is capable of murder . . .

But Paul admitted to it. He admitted to providing the medicine that killed Ollie. Or at least, that paralysed him. Surely two of my brothers can't have killed someone?

My brain is swirling, struggling to make sense of it all. Thoughts are flying thick and fast, confusing me with theories and answers to the one thousand and one questions I have.

I realise I'm standing still in the middle of the living room in my cottage. How long have I been here? How can my brain be this frantic and my body this still?

I sit at my laptop, finding the footage from Saturday night. The night of the party when Iggy walked into the wing alone and Steven complained about the estate not really being for me. And when Mrs Davies said his secrets could come out.

The conversation outside when Steven said he was only fourteen. When Mrs Davies was trying to encourage him to put me in favour with Granny. I get it now. She wants vengeance for Jamie's death. For my father's death. But she doesn't want it for herself. She wants it for me.

When she talked about the secrets coming out I thought she meant the usual stuff. I thought Ollie must have overheard something . . . business as usual. I know exactly what my siblings are like. Corrupt business and bribery. Paul's drug taking. Caitlin's insatiable appetite for non-marital sex. But it wasn't anything so staid. It was murder. It was actual murder.

He was only fourteen. But it was driven by hate. She told me exactly what had happened.

Steven walked in on them. Your mother and my Jamie. They were having sex in the cottage, in Iggy's place – before it was Iggy's place of course. Steven was fourteen and full of teenage angst and hormones. As the eldest, he was always keen to take control. To show that he had it in him to manage the place. He saw Jamie as a threat to that. Seeing your mother in the throes of passion with him knocked Steven into third place – in his eyes. Your mother always loved Steven but he was impossible. A dark and gloomy presence since he was a young boy.

Anyway, when I saw him heading to the cottage I tried to catch up with him. But he burst in before I could stop him. I heard him screaming at your mother. Saying he hated her, she was a slut, a slag. I'd never heard him so full of venom. And that's saying something, believe you me. I walked in and tried to call him, but he told me to fuck off back to the 'servants' quarters'. I was angry but not shocked at that. He'd always jostled for position even as a toddler. And then he turned on Jamie, calling him a peasant. Saying he was infecting his mother. His slag of a mother, he repeated. Of course, Jamie, as a grown man, jumped up to deal with Steven. He shouted at him, telling him how dare he speak to his mother like that. Reminding him that he didn't know the truth. That he didn't understand life.

Steven spat something back at him – called him a fucking peasant again or something to that effect. And Jamie leaped forward but I stood in between them. To this day I regret that, because it emboldened Steven. Made him think he was invincible. I guess he thought he could say what he wanted and there would be no consequences. I mean, how could there be? We didn't want anyone else to know about the affair.

Of course, not long after this happened, and just before you were born, we endured the fire. The damage to the smaller cottage next to yours. But it wasn't an accident. It wasn't just a jackdaw nesting in the chimney. It was arson. Arson and locked doors. And that's what killed my boy. My Jamie.

Mrs Davies cried as she told me this, but her tears soon stopped and her look of sadness was replaced with one of rage.

I saw him locking the door. And I knew I needed to

confront him. I decided I would record him on my Dictaphone. I carried it for secretarial purposes. It came everywhere with me. And at first I thought what he was doing was just a childish prank and I would get him to own up to it on tape to share with your mother. So I pressed record and apprehended him as he was locking the cottage doors. I slid it back inside my pocket and then I asked him for the key. We started arguing. He was saying terrible things about your mother, about Jamie. About how thick his father was. He had such disdain for simply everyone around him.

I said I knew Jamie was in the cottage and he needed to let him out and this strange smirk appeared on his face. It was a look of pure evil, Kassie. And it was then that I noticed the flames, licking at the windows from inside. I turned to look and banged on the window, shouting for Jamie. But there was no answer. When I turned back around, Steven had already fled. He was too far away for me to catch him. I was torn. Should I chase Steven for the key knowing full well I wouldn't be able to keep up with a fourteen-year-old boy? Or should I try to find another way in to save my boy?

I called 999. Of course they told me to hang tight and wait. But I couldn't wait for them. Not if there was a chance of getting in and getting him out alive. So I looked around and found a brick and threw it as hard as I possibly could. But I couldn't break the glass. It was thick, enforced stuff. I kept banging on the door, calling Jamie's name and running around to the other doors and windows, desperately trying to reach him. Finally, I spotted him. He was on the sofa, unconscious. A glass of red wine spilled on the floor next to him. It was clear then, what had happened. This wasn't just some prank gone wrong. Steven had spiked his drink, set the fire and locked him in. That's not carelessness. That's not a punch gone wrong. That's pure evil. That's pure, manipulative evil. Steven was callous – psychopathic – from a very young age. I mean, he was a child, Kassie! A kid.

Anyway, I could hear the sirens approaching and as I looked towards the road I saw your mother running out towards me across the lawns from the big house. She knew Jamie was in the cottage and she could obviously see the smoke now as it was billowing up high. It happened so quickly. And she ran to the door, desperately pulling the handle up and down, pushing on it, banging her fists on it over and over and over and wailing. Deep, animalistic wailing. The sirens got louder and I turned to see the engine driving over the grass and towards the cottage. I grabbed your mother and held her tight as she fell into me like a dead weight, bawling.

Kassie, she was never the same again. The glow he ignited in her vanished as soon as she knew. As soon as she realised she was not breaking into that cottage. And she lost her will. That's why she didn't survive the pregnancy. She was too unwell. She wasn't eating. She was weak and frail. It wasn't you, Kassie. You didn't kill your mother. Steven did. He destroyed her.

Steven destroyed your family. Our family.

When she told me this I felt every emotion like a punch in the gut, one after the other. I never got to meet my father because of Steven. And I never got to meet my mother. Not because of me, but because of *him*.

Jamie, my father, was a gardener. He looked after the goats we used to have. Before Iggy was born. She was the last. I know who I am now.

But Steven. I feel like his very name is poison. This whole family is poison.

Steven needs to pay for what he did. Caitlin needs to pay for manipulating Granny and everyone else around us. I am surrounded by pure fucking hate and greed. They need to be stopped.

And I want to be the one to stop them. I owe it to my parents.

Chapter 45

Monday 25th August

16.13

Screaming. Loud, ear-piercing screaming. Like a baby crying but . . . it's not human.

Waaaaaaaaaahhooooo.

Waaaaaaaaaahhhoooooooooo.

The camera is moving frantically from side to side. In front of it, hay is on the ground. It's inside a building. Inside the pen. A face blurs the camera, obscuring everything with beige, too close up and out of focus. Then it moves backwards again, warm brown hair and freckles coming into view. The face sniffs. A hand wipes leaking eyes.

The camera yanks around wildly. It appears to be tethered.

Waaaaaaaaaahhooooo.

Waaaaaaaaaahhhoooooooooo.

A voice. Human this time.

'Do it.'

A hand picks up a knife. Sniffling, sobbing sounds. Human this time.

'You have to. It'll ruin us all.'
'I can't. I can't do it. I can't do it.'
'You have to do it.'
'I can't.'

Flesh. Arms. A struggle. The camera jerking forward. Backwards. Forward.

Waaaaaaaaaaahhooooo.

Waaaaaaaaaahhhooooooooo.

The camera jerks backwards over and over again. More screaming. Scratching. A struggle as hands grasp and grapple. Screams. High-pitched, terrified screams. The glint of a knife catching the sun. Sharp and clean silver.

'I'm sorry, Iggy.'

Chapter 46

Kassie

Monday

I fly out the front door and race around the corner of the house, skidding on the gravel. My heart is pounding; I can hear it in my ears, feel it hammering in my chest. I fall onto rough ground. My knee smarting, I don't even look at the damage. I pull myself up and fly into the paddock and through into Iggy's place. 'Stop!' I scream. 'Stop!' I race over to Iggy.

Paul sits there still. A knife in his hand. Then he drops it to the ground. He is shaking violently.

Paul stands, trembling, then drops back down to his knees, folding forward, the top of his head hitting the ground and his arms splaying out either side of him. He looks like he is praying.

I hold Iggy's face in the crook of my arm, attempting to calm her. I stand in front of her and crouch down, inspecting her. There is no blood. There are no marks. She is simply terrified.

I look back to Paul. 'What the fuck!? What were you thinking?'

He simply remains where he is, his head now banging over and over onto the ground, bits of hay sticking in his hair. He is wailing. Pained. Looking straight into the ground.

'I didn't want to. I said I couldn't. I told you I couldn't do it.' He is screaming into the empty room behind us.

Who is he talking to? Is he talking to me? Is he hearing voices? What is he talking about?

I untie Iggy and cuddle her. She rubs her face into mine, her wiry hair mingling with my messy bun, pulling it loose. But I don't care.

'I thought I was losing you,' I say. 'Darling baby girl.'

Paul sits up now, hitting his head with the base of his palm over and over and over, his forehead pinched in anguish. I watch him, Iggy still pushing her face into my hair.

'Paul. Paul. Look at me.'

He carries on hitting his forehead. 'Paul!' I shout. He looks up at me, his eyes vacant but for a glint of a tear. His face is blotchy and puffy. Redness fighting against his freckles, eyes swollen like wet paper.

Then the door to the back of Iggy's place slams shut.

Someone else was here.

Chapter 47

Paul

Tuesday morning

I open my eyes and see daylight for the first time in . . . it must be days. It's like a tinted film has been removed from my eyes. I look down at where I'm lying. I'm not in my room. And the sound of Iggy screaming replays over and over in my head. What was I doing?

What was I thinking? What the fuck have I done this time?

And Ollie.

It hits me as though it's the first time. It hits me like daylight seeping through the curtains when you're still partying. A reminder of reality. A shot of it straight into your veins.

I can't hide from it forever.

I sit up slowly, my head and heart pounding. I realise I am in Kassie's spare room. I feel cold, feverish. I wrap my duvet tight around me and look for my phone. I can't see it. My clothes are on a blanket box at the bottom of the bed.

Mucky, creased and full of bits of hay and dirt. I swing my legs round and wince. Then I stand up and walk towards the door. It's locked.

An immediate rush of panic hits me and then my logic catches up. I fear it's been missing for some time. I've been on a mind-bending twisted fucking horror trip for, what? Days now? I look out of the window and can see visitors swarming around in the distance like worker ants. All eager to explore this place that's become our mundane reality. The place that I'm lucky to live in but that I drown out with intoxicants.

Spoilt fucking stupid rich boy. Stupid stupid rich boy.

I glance to my left and look in the mirror. My hair lies flat against one side of my head and sticks out in wisps on the other. My skin is baggy and red, my eyes disappearing into puffs of surrounding skin. There is a bruise starting to show in the centre of my head near the hairline. I touch the area and wince. It's sore and tender. How did I . . . ?

Spoilt rich boy. Spoilt stupid rich boy.

It's only my own voice I hear now.

Outside, a family have brought a blanket. A mum, a dad, two boys. The blanket's settled in the centre of the lawn. The older boy's standing with his hands out as his dad opens a tote bag, removes a frisbee. A wholesome scene of family life. The fountain creating a refreshing scene ahead of them. I stopped hearing the trickle of that fountain the night all that shit with Caitlin happened. It became a leaden fucking ball and chain of a memory.

I can see Kassie making her way towards the cottage. She's got her hair tied up in a yellow and paisley scarf. I have a flashback to the greenhouse. Kassie holding out her hand. She's the only one with even a grain of compassion.

I wait until she gets a bit closer and tap lightly on the window, not wanting to alert the public to my presence. Not wanting to poison their view. Kassie spots me and I wave her towards me. She holds a finger up to indicate she'll be one minute. Her face is hard. She's not the sister I had on Saturday morning. I'm not the brother she had then.

In my mind, Iggy screams again. There was a knife. Oh God. I've no idea if I hurt her. If she's still . . .

I need to speak to Jack. To find out what he remembers.

Panic shoots through me and I feel as though I want to rip my own skin off and run away from myself. Again.

There's a knock at the door then I hear a key turn in the lock.

'Yeh,' I say, clearing my throat when I realise how pathetic and gravelly it sounds. My chest is still hammering.

Kassie comes in and moves towards the bed. She perches on the edge of it but doesn't look at me. Her back is to me.

'Is Iggy OK?' I ask.

She nods her head. 'Uh-huh.' Her voice is quiet. Distant.

'I don't know what happened. I can't remember. I know there was something . . . I know I was about to . . .'

Her voice gets suddenly stronger. 'You took a knife to her. You were going to fucking kill her. My baby girl.'

A tear dribbles down my face. I wipe it harshly with the back of my hand. 'I don't know what I was doing.' I realise it sounds like an excuse. 'I mean. It's my fault. I get that. But I don't know what was happening. Or why. I'm so relieved you came just in time. If you hadn't . . .' I feel as though someone is looking out for us. The angels? Protecting us from whatever's out there.

Kassie clears her throat and, still looking away, she says, 'I was watching you on the camera.'

I tilt my head to the side. 'Camera?'

'Please, Paul. Promise me you won't tell anyone.'

I sit up straighter on the bed and clear my throat again. 'What camera?'

'On Iggy's collar. There's a camera.'

I take this in. 'Why?'

'Well, I thought, at first, it'd be good, you know, to capture how she sees the world. But then, she captured a lot more than hay and birds and . . . well, I thought I could capture some evidence. To use against Steven and Caitlin.'

'But. You never told me.' I feel a level of fear rising up in me. 'That's a violation.'

'You've absolutely no leg to stand on here. Not after what you've just done.'

I swallow. Of course she's right. 'But I was out of my mind. I never intended any harm. But you could have told *me*, Kass.'

Kassie shrugs. 'I'm sorry. But if I hadn't done it, I would have never found out.'

'Found out what?'

'Well, I wouldn't be sitting here now, with you, if I didn't know that you weren't doing whatever it is you were planning to do to my girl off your own bat.'

I think back to the moment. I desperately want to erase it from my head. I love animals. I've never harmed an animal in my life. But it does feel shadowy, as though there was something or someone else there. Does she mean because my brain wasn't my own?

Kassie says, 'It's on camera. It's all on camera.'

Chapter 48

Kassie

Tuesday

After hearing the door slam shut and rescuing Iggy, I had walked Paul back to the cottage and tucked him in bed in my spare room – making absolutely sure he swallowed four diazepam. Then, leaving him in bed, I watched the rest of the tape from the comfort of my sofa in the cottage, Iggy by my side at all times. I sat up, hit play on my MacBook, which rested on my chunky wooden coffee table in front of me. And there, just as I was taking a sip of chamomile tea, I was rocketed out of my calm. I saw the missing piece of the jigsaw puzzle. The bit that played on as I ran around the side of the cottage to save Iggy from Paul.

But I wasn't saving her from Paul.

It was all on there.

The knife was being held to his throat. To *Paul's* throat. He was completely delirious, off his face still. Seeing reality morph into hell. And being pushed to take my baby girl from me. Being *forced* to take my baby girl from me. Being told that she was the devil. It was her or him. But she was the one that was going to destroy everything. A demonic creature. A narrative provided by someone else, the same person holding the knife to Paul's throat.

Steven.

Of course it was.

The brother who hates me because I'm not a real Morland. The man who killed my father.

I won't let him get away with this.

He's not just ruining me, he's ruining Paul too. Destroying his mind. It's not just the drugs, it's the manipulation. The hate. Paul has grown convinced that he is single-handedly ruining this family with his behaviour.

When I told Paul what I'd seen on tape he sobbed. He was so relieved and yet so horrified at the reality of who our big brother is. What else is Steven capable of? Steven with his stiff suits and stiff mannerisms. All calm and cold and heartless.

I rewind the footage to the first day the public were let into the grounds. The conversation between those two women about one of our staff leaking the footage of Paul off his tits and naked at the bus stop. But there's no clue on there as to *who* it might have been.

But what if it wasn't a member of staff at all? What if it was one of us?

I call Mrs Davies and tell her about what almost happened to Iggy. She audibly gasps when she hears about it all. 'Is Iggy OK? Is Paul OK?'

'Yes. Thankfully. I managed to stop it before it went too far.'

'But how did you know?'

I explain about the camera I have hidden around Iggy's neck.

'You've been filming everyone?' Mrs Davies asks. 'Kassie, isn't this a violation?'

'Look. It's, whatever it is, can we talk about my morals later? There are more important things. There's no line Steven won't cross, is there? I mean, who is this man I've lived with all my life?'

'He needs to be stopped.'

'There's something else,' I say. 'On the footage. That I found.'

I sit up on my bed and lean forward, playing the sound of the tape down the phone to her. 'The bit about someone from the estate following Paul and filming him naked. Do you think there's anything in it?' I ask.

She exhales wearily. 'Yes,' she says. I feel my eyes widen. 'Kassie. Sweetheart. There's so much to come out. There's so much to say.'

The other end of the phone goes quiet and I can hear her rustling around. A door closing. She's obviously going to speak somewhere more discreetly.

'It was him, wasn't it?' I ask. 'Steven shamed Paul.'

'No. It was Caitlin.'

'What?'

'It was Caitlin who filmed the footage of Paul and released it.'

'But why would Caitlin . . . ?'

I hear Mrs Davies exhale wearily. 'She's been playing you all off against each other. She's not who you think she is.'

'Believe me, I've never held a high opinion of her,' I say, my breath catching as I try to keep up with what I'm discovering.

'She was a terrible big sister to you,' Mrs Davies says. 'Always was. Never protected you.'

I take a deep breath. Mrs Davies doesn't even know the half of it.

I break the silence. 'I never thought she might be the one to shame Paul, though.'

'Paul looked up to her. Perhaps a little too much,' Mrs Davies says. 'It was . . . unhealthy. Still is. Caitlin's got a hold on him.'

I think back to their conversation in the ice house. 'Is he . . . is he in love with her? I mean, not in love, like, is there something I'm missing here?'

'I've always had my suspicions. But the power imbalance, it's huge. Paul never really had a mother. Caitlin took on every female role she could play. It's what she does, after all. Play up and manipulate. And my God, can that woman manipulate. She's a page straight out of Lady Morland's book, I'll tell you.'

'How do you know all this?'

'Because, Kass. I'm not one of you. I can step back and see what's really going on. And because I listen. In this house. Besides, you were there, when she was making her so-called accidental remarks to Granny about Paul and Steven.'

'But Steven,' I say. 'Steven's just . . .'

'Just what, love?'

'If Steven was prepared to do that to Iggy, and to Paul, you don't think he could have . . . ?'

'Ollie?' Mrs Davies asks. 'It had occurred to me.'

'But why? What made you think that?' I wonder why I'm even thinking it. After all, Paul admitted to giving him that strong liquid medicine. It could have easily been a case of him losing control, falling, breaking bones, being unable to move.

Appearing to be dead.

Us, moving the body.

I shudder. I'm not innocent. None of us are innocent. Blood or not, I've behaved like a Morland.

Mrs Davies goes on to explain about the conversation Ollie overheard during the party. It was before Ollie went on to DJ. Before everything got completely out of hand. Steven knew he'd overheard them talking. About me not being a true Morland. But I still don't understand how that's a motive. I know Steven has the potential to harm – but where is the motive here? And also, Paul kind of did own up.

'How does this tie in with the whole trip killer stuff Paul keeps freaking out about?' I ask.

'I honestly don't know.' I hear Mrs Davies sigh down the phone. 'Maybe it doesn't. Maybe we're clutching at straws. Trying to create our own narrative because we don't want to believe Paul could have been responsible. Maybe we're just being biased.'

'Either way, Paul never meant any harm. I know it.'

'It doesn't matter now though, does it. If we had just called the ambulance at the time . . .'

'And now we're all complicit.'

'Exactly. And there's a dead body at the bottom of the lake.'

'But maybe that's not the only evidence. Maybe . . . maybe we can find something on Iggy's camera footage? And if it's not there, maybe we can make some.'

'We have enough to put Steven away, Kass. There's more I need to tell you. There is a motive as far as Steven's concerned.'

'How so?' I ask.

'We weren't just discussing your lineage when Ollie overheard us. We were discussing how Steven got rid of my Jamie, your father.'

Chapter 49

Paul

Tuesday

I eventually get out of my pit and walk into Kassie's living room. My body feels weak and my legs like jelly. But Kassie's cottage is the antithesis of the main house. It's more like a home than anywhere else on the estate. I sit on the sofa and she brings me a cup of tea. 'You still cold?' she asks, clearly worried about my continued shivering.

'I don't know. Must just be the comedown.'

'Here,' she says, chucking me a throw. 'I'll stick the fire on too.'

'But it's not even September yet.'

'Who cares, you're not well. And I need you back to full strength. We need to have each other's backs.'

Then she stands, turns and kneels in front of the fire on the rag rug. That was something else my clever little sister made. She's more talented than the rest of us put together.

I watch as Kassie carefully places logs, newspaper and firelighters into the basket before striking a match on a huge box and taking a flame to it. It crackles and glows, flames rising high from the paper before simmering back down and focusing its energy on working through the wood.

I pick up her MacBook that she's left on the table. She said she wanted me to watch something that she'd found. The program is open so I click play. 'Sorry, what time am I looking for again?' I ask, forwarding and rewinding the footage on Kassie's MacBook as I continue to judder beneath the blanket. The air outside has plummeted somewhat, but this is definitely not just caused by a mild change in weather. I feel my jaw clench and my muscles twitch as I attempt to still myself.

'It was somewhere between eleven and twelve,' she says, turning round to look at me, box of matches still in her hand in case the fire hasn't caught its wind yet. 'Just, be warned, you might not like seeing yourself like that.'

I take a breath and finally get the tape to stop at the right time. I focus in on the screen.

There's Naomi, talking to me. We're not front and centre of the frame, and I can't hear what's being said, but I certainly can't remember it either. I feel ashamed. I vaguely remember a strange conversation with her but not on the lawn. Maybe that was earlier. And she doesn't have her angel wings on here.

Then I have a flashback – I remember seeing them at the bottom of the pit in the ice house. And dragging them back out again. But how did they even get there?

I narrow my eyes and try to focus on what we're doing on the screen, rewinding it and rewatching it, zoomed into a now-fuzzy frame. 'Did you see Naomi around this time?' I ask Kassie. She stands up, placing the matches on the mantelpiece.

'I saw her a little before then, I think it was. She was a bit pissed off with you, to be honest.'

'Not surprised. What had I done?'

'Not sure. But it wasn't long after you charged out of the kitchen in a vile mood. After you'd necked a load of truffles. And swiped the cooking whisky.'

I rack my brain as I remember snippets and thoughts and feelings. I try to piece them together. I was angry – but not with Naomi. With Caitlin. And then there was Naomi with a bottle of wine, under the cloisters. Did I reject her? Why would I do that? Was I cruel to her? I can't recall the conversation, it's more a feeling and a series of still images on a carousel.

'Do you know why I was so angry?'

'You'd been looking for Ollie. In the house.' As Kassie says this it's almost as if there's a dawn of realisation that passes over her face. Was I angry with Ollie – not Caitlin? Did I purposely hurt him?

Was it because he was with Caitlin?

I can't control my feelings about my sister.

But how can I explain that to Kassie?

'Why were you so wound up then? Had he said something to you?'

The look on Kassie's face unnerves me. Can she truly believe I killed him out of vengeance? It was an accident. It was.

Wasn't it?

'I don't know! I was just pissed off that he was fucking around with Caitlin when we were paying for him to do a job. And the guests were sick of the loungey chilled shite he was playing by that point!'

Kassie tilts her head to one side like an inquisitive dog.

She doesn't believe me. And who can blame her? I don't even know if I believe myself.

I glance over to the window where I can see Iggy grazing in the paddock. 'Aren't you worried he's going to try something again? With Iggy? Aren't you worried *I* might?'

'I don't want Steven to know that I know about what he did to you and Iggy. I've just got to act normal – but keep a closer eye on her. And on us.'

I look back at the footage of Naomi and I chatting at the party. 'She doesn't look angry in this though?' I say. 'She looks . . . she's stroking my arm. But she looks . . . concerned, maybe? It's hard to see.'

'Let this bit play out and see where she goes,' Kassie says. 'Honestly. It's rather revealing.'

I let the footage play on. I can see myself lifting an arm, pointing towards the Hall. Not our wing, but the main entrance. Where the hellscape was taking place. Naomi looks over, pats my arm once more and leaves.

'Why do you think she's heading to the Hall? Why do you think I was pointing to the Hall?'

'I've no idea. But it was down those stairs, at the back of the Hall, that we found Ollie.'

I pick up my phone and dial Naomi's number. The phone rings several times before I hear her voice.

'Hello.'

'Naomi. It's Paul.'

There's a brief silence. 'Paul,' she says, her voice flat.

I have no idea what to say. I wouldn't have blamed her if she'd just hung up on me immediately. But she doesn't. Kassie sits with me as we speak. I try to keep my voice low.

'I'm so sorry. About the other night. I was so wasted. If

I said anything to you that was . . . well . . . if I was at all out of order. I'd make it up to you, but, to be honest, if you think the best way of me doing that is staying away, I totally get it.'

There's another silence, meanwhile Kassie is waving her hand frantically, encouraging me to get to the point.

'I'll. I don't know, Paul. Let's . . . see,' Naomi says, her tone flat. 'It wasn't exactly the best introduction.'

'I get that.'

'Anyway. Is that why you called?'

'Yes, to apologise. But also, there's just one thing, a favour really, I want to ask. And I know it's cheeky of me, like, really fucking cheeky, but do you remember talking to me, at around half eleven or so. At the party? I pointed to the Hall and you went over.'

'Yeah. You were worried about the DJ.'

I let the oxygen back into my lungs. 'What was I worried about? Specifically?'

'You said he'd had a bad trip. Not that you were in any fit state to judge, given yours seemed to be just as bad. Is that all?'

'Yes. No. I mean, why did I point to the Hall? Did you go there? To see him?'

She sighs. 'Yes, I just went over to check on him because you were so panicked about him for some reason. But Steven was looking after him so I left them to it.'

'Steven?'

'Yeah. He was giving him a drink of water or something. I guessed he was trying to sober him up or something. I don't know. I mean, he'd had a trip, he wasn't just pissed. Anyway, I decided I didn't need to intervene. He was in safe hands, so . . .'

My heart is pounding hard in my chest. Kassie can tell I'm agitated.

'What?' she mouths at me in a low but frantic whisper. 'What's she saying?'

'OK. Thanks, Naomi. And, well, you've got my number. Don't blame you if you never want to use it again of course.'

'OK. Well. Have a good day.'

She hangs up and, even in the midst of what I've just discovered, I feel pissed off. Ashamed. Fucking it up. As per.

'Well?' Kassie says. 'Spill.'

'She found Ollie with Steven. He was looking after him.' I use air quotes. 'Giving him water.'

'Oh my God,' Kassie says. 'You know what this means? You didn't kill Ollie. It was Steven. Of course it was Steven.'

Chapter 50

Kassie

Tuesday

I receive a WhatsApp from Steven to the family group:

> Family meeting. Living room. Ten minutes.
> Granny's here.

She must have made her decision. She must be ready to announce who is inheriting.

But I'm going to head to this family meeting armed with knowledge that could destroy Steven. Knowing full well that, should Mrs Davies and I decide, we can use that recording of him however we please. And now we know that he was 'helping' Ollie and, in Naomi, we have a witness to testify to that. So if he inherits, we can blackmail him. We can get him to cough up and share.

Or leave.

When I walk in everyone is sitting around in silence.

The only thing making any sound is the screamingly bright yellow of the walls. I can almost feel it buzzing. Paul is already here, he must have left the cottage after I unlocked the door. He still looks pale and shaky. He's sitting in his jeans and T-shirt, knees up on the sofa. I join him in solidarity and lean my head on his shoulder. He squeezes my arm. It is a silent understanding. An acknowledgement of what we have both learned recently. Of how we need to stick together in this snake pit of a family we've been born into.

Steven is silently hovering by the bureau next to the door where we keep our emergency stash of cigarettes. He is fidgeting, an air of being on the edge, and circling his finger around the top of his whisky glass profusely. He's not looking at any of us. I shudder, realising that I'm no longer just in a room with my family, but in a room with a murderer. No, not just a murderer – a serial killer.

You watch those programmes, on TV, true crime documentaries and the like, where relatives of serial killers say they had no idea. It seems Steven has killed at least two people – and he almost killed Iggy purely out of spite. What might he do next?

Even Caitlin is quieter than usual, pacing around in front of the TV, furiously scrolling on her phone. I can tell she isn't actually reading anything. She's using it as a fidget toy.

Granny is sitting primly in the armchair, with her ever-present shadow Dennis loitering behind her. Granny clears her throat haughtily. 'OK. I've made my decision. It's done.'

You could hear a pin drop. All eyes are on Granny as she tortures us with a pause reminiscent of a quiz master.

Finally. She opens her mouth. 'I have decided to hand over the estate management and purse strings to Caitlin. Or more precisely, Caitlin and James.'

Steven takes a long drag on his cigarette and turns his back to the circle. Caitlin grins from ear to ear and Paul sits without even a hint of a change in expression. My heart, on the other hand, plummets. If it was Steven, I had a way around that. But Caitlin and James? How on earth am I going to stop that one from happening?

'I must stress,' Granny adds, 'that this is very much dependent on James and Caitlin remaining committed to one another – legally and emotionally. And if anything changes in the marriage, well, it will be written into the contract that I can review the decision.'

Caitlin nods. 'Of course.' And I hear Steven mutter something under his breath.

'So I think that's all from me,' Granny says standing up and smoothing her skirt down. 'Dennis?'

'Yes, Lady Morland?' he says.

'Can you get the paperwork in motion? And arrange a driver for me.'

'I can drive you today. Not a problem, Lady Morland.'

'Caitlin – I'll be in touch with the paperwork. I'll need James on hand to sign as well.'

Caitlin nods. 'Yes, of course.' And Steven shakes his head and lights another cigarette as Granny and Dennis both leave the room and close the door behind them.

There's a moment's silence. But it doesn't last long.

'So,' Caitlin says, standing up out of her seat and addressing us all as if giving a lecture, 'I'm sure we can all agree this is the most sensible option. You'll still get your allowances – although James' accountant will be wanting to go through your personal expenses with you. But I'll manage the running of the estate and the lump sum.'

'All planned out,' Steven says. 'Seriously, just how long have you known?' He shoots a look at Paul. 'Have you nothing to say?'

Paul shrugs but says nothing.

Steven looks disappointed. 'What about you, Kass? Not that it was ever going to be yours in the first place. But now, it seems, it's going to our good friend James.'

I follow Paul's lead and shrug. This isn't over yet. We can still create some chaos. Paul has video footage. Of Caitlin and Ollie. But maybe we need to go further. Maybe Caitlin and James themselves have an arrangement? An arrangement to stay married for reasons other than their non-existent love.

'The estate is not going to James,' Caitlin says to Steven. 'It's going to me.'

'It is going to James because – let's face it – she'd hardly give it to you and you alone. Your marriage was practically arranged for this very moment.'

My ears prick up at this. 'What do you mean arranged?' I ask.

'Nothing,' Caitlin says, leaning back against the arm of the chair.

'I mean,' Steven presses on. 'That James' introduction to this family was always on the cards. Granny made sure of it.'

'But I don't understand,' I say. 'Why is she so bothered? I get he's rich, but so are we.'

Steven sighs. 'We're only as rich as James' family allows us to be.'

I glance over at Paul who shrugs and shakes his head. He leans forward. 'OK,' Paul says. 'Just stop with all the vague shit. What, exactly, do you mean?'

Caitlin exhales, rubbing her nostrils. 'He means that, when Dad was unwell, we got into money trouble. James' family bailed us out. We're indebted to them.' Caitlin looks down to the floor, her sparkle fading. 'And Granny decided that *I* should be the one who pays that debt back. Anyway,' Caitlin says, clapping her hands and plastering a smile back on her face, 'what's done is done. So I will be moving back to the estate. Part time at least. With James.'

'But I thought James was in a huff with you?' I say. 'He's not even here.'

'He's fine,' Caitlin says smiling. 'All good.'

'So, what exactly does this mean?' I ask. 'You get control of the management, but eventually we all still get a stake, right?'

Steven lets out a fake laugh and turns to face the wall. Then Caitlin adds, 'Well, in theory, yes that *can* happen. But with it being in my name, I am at liberty to make whatever decision I choose regarding who gets what and when. But don't you worry, sweetie, I've always been fair.'

'Oh please,' Steven says. Paul still sits silently brooding.

'OK. Well, it is what it is,' I say. 'I guess we should celebrate the uncertainty finally being over at least.' I look at Caitlin. She's the one in control now. I need to work on her. I need to talk her out of taking my cottage. 'Why don't you come over to the cottage later,' I say. 'I still have lots of herbs left over; I'll make us some cocktails. We can, I don't know, try to work out what's what.'

'Whatever,' Paul says.

'Count me out,' Steven says.

'If you want your allowance, I'd play along if I were you,' Caitlin snaps. The dynamic between them has changed in an instant. Steven sneers at her and walks towards the door.

'One hour from now. At Kassie's cottage,' she calls after him as he leaves, slamming the door.

Chapter 51

Kassie

Tuesday

Paul lies back on my sofa, while Iggy sits on the rug by the fire. They still aren't comfortable with one another after everything that happened, which breaks my heart a little.

'I can't believe we have to entertain her,' I say. 'Like, she's got complete control over everything we do now.'

He shrugs. 'Has anything really changed? She's always been in control. The only person who's going to feel a change here is Steven.'

'I guess,' I say. I go back to the kitchen counter to remove more mint leaves from the stems of my small indoor plant for the cocktails I'm going to make later on. Caitlin demanded something special so she'll get something special because that's the way of the world now.

I place the green fragrant leaves in a small ceramic bowl next to the sink, four vintage crystal glasses lined up neatly, waiting to be filled. I thought I'd try something a little different, to add a bit more spice to the traditional mojito, so I've got a spicy mix of ingredients stewing on the hob, too.

Knowing what I know now about Steven fills me with a mix of dread and excited anticipation. Who knows what he'll be planning now this has happened – but if he is we'll throw him a curveball because we're onto him. If he even tries anything on me, Mrs Davies has that recording stashed. It feels like I've life insurance in his presence.

And Caitlin's shrewd, but I haven't told her yet about our discoveries. So I'm not convinced even she knows what our big brother's capable of. They're both working blindly, in a way. Both playing with fire. They could still fuck each other up.

I can't pretend it hasn't crossed my mind that calling the police and dredging up Ollie's body might be exactly what we need to reset things. But then it risks me, Paul and Mrs Davies losing our liberty too. We're all caught up.

Maybe that's only right, though. Maybe that's exactly what should happen?

I consider Ollie's destiny. His weighted body floating beneath the dark murky water, tangled in weeds and debris. Perhaps it was being swept downstream right now. Perhaps it is caught in the bulrushes – protruding bone entwined with roots and dirt. In some ways, he can evolve into part of the land. The wildlife. In some ways, he might be freer than any of us now.

But his destiny wasn't ours to decide.

As the evening air is still, I take Iggy out to the paddock rather than locking her in her little pen for the night and let her roam around the grass and chew on the hay until her heart's content. She looks at me as I go to leave and I walk back to her, moving in for a cuddle. I can feel her furry cheek on my smooth skin and my heart feels like it could dance knowing that she's still here, still with me after everything. I pull away and stroke her head. 'You're a good girl, Iggy Pop,' I say. 'Such a good girl.'

I still can't believe the danger she was put in. I still can't believe how anyone could look into those teeny little eyes and want to hurt her. To extinguish her beautiful soul. I stand back up and leave Iggy to wander about the paddock when I spot Caitlin in the distance making her way over. But she's not alone.

James is by her side. And now I know about the debt it all makes sense. In fact, a little part of me almost feels sorry for her.

Almost.

I watch my sister as she strides over in an elaborately patterned kaftan-style jacket, white vest and white trousers beneath it. She looks radiant. Money'll do that to a sociopath. It's probably the only thing that can make her sparkle so effortlessly. James, meanwhile, looks as beige as ever. Even his hair can't be arsed as it flops helplessly into his face.

'Kassie, darling,' Caitlin says, kissing me on both cheeks as if we hadn't just seen each other an hour earlier. She hands me a bottle of champagne.

'Thanks,' I say. 'I've made us some cocktails too, like you requested. A twist on the classic mojito.' I can already feel the shift in dynamic. And she is already exuding it. She simply loves her new role.

'Oh how wonderful. Thank you so much,' she says.

James steps forward and moves to kiss my cheek. His face is all red and ruddy. 'James,' I say, with mock delight. 'Where have you been? We've missed you.'

He glances to Caitlin and back at me. 'All will become

clear,' he says, tapping his finger to his nose. 'All will become clear.' People who repeat their own sentences like that make me want to hurl.

'I literally can't wait,' I say. 'Paul's already here. He's been chilling out watching the soapbox challenge. He's still not feeling grand, but he's happy as a pig in shit as long as he doesn't have to move.'

'Good. Good. Excellent,' Caitlin says, and we lock eyes, smiles tight across our faces in a display of faux sisterhood.

'Right-y-o then,' James says clapping his hands as though he's giving the marching orders. I notice Caitlin roll her eyes. Whatever has happened between them over the last couple of days, she clearly still despises him. This is all about money and property. Something that I once, rather foolishly, believed I might have a stake in. Perhaps it's for the best. This place is cursed.

It takes all my might not to laugh or roll my own eyes at James and his over-the-top upper-class ways but I somehow manage to pull it off.

'Come on in,' I say. 'I'll grab you both a cocktail. Where's Steven?'

We walk side by side from the paddock and towards the lilac cottage door and stand in front of my picturesque corner of Morland Estate. 'I do wonder if we might shake this place up a bit?' Caitlin says. 'You could move into Mrs Davies' cottage, Kassie. Then we could create a rental here. It would be great for business. It's the perfect spot.'

'And Mrs Davies?' I ask.

'Well, she's been here long enough, don't you think? I'm not sure it's right having staff living here on the estate. I'm not even sure it's right having the same staff all this time.'

I say nothing but mentally bank her little plot twist. She

doesn't really want the cottage, she just wants to take it off me. Because she can.

Because now, she can do anything.

We walk into the house and James sits next to Paul who is still watching the soapbox racing.

'Oh I love this,' James says, trying to craic on with Paul. 'Any strong contenders yet?'

'These guys have potential,' Paul says of the all-female team on screen, without looking at James. 'All-female engineers.'

'Women drivers eh? They'll probably miss the first bend. And what's with all the pink?'

Paul now looks to his left and his top lip curls up in James' direction.

'They're probably trying to make a point, darling,' Caitlin says walking over to James and placing her hand firmly on his shoulder. A clear signal that he needs to pipe down.

I stoke the fire and Caitlin wanders over towards me, her kaftan-like floral cover-up flowing behind her like a silk wave of calm. I hate how she can be so calm when she's clearly planning on taking everything from all of us. Who knows if any of us will even be living here by next week. I wouldn't put it past her.

'Seriously, darling,' she says. 'A fire. In August?'

'It's not for me, it's for Paul,' I say, nodding in his direction where he is still sitting in a tense position. 'He's had the shivers, some kind of fever or something. I don't know. But I thought it was better than putting the heating on. At least he can lie in front of it and soak up the concentrated heat.'

'It's a comedown, that's all. He's had enough of them. You're so overprotective, Kass.' She laughs as she says it and I can see Paul's dark expression as his eyes bore into her.

'Not like this,' I mutter under my breath. She hears me but chooses to ignore it.

Paul is looking increasingly uncomfortable and pissed off on the sofa. Both Paul and James stare straight ahead at the TV screen, now sitting in silence other than for the sound of on-screen cheering and an overenthusiastic commentator.

I grab Caitlin's arm and pull her in the direction of the hallway. There's still one thing I don't understand about Ollie's death and what happened the night before.

'What's up?' she says. 'What can't wait until we all at least have a drink in our hands?'

'I found Ollie's phone. In your room. Remember?' I search her eyes for any hint of recognition or panic. She keeps a straight face.

'So?'

'What do you mean, "so"?' I air quote angrily. 'A man dies – a man who *you* brought here, who you fucked, who your husband *knew* you were fucking, and his mobile phone is in your bedside drawer.'

She leans the back of her head against the wall and lets out a deep, lazy breath, her chest deflating dramatically. 'I needed to know, Kass. Not that any of it matters now, but I needed to know if he was serious. About me. I needed to know if he was seeing anyone else.'

'What? As in . . .'

'Shh!' she says. 'James is out there.'

'It's hardly news to him though, is it. Given that's why he disappeared the night of the party.'

I know that Caitlin wasn't responsible for Ollie's death. I know it was Steven. But there's still something that doesn't add up. 'So,' I whisper now, even though there's no point, 'you were actually in love with him? Is that what you're saying?'

'I don't know.' She sighs. 'That's probably a bit overdramatic. But yes, I liked him.' I look into her eyes and there is a flash of sadness.

'Did Steven know you loved him?' I ask, wondering if that might have been Steven's real motive. Did he know Granny was going to hand over the estate to Caitlin and James and that's why he did it? To spite her? To hurt her in the worst way possible.

She sighs. 'He told Granny.'

I frown. 'Why did he tell Granny?'

'Oh do keep up. Because if Granny knew, she might not trust me to run the place and keep James onside. Which I almost didn't, if you remember.'

'Didn't what?'

'I almost didn't keep James onside. He saw me kissing Ollie in the house. He had already tried to pay him to stay away.'

'So why did you need to know if he loved you? Why did you need to check if there was anyone else? You had James. Why shouldn't Ollie have . . .'

'I just needed to know. All right?' She shuts the conversation down by walking back into the living room.

I follow her, feeling a blast of warmth. It is, admittedly, heating up a little too quickly for this time of year.

The TV programme has switched from soapbox racing to football, which I know Paul hates, but he is staring at it vacantly to avoid conversing with James.

'Paul, if you stay close to the fire to keep you warm, I'll open the window so the rest of us can have a breather.'

'Sure,' he says, his face staring at the TV but clearly not taking anything in. 'But it's fine, you know. I don't need wrapping up in cotton wool.'

'I can see you trembling,' I say, stopping him from making any more of a fuss about the fire. It has to stay on. 'Music?' I say, clapping my hands. 'Any requests?'

'Whatever,' Paul says.

Caitlin shrugs. 'I'm easy. I'll let you take charge of that one.'

I smile, but inside I'm spitting in her eye. This is just the start. Wait until the papers are signed, she's going to get much, much worse.

I stick a playlist on Spotify, some classic and new indie tunes.

'Still on a bit of a comedown, sweetie?' Caitlin asks Paul, nudging him up on the sofa and sitting far too close to him. He is now sandwiched in between her and James. I can see him squirm as she does it. 'You really need to start taking control of your life, darling. You can't let substances control you. Terrible things happen when you're that intoxicated. As we all know.'

Caitlin still thinks Paul is responsible for Ollie's death. But then, given what she's just told me, about wanting to be with him, why is she being OK around Paul? If she thinks it was him who overdosed Ollie on that antipsychotic – how can she even stand to be in the same room as him?

Perhaps Caitlin's idea of love is different to everyone else's.

The front door swings open and Steven stands, swaying. He's trying to cover up how much he's had to drink but he's clearly been drowning his sorrows big time. He walks in and falls backwards into my armchair, eyeing James. 'James.' He nods.

'Steven.'

Steven doesn't even acknowledge the rest of us.

'Right then,' I say, cutting the ice. 'Now everyone's here, I'll grab us all a cocktail.'

'Your cocktails went down a storm the other night, Kassie,' Caitlin says. 'Maybe we should find you a longer-term estate role in hospitality, hm?'

I smile through gritted teeth then leave them sitting in the lounge in what would be silence if it wasn't for Caitlin yapping on. 'I've got big plans for this place, and you're all going to contribute. You're all going to get a say, you know. A small one anyway.' I can hear her whooping with laughter. 'I'm genuinely, *genuinely* excited about us all working together on this. And, I'm sorry, Steven, but it truly is time for those custard yellow walls to go . . .' She breaks out into more shrill laughter that cuts through me like glass.

I ignore her gibbering and pour the cocktails, using the sieve and fresh mint leaves. I carry the first three in for Steven, Caitlin and James. 'Here you go. A mojito with fresh mint and a spicy little twist.' They both take them and sip. 'Ooh Kassie, this is delicious,' Caitlin says, although I'm not convinced she's in love with the taste. Steven necks his back in one go to show his disdain for all the effort I've put in. James merely thanks me and sips on his quietly.

'Anyway,' Caitlin continues, totally in her element. 'We're going to turn this place into guest cottages.'

'So you really are evicting me?' I say.

'I said you could have Mrs Davies' cottage didn't I?' Caitlin says the last two words shaking her hand in front of her dismissively.

'You don't think this place means something to me? It can't be that important to turn it into a guest cottage surely. The income won't be all that.'

'We need to make sure the estate is working as hard for us as it possibly can be,' James says.

'Us?' Steven mutters under his breath, then he lets out a sarcastic laugh. James holds his cocktail glass in one palm, twisting it nervously with his other hand.

'But, darling,' Caitlin says taking in the space around her. 'This place is ripe for investment.'

'It's. My. Fucking. Home,' I say.

'Except it's not. Not really, is it,' she says, wrinkling her nose at me, a sickly smile on her face.

I silently sigh and walk back to the kitchen to retrieve the final two cocktails. I hand one to Paul and perch on the arm of the sofa next to him sipping my own.

'So, I'm thinking that we should probably discuss how this is all going to work? You know, once I sign the papers?' Caitlin says, continuing to sip her drink and wincing slightly. Perhaps it's too sour for her, she needs sweetening up. 'We maybe need to put some timelines in, targets for when we change things up. And, obviously, James will be a part of that.' She looks over to her husband.

James closes his eyes and raises his eyebrows. 'Yes, yes. I have some ideas too. I think we . . .'

'Can we just cut the shite now?' Steven snaps. 'It's out in the open. We know exactly what's happening. We know Granny's basically just secured our family debt.'

'Well that's not quite . . .'

'James. We *know*. And our sister has never been able to hide the fact that she despises you.'

'Steven!' Caitlin snaps. 'That's so not true.'

'If Granny hadn't found out about you and Ollie, he'd still be here,' Steven says.

'What are you talking about?' I ask, confused as to why

Steven has decided to bring up the very thing that could take away his liberty.

'Ollie. Ask James why he was so broken?' Steven's starting to slur now. James, however, looks completely baffled. His eyes are wide but not in a knowing way.

'Steven,' Caitlin says, as calmly as she can. 'James had nothing to do with Ollie's death. We know it was Paul. And we know it was an accident. So we just need to move on . . .'

'Ollie's dead?' James says. Caitlin's eyes widen. She's dropped herself in it. She hadn't considered how to tell him.

'Yes,' Caitlin says. 'Dreadful accident.'

'But. How?' James asks, genuinely perplexed. Caitlin shakes her head and then lowers it. 'There was an accident with some medication . . .'

'Actually . . .' Paul says, sitting upright.

'Paul,' I say, trying to silence him. I don't want Steven to get a whiff of what we know. Not yet.

'No, Kassie. I won't keep quiet on this.' Paul stands and walks over to Steven. Steven levels up to him, although he is starting to sway a little on his feet. 'We know what really happened. We know you were—' he uses air quotes '—"looking after" Ollie.'

'What the hell are you on about?' Steven says, his sharp nose in Paul's face. 'You've been away with the fairies the last few days.'

I see Paul straighten up, squaring up. 'Naomi told me. She went looking for Ollie because I was worried about him. And oh, how funny, she found you looking after him. Giving him water.' He air-quotes the word 'water'.

'And,' Steven says, 'the guy was off his face. Completely fucking mashed. I wasn't particularly bothered but I didn't want him chundering all over the Hall.'

'But it wasn't water though, was it, Steven?' Paul says. I realise there is no way to stop this now. Although, it probably no longer matters.

Steven is looking increasingly green. 'Yes, Paul. It was water.'

Caitlin is starting to look concerned.

'What the hell is going on?' James says, looking at each of us in turn. 'How is Ollie dead? Will somebody just tell me? I honestly have no idea what any of you are talking about?' James says, gulping down the last drops of his cocktail and placing his now empty glass on the side table.

'Paul's admitted it,' Caitlin says. 'Paul told us in his own words what he did to Ollie. And the thing is, he says it's an accident, but really, Paul, was it? You knew about Ollie and I. And you couldn't stand it. You couldn't stand it because you've always been so fucked up about me. All that stuff at the fountain.'

'Shut up shut up shut up shut up,' Paul says, holding his hands to cover his ears.

'What happened at the fountain?' I ask.

'I saved her life,' Paul cries.

Chapter 52

Kassie

Tuesday

Paul is pacing frantically in front of the TV, repeating himself over again.

'I saved your life, Caitlin. I saved your fucking life.'

Steven is back in his chair now, nodding and barely part of the conversation. 'You don't have to get that fucking intimate with someone to save their life. Your own sister. Your own sister,' she shouts. 'You've always been fucked up.'

'You don't know,' he shouts. 'Because you were unconscious. You were on your way out. You were fucking out, Caitlin. Lights out. Goodnight, Vienna. You and your fucking benzo bullshit.'

Caitlin looks at me, releasing a laugh as Paul heads towards the hallway. I jump up to go and stop him but Caitlin grabs hold of my arm. 'Is he tripping his tits off again, Kassie? What have you given him?'

I side-eye her quickly, trying to keep my focus on my brother who has left the living room. I have no idea what he's talking about but I haven't seen him that angry at Caitlin ever. But what Caitlin's saying now? Why would she say something like that if it wasn't true?

James leans into Caitlin, whispering something into her ear.

Paul shouts from the kitchen, 'I was trying to save your fucking life, you stupid ungrateful bitch. And you fucking know it.'

Steven belches and moves forward to pick up his empty glass. He tries to take a sip, realises its empty and holds it to his eye. Then he places it back down onto the side, almost missing the edge of the dresser. He's beyond pissed now. Good.

Steven randomly starts clapping sarcastically and almost falls sideways. He belches again. 'You can't even keep your legs shut for your little brother, Cait. James, what have you married into?'

'Don't call me Cait.'

'Caitlin, what is all this?' James says.

'You're not even bothered that James knows the truth, are you?' Steven carries on laughing.

'I was unconscious. It's Paul who needs to be held to account.' Caitlin's eyelids droop slightly as she says this.

'You OK, darling?' James asks.

'She could do anything and you'd still forgive her, wouldn't you?' Steven says to James. 'Perhaps if you had more of a backbone she wouldn't be fucking everyone in sight in the first place. You're too flaccid, James.'

Caitlin gasps. 'How *dare* you.'

Paul re-emerges and continues to stand in the same spot he was last in. He is staring Caitlin down now, just as Steven is. James looks like a rabbit in the headlights.

'Fuck you, Steven. And fuck you, little brother. You both better sort yourselves the fuck out or I swear . . .'

'You'll what?' Steven says, his voice slurring lazily. 'Take what's mine? Already done it. I mean, really, sis, I've nothing to lose.'

I panic when I hear these words. Because I know what he's done. I know what he did before he had this news. What's to stop him going for any of us? Going all out for himself? Aside from how completely inebriated he is, I guess. Perhaps that's a blessing. I keep remembering my insurance policy. Mrs Davies has that recording. If he tries anything, I spill.

'You wouldn't even be here if I hadn't given you that coke . . .' Paul says, but Caitlin interrupts him.

'You really want to go there, Paul? Now? You didn't have to shoot it up your sister's ass though did you? You might have saved my life but you took Ollie's.' She starts crying now. Crocodile tears. She's using whatever she felt for Ollie to her advantage.

James repositions himself and puts a protective arm over Caitlin. Their relationship has to be financial. How can he forgive her like this?

'He's not the only one round here with form for hand-feeding people drugs,' I spit, incensed at Caitlin's faux vulnerability. 'You seem to have forgotten about spiking my drink and leaving me with some guy. I was barely fourteen.'

'Oh, Kassie. Just because you're ashamed of what you did.'

'I am *not* ashamed. Because I know what really happened. I've had years of therapy.'

'Pay those quacks enough money and they'll tell you exactly what you want to hear,' Caitlin says dismissively.

'You just don't care, do you?' Paul shouts.

'She's talking nonsense,' Caitlin says.

'It was rape, Caitlin,' I cry. 'And you orchestrated it.'

'What? Sorry, what? Caitlin?' Paul looks over to her and then back at me. There are tears forming in his eyes. 'Kass. What happened?'

'I was educating you, Kass,' Caitlin says.

'Educating? Crikey. Well, I mean you did give me the talk, didn't you.' I turn to Paul. 'According to Caitlin, she lost her virginity aged thirteen. Called it an eye-opener. She told me it was the only way to assert myself in life and that I should waste no time in losing mine. I was fourteen at the time. I hadn't even had a boyfriend yet, not held hands or anything. Then she introduced her boyfriend's younger brother to me.'

'Kass, you're twisting things,' Caitlin says.

'You spiked my drink with vodka, Caitlin,' I say. 'I thought I was drinking home-made lemonade. And then all I remember is that I woke up the next morning, found blood in my knickers, puked my guts up all over the toilet bowl. I assumed it was my period starting. It was only when it didn't show up again for several months that I realised perhaps it wasn't. Besides, periods didn't make you sore, did they? Not down there.'

'Oh, Kassie.' Paul walks over to me and puts his arm around me. He is shaking, but he now knows he isn't the only one Caitlin's had a shot at destroying.

'He was sixteen, the guy,' I say. 'But worse than that, Caitlin was twenty-three. My twenty-three-year-old sister orchestrated putting me in harm's way. But who could I tell?'

A tear wobbles from each of my eyes and I sniff hard.

But then I notice Steven slowly falling sideways onto the carpet. 'Look!' I say. 'What the hell is up with Steven?' He collapses to his knees and starts rocking back and forth, clutching his stomach.

'Too much to drink,' Caitlin says, looking around her. 'Where's Mrs Davies when you need her?'

'I'm quite capable of getting him a plastic bowl,' I say, running into the kitchen and scooping the washing-up bowl from the sink. I place it in front of him and he continues rocking and groaning and belching.

'Ugh, Steven,' Caitlin says. 'Can you go back to your room or something?'

By this point Steven's eyes are rolling and he falls backwards, his head hitting the painted floorboards beyond the edge of my woven rug. 'My stomach. Shit it really hurts,' he says.

'What is up with him?' I ask. 'This is way beyond.'

Paul looks over and shrugs. 'I'd say he needs to stop calling me out for overdoing it. At least I've never keeled over before 7 p.m.'

'Steven, mate,' James says, gently shaking him. But then Steven hurls orange vomit all over James' chinos and I almost burst out laughing. James looks like he could hurl himself at that point. He takes a tissue from his pocket and holds it over his nose.

Caitlin shakes her head, but then her face looks pale, too. Then I notice her chest heaving. She walks backwards, staggering a little, and leans a hand against the wall, steadying herself.

'You OK, Caitlin?' I ask. 'You look pale.'

'Yeah, just . . .' I see a movement ripple through her body like a Mexican wave and then she runs into the bathroom.

James runs after her and we can hear Caitlin hurling over the top of the music.

'Fucking lightweights,' Paul says.

'I don't think it's that,' I say as we take in a surround-sound chorus of spewing. 'There's something really wrong with them all.'

Chapter 53

Paul

Tuesday

Caitlin is puking in the bathroom. Steven sits up, hushed and lolling, his eyes half shut. I can literally see his stomach and throat muscles lurch. I leap towards him and push the washing-up bowl back into place. 'Jesus, this is fucking grim,' I say. 'Kass, why don't we just boot them out and me and you hang out?' Paul says laughing now. 'It'll be way more chilled.'

'I can't boot them out while they're both puking. I mean . . .' Kassie glances towards the bathroom where we can hear Caitlin's guts hitting the water in the toilet.

'What the fuck is up with them?'

'Perhaps they're purging all their evil.'

'Might as well put your feet up, Kass; it'll take a while to get it all out.' I laugh. 'I'm gonna get another cocktail.'

'No!' she shouts at me, making me jump. 'I mean, you can't seriously want to drink a cocktail surrounded by all this?'

'Lighten up. They're just wasted.'

'No, Paul. No cocktails.'

'Why are you acting strange all of a sudden?' I say, confused.

Caitlin walks back in with James propping her up. He's practically having to drag her half-conscious, across the floor. 'What's up with her?' Kassie asks.

'She's been vomiting.'

'Yeah, we know that,' I say. 'Sounded like something from *The Exorcist* in there.'

'And I'll be honest,' James adds, 'I'm not feeling too great. I'm wondering if we've all eaten something.'

James sits back on the sofa and Caitlin collapses onto the floor in front of the fire, moaning and rolling around, clutching her stomach. She's lost all sense of dignity. But something inside me feels scared for her. I've never seen Caitlin like this. Even at the fountain that night. She was unconscious, but she wasn't messy. Not like this.

'I'm so sorry. So so sorry,' Caitlin is wailing.

'It's OK. You've nothing to apologise to me for,' James says, trying to comfort her. 'I think we must have eaten something.'

She sits up suddenly looking startled. Looking vacant, staring at nothing. 'I had no choice. He . . .'

Kassie moves closer to Caitlin. Meanwhile James rushes out to the bathroom.

'What did you have no choice in, Caitlin?' Kassie says, holding both Caitlin's arms.

'She's just talking shite,' I say. 'Ignore her.' Part of me feels worried. Will she say some bullshit about the night at the fountain? It's all out there now. But I know she knows I feel something unnatural for her. She's always known.

But she made it that way. She made it happen.

Caitlin sits, her eyes lolling and Kassie strains to keep her upright. To keep her talking. But I don't go to help. I don't feel as though I can be anywhere near her right now. 'What did you have no choice in, Caitlin?' Kassie asks again.

'I didn't want to. I didn't want to do it.' She's wailing now. I lean in more closely, trying to make it out.

'Do what?' I ask.

'Granny knew. She knew,' she says, then she starts repeating the words in a frantic whisper. 'She knew she knew she knew she knew.'

I look at Kassie and whisper loudly, 'What's she talking about?'

Caitlin's head snaps round. She looks demonic. Possessed. 'She knew I was in love with him.'

'Who?' Kassie asks, and a part of me dares to wonder. Was the feeling, as dark and absurd and complicated as it was, reciprocated?

'In love with who?' Kassie says again.

Caitlin pukes on the floor, hitting Kassie's jeans as she kneels in front of her. She goes to wipe her mouth but misses. She's completely off her face. This isn't food poisoning.

'She said I had to get him out of my life. For the estate.'

She collapses forward onto the floor and sobs.

'I loved him,' she says. 'I had no choice. I never wanted to kill Ollie.'

Chapter 54

Kassie

Tuesday

Caitlin's admission takes my breath away. It's not just Steven – it's Caitlin too. They're both capable of murder. They both *murdered* somebody. Right here, on our estate. In our home.

'But how did you move him?' I ask.

Caitlin mumbles something barely audible. 'Dennis.'

I feel another lightning strike of shock hit my gullet. 'Dennis? But–'

'He'll do anything for Granny,' Caitlin says, letting out another groan and clutching her stomach.

'But how did he know about the secret cellar?'

'I reported the loose tiles,' Paul says, his voice becoming quiet and faint. 'On the day of the party. Almost tripped up over one of them.'

Things are making sense now. It wasn't Paul at all. Of course it wasn't.

The whole place is starting to smell of smoke and sour sick.

I stand and look around me. It's carnage. But Paul is also looking woozy now and I can see sweat starting to bead on his forehead and above his top lip. 'Paul?' I say, panicked, given what his body has already been through this weekend. He looks disorientated. 'Paul. Paul! Do you want some fresh air?'

Is he relapsing or something?

He nods and I go to stand him up and walk him to the front door. I grab a throw en route and hold it haphazardly under my arm in case it's a fever and he gets chilly again. It's getting dark outside now and I walk him a few steps away from the cottage towards the paddock where Iggy is. I position him on the grass and throw the blanket over him. He lies on his side but then suddenly sits up. 'I'm going to be sick,' he says, and pukes all over the grass.

'Paul. Paul, listen to me. Did you have another cocktail?'

'Just whatever was on the hob. It was rank by the way.' He pukes again, spattering the grass.

He must have just got it when he stormed out of the room before. When all that stuff about Caitlin came out. Shit shit shit. It wasn't even watered down with anything. That'll be so strong. I feel cold prickle throughout my entire body.

'I'll get you some water, just . . . just stay there.'

I race back into the house where Steven, Caitlin and James are all now practically comatose. I take my phone from my pocket and dial Mrs Davies' number.

'We've got a problem,' I say. 'Everyone's puking up. Even Paul.'

'What? Why?'

'They all started puking, and then Paul did too. He's been so ill these last few days I'm worried if his body can handle it. Can you come get him? He's outside. On the grass near the paddock.'

She confirms that she's on her way and I put my phone back in my back pocket. Then I walk back across the living room, my horrible siblings and hapless sap James all groaning and looking as though they're tripping their tits off. It's like they're all together, all in this same state, but separate from each other too. They can't even communicate. They can't say anything now.

I move over to where Caitlin is lying down on her back in front of the fire, her eyes closed and her hands on her stomach. Her mouth is twitching and she's breathing calmly. I stroke her head. It's cold and clammy. Her kaftan is all tangled tight around her so I pull it out to make her more comfortable, spreading it loosely around her. I lean into the fire, which has become way too hot for the cottage, and I poke it with the iron. Sparks fly up and the flames grow in ferocity. I place the iron back on the stand and grab the tongs.

I stick the tongs up into the chimney and hear a loud, shuffling and cracking sound. A huge piece of debris dislodges from the chimney, hits the fire and bounces onto the floor. Within seconds, it's set Caitlin's silk kaftan alight.

Flames dance all around her and creep closer and closer to her body. It takes mere seconds before the flames latch on to other materials, multiplying and ripping through my home.

The heat is like nothing I've felt before. It's as though the flames are on my skin, in my lungs. I gasp and start spluttering.

I look around me and Steven and James are both completely out of it in various positions on the sofa and the floor. They're not responding to what is happening. As the flames get higher I panic and realise I need to get outside and call for help. I run out the door, struggling to catch my breath. My chest is burning. I find Mrs Davies rushing around the side of the house and remember that Iggy is in her paddock. She'll be getting frightened if we don't move her soon.

'We need to get Iggy back to the main house,' I say, breathless.

'But, Paul.' She gasps. 'Where did you say he was?'

I realise then that this is the spot I left him in. The blanket is gone, but the pile of vomit is there, soaking into the grass. Paul is gone.

We both look back to the cottage, flames licking up beyond the windows. 'Oh my God!'

I watch in horror as I see Paul race to the front door, slipping over before he reaches it.

'Paul! Paul!' I'm screaming his name and running towards him. Mrs Davies' voice is behind me. 'Don't, Kass! Please. I can't lose you!'

I turn around. 'Get Iggy. Meet me back at the house. In our wing. Just take Iggy inside with you. Call 999. Quick.'

She reluctantly grabs Iggy as Paul stands himself back up and throws himself on the front door. It opens and within seconds he's inside. 'Paul! No!' I scream again.

I can hear his desperate voice from inside the cottage. 'Caitlin! Caitlin!'

Oh my God. He's gone in there for her.

I stand frozen for a few moments, unsure what to do. I can't believe he's gone in there after Caitlin. But he's vulnerable. And I need him. I can't lose my last surviving sibling. The only one I ever loved.

I kick the front door open but the flames are too close and I'm hit with a wall of intense heat, scorching my face. I can't see anything in front of me. The smoke is thick and black. I step forward, then take another step. But there's no use. I hear a creaking sound and then an almighty crash. I gasp, and it feels as though my lungs are being singed. Like the flames are literally raging inside of me.

'Paul!' I wail. It comes out like an animal noise. A sound I don't think I've ever made before. Then there's another crash. The sound screaming in my ears.

There's nothing I can do.

Chapter 55

Kassie

Tuesday

'Have you called them?' I ask, desperately after racing into the main house. 'We need them here. We need them now.'

'Yes, yes, of course. Is he . . . ?'

'He's in there. Oh God, he's in there.' I break down and she puts her arms around me and I sob. 'What was I thinking? I didn't keep an eye on him. I let him wander out. We need to get him out, Mrs Davies.' My body automatically veers towards the door in an attempt to get back outside and to the cottage. Mrs Davies holds me tighter, Iggy in her other hand.

I look into Iggy's kind eyes then bend down to stroke her head.

I can hear sirens in the distance, wailing, getting louder and louder as they approach Morland Hall.

'They're here,' Mrs Davies says, looking out of the window.

We race outside, locking Iggy in the house, safe and sound. Just as Paul should be right now. The pain he's been through, I was the only one he trusted, the only one he could confide in. What have I done?

The blue lights create a pulsing bright glow all over the entranceway. I can see someone in uniform jumping out of the fire engine. We run towards him. I am breathless. I point towards the pathway that leads towards the cottage. 'It's down there,' I pant. 'The cottage. My brother's in there.'

I realise I have only mentioned one person. My brother. Paul. Will they realise how strange that sounds when they discover more than one body?

Body.

Bodies.

My stomach lurches and I puke up everywhere, Mrs Davies rubs my back as I do. 'Help is here now,' she says calmly. 'Everything may still be OK.'

'You don't understand. I went in there,' I say, starting to cough. 'I couldn't see. It was completely black. Aside from the flames. Smoke everywhere. Things cracking. The house was coming down. I've killed him. I've killed my own brother.'

She continues rubbing my back and holding her other arm around my shoulder. I make a start to walk towards the cottage but she holds me steadfast. 'Leave the professionals to it, Kassie.'

I am crying now. Desperate. But what can I do? I watch as the fire brigade race towards the burning cottage, the sky flickering with blue lights, orange flames and thick, black smoke against the petrol blue sky. Mrs Davies moves in front of me, holding my shoulders in her hands, firmly.

'Remember the plan,' she says.

But I can't. I can't think about it. I deserve to rot in hell for this. 'I can't,' I cry. And then I'm coughing again.

She shakes me hard. 'Kassie. You have to. You must. You were all drinking and then . . .' She looks me straight in the eyes and my head lolls to the side, more tears falling. She shakes me again and I look back at her. Mrs Davies. My grandmother.

'We were all drinking,' I say, remembering the plan. 'Something jumped out of the fire, hit Caitlin's clothes.'

'Yes, and . . .'

'And we all tried to help her. She was screaming but by then the flames and smoke were too much. I had to leave.'

'That's right,' she says. 'And then we called emergency services.'

I nod my head.

'You need to stay on track, Kassie. You need to keep your head.'

'But Paul . . .' I cry.

'He was never going to be free of Caitlin, was he?' she says, sighing. 'He was tied to her in every way. She's had him trapped since they were kids. And she's had the final say.'

My eyes flick from side to side, trying to work this all out. Why would he let Caitlin treat him like that then risk his life for her?

'I never gave him a cocktail. I made sure. I was absolutely sure. But I think he must have got hold of one maybe?'

'See then? It wasn't your fault.'

'Of course it was,' I snap. 'I orchestrated this.'

'*We* orchestrated this,' she says.

I had come up with the plan involving the psychoactive plants. Harvesting the soul vine and chacruna that I'd been growing. That they knew I'd been growing. The stuff that Paul wanted us to use at the party. But it's dangerous stuff.

You absolutely have to be in the right environment. You have to be safe.

A ceremony is supposed to enlighten, to purge, to remove all sin.

But I wasn't using it as intended. It was sacrilege, really. I should have known it would all go wrong.

I think about Caitlin's admission before she died. She and Steven will have gone on a psychological journey before the flames took them to their final destination. I can't imagine what they'll have seen though. It'll take more than ayahuasca to help Steven and Caitlin find awakening and compassion. Their horrible, narcissistic lives will have flashed before their eyes. I hope it's a comfort to them. A reminder that nobody's going to be missing them.

I wonder what James saw. He's as clueless now as he was before.

But Paul. Sweet Paul. Racing in there, looking for Caitlin. For her. Why was he so fucked up about her?

Dennis walks into the room. 'They've made it safe, but they've cordoned it all off. Nobody can go inside.'

'OK,' I say vacantly.

'Have the police finished inside?' Mrs Davies asks, her arms wrapped tightly around me as I sit on the sofa in a blanket.

'No. They're still working through everything with some of the fire officers. Forensics are here too.'

I am frantically biting at the skin around my thumbnail, which is beginning to sting. I pull it away from my face and, as my vision clears, I can see a small bubble of blood pushing its way out. I wipe it on my jumper and bury my hands beneath the blanket Mrs Davies wrapped me in earlier. Everything inside my chest is tight. Everything inside my stomach is upside down. And my brain is racing at a million miles an hour. Pedalling back and forth, going over and over everything. How did I fuck this up so monumentally?

'Is anyone . . . ?' I ask.

'I'm sorry, Kass,' Dennis says. 'Nobody made it.'

My chest feels like it could explode in pain. My heart feels like it's snapping into a million pieces. 'No,' I scream. 'Nooooooo!'

Mrs Davies holds me tight and rocks me. 'There now. There now. Sh. Sh. Sh.' And my sobs quieten but they don't stop. I don't think I'll ever stop.

'Have you informed Lady Morland?' Mrs Davies asks.

'Yes. She's going to come anyway. To see Kassie and discuss the estate,' Dennis says.

'Huh. She's got her priorities in order then,' Mrs Davies mutters under her breath. 'Can you give us a moment please Dennis,' she says, and I hear his footsteps, the door shutting behind him.

I cry. My body jolting. Mrs Davies hugs me tighter. 'I've lost them all,' I say. 'And now I have to live with what I've done.'

'It wasn't your fault, Kass. It truly, truly wasn't.'

But we both know that's a lie. We both know that Paul is dead because of me.

'I've got to live with this. On my own. Alone.'

'You won't be alone. Not ever again, Kassie,' Mrs Davies says, holding me close. I can feel her heart beating in her chest. I lift my head, leaving a damp patch of tears on her shirt, and I look out of the window. Where only days ago there was dancing and drinking and fairy lights, now it is empty but for blue lights flashing against the dark sky. I feel like I need to burst out of my skin and get swallowed up.

I wanted to clean things up. To make things right. It wasn't supposed to end like this.

But the estate is full of bodies now. Full of death and darkness. And that's down to all of us.

I'm a Morland. Always have been. Always will be.

Epilogue

Monday 28th October

09.30

Feet walking past the camera. Some running, some skipping, some walking. Laughter can be heard. Directly in front of the camera is a wood gate, intricately carved pumpkins sitting on the ground. People walk towards the gate, their hands reaching in towards the camera.

'Can you name the animal, Ellie?' an adult voice says.

'It's a goat.'

'Well done! And what do goats eat?'

Another adult voice chips in, 'You know I'm not even sure I know the answer to that.'

Adult number one whispers back, 'We'll just stick with grass.'

They laugh. 'Do you want to feed the goat, Ellie? Where's your brother. Michael! Michael! What's he doing over there?'

The space in front of the camera opens up with the two people moving to either side and further away towards the distance. Towards the little boy standing in front of the water, his arm pointing towards it.

'Mummy. Mummy! Look what we've found.'

One of the adults, a lady, races over to the young boy. 'What is it, Michael?'

'It's a Guy Fawkes floating in the water.'

The woman grabs the little boy and pulls him in close. 'Trudi. Call 999.'

Acknowledgements

This book was inspired by a trip to Seaton Delaval Hall with my good friend Kassie where we learned all about the legendary parties that took place in the grounds of the estate in its Georgian heyday (although I must say and caveat, the Delavals DID NOT influence my criminal, narcissistic and repulsive Morlands!). So I must thank the National Trust staff and volunteers who spent time telling us tales about the historic goings on in the estate.

Huge thanks of course to my wonderful editor Billy who has been a dream to work with – we've had so much fun exploring the twists and turns of the book together. And of course, big thanks to the wider team at Avon for all their support and creativity.

Thanks also to my agent Jo for seeing the potential in my excitable idea for this book after my visit to Seaton Delaval Hall – and for being there with me every step of the way.

Love and thanks also to my gorgeous husband Chris and brilliant stepson Sam, my mum, my sister Julia, my bestie Jayne and the Keldy gang - Kass, Samantha, Sarah, Sarah and Suze.

***This is not a love story. This is the story of
how I killed Harry Collins . . .***

Love Lucy Roth? Read her wicked feminist thriller, *When Sally Killed Harry* – perfect for anyone who wishes they could take their revenge on The Tinder Swindler or Sweet Bobby . . .

'I absolutely loved everything about this book – it's the best fun, with such whip-smart characters and a compelling story. I couldn't put it down (I barely slept!). Lucy Roth is officially brilliant and I am obsessed!'
Lucy Vine, author of *What Fresh Hell*

'A razor-sharp revenge thriller with bite, brains and a body count. Cold-blooded and wildly funny, it's the perfect beach read to pair with blazing sun and a chilled drink'
The New York Observer

Available in paperback, eBook, and audiobook now!

There's no smoke without fire...

As someone who has suffered abuse, Maddie protects women by murdering the men who attack them – men she calls 'fleas'. Fleas are men who follow women home. Abusive husbands who refuse to walk away. And then there's the Manchester Maniac: a serial killer stalking the streets of Manchester, determined to murder people like her.

But Maddie can't get away with it forever. Years later, in the interview room of her prison, she comes face-to-face with a very important visitor. Someone she's going to tell all to, about how she caught one of the UK's most prolific serial killers, and how she got caught as one herself...

This emotional and chilling thriller in the vein of *Promising Young Woman* is perfect for fans of Alice Feeney, Helen Fields and Jo Callaghan.

Available in paperback, ebook, and audiobook now!